THE
CHURCHILL PLOT

ALSO BY DAVID R. STOKES

The Shooting Salvationist
Camelot's Cousin
November Surprise
Jack & Dick
Jake & Clara
Firebrand
In the Arena
How to Keep Calm & Carry On
The Simple Life
The Bothered Butler
Got Any Rivers?
Flour Power

THE
CHURCHILL PLOT

A Novel

David R. Stokes

To my late father-in-law Reverend Robert E. Holland, in fond remembrance of countless conversations about history, politics, faith, and the occasional conspiracy theory.

"O death, where is thy sting? O grave, where is thy victory?"

— First Corinthians 15:55

PROLOGUE

JANUARY 15, 1965

EDMUND MURRAY STOOD WATCH. He had been working as a bodyguard for fifteen years; although if you asked him, he would tell you that he preferred the term "protection officer." This tenure included a period of time when the man he protected was the most powerful in the realm—the Prime Minister of Great Britain. Heady stuff for a lawman. But those whirlwind days were long gone, and now nearly ten years had passed.

It was demanding work, and Murray was thankful for an understanding wife. He still owed her a honeymoon, and he smiled briefly at the thought that they had been married for nearly twenty years without a romantic holiday. But that was the only time on this particular day that his face would even drift in the direction of a smile. Murray was a detective sergeant for Scotland Yard, and he had been on this unique assignment since way back in 1950, but today, the end of his assignment was now sadly in sight.

Not that he was ungrateful. Certainly not. He had been an eyewitness to history with a front-row seat to great events. Like on this day, when he stood in front of a surprisingly average looking house located at 28 Hyde Park Gate in Kensington, West London. It was cloudy and cold—not below freezing, but the mist that fell intermittently seemed cold enough to morph into snow. Three men approached.

One of them spoke to Murray. "Sir, we've been sent by headquarters and told to report to Detective Sergeant Murray. You him?"

Murray looked them over for a moment. Unlike him, dressed in his usual dark business suit, they wore the everyday working uniforms of police constables accented by polished silver buttons. He replied, "Indeed, I am."

"What do you want us to do?" one of the men asked.

"Well, officers, not much happening at the moment. Just stand here with me and look official. And whatever you do, don't smile. This is likely going to develop into quite the sad day," Murray instructed, with the confident voice of a man in charge.

In perfect unison, the officers replied, "Yes sir."

They had been sent to the site because the crowd gathering in the street around the famous address was growing. And it was likely going to get much larger. Some in the crowd were there in their own official capacities—journalists and representatives of the BBC. Others were just ordinary people who were curious and hungry to connect with something extraordinary. The officers tried in vain to keep the glare of a few television lights from their eyes and to stay warm as the mercury crept down the thermometer. Occasional moments of drizzle suggested more substantial rain to come. Two of the men longed for a cigarette, but not Edmund Murray. At any rate, there was no break for them looming on the horizon.

Just a whole lot of waiting.

✳

At one point earlier that morning, the front door of the Georgian-style house had opened slightly, and Detective Sergeant Murray leaned in. A woman's voice could be heard. "Mr. Murray, one of the doctors will be out shortly after lunch, with a statement."

"Thank you, ma'am," the officer replied, with a slight tip of his hat. But that hour had come and gone, and there was no statement. Murray was quite familiar with how the whole world of Winston Churchill dealt with the concept of time. The great man seemed to thrive in a dimension where clocks were simple wall adornments and calendars were mere suggestions and not to be taken all that seriously.

Though the curtains were drawn over most of the windows, some in the crowd could see wallpaper with a floral pattern through two of the portals that had not been completely covered. People strained their necks to see around those standing in front of them to look through the windows. Occasionally there would be a whisper, like the one from one lady, "I think I saw something. Is that him coming to the window?" But their minds were playing tricks on them.

"I was just here a month or so ago. That was a much happier day," another lady in the crowd said to no one in particular. "It was his ninetieth birthday. He came to the window and smiled. Then he flashed that victory sign. We all cheered. It was a lovely thing," she continued. She brushed a tear from her cheek.

"Don't go looking for any victory sign today," a man standing near her said in a quiet response. Several people nodded in somber and silent agreement. Some bowed their heads and their lips moved in private prayer.

Meanwhile, in one of the rear rooms of the house, two doctors attended to its famous resident. They had no words of reassurance for the man's wife. "We are very sorry," one doctor said to Clementine Churchill, speaking for both of them, "but this latest episode looks to be too much for him to overcome. It's just a matter of time, now."

"How much time?" Mrs. Churchill asked.

"Could be hours. Could be days. Very hard to predict in such cases," the other doctor replied. "We know he's been long thought of as an English bulldog and such, but even the strongest of their breed reach an end at some point."

"How is this different from the other episodes?" Clementine asked.

"It's a matter of degree, simple as that," the first doctor said. "It would appear that your husband is getting ready to meet his Maker."

The woman Winston called Clemmie began to weep and said in a wavering voice, "He's always wondered if his Maker would ever be prepared to meet him." She walked back into her husband's room, now fully convinced that he would soon be gone. Meanwhile, the crowd outside continued standing without growing restless, collectively lost in the significance of the moment.

Also in the crowd outside the home of Sir Winston Churchill that day were two men sent by the Soviet Embassy in London. The Soviets were very interested in what was happening. In fact, they had been waiting for this moment for many years.

Every hour one or the other of the Russian men went to a pay telephone a block away to ring a report to someone. Soon other comrades would arrive at the scene, then others. The Russians watched in shifts. As with all the others, they were waiting for the final moment. But their part in the vigil had nothing to do with respect. Not at all. The Russian men, and those for whom they worked, had a very different agenda. Even in his most lucid moment, Winston Churchill, a man with a keen sense of history and the times, could have never grasped the reality of a plan that had been around and waiting for more than a dozen years.

A plan that depended on his death as a *trigger*.

For days, the story of Winston Churchill being near death would be front-page news not only in Great Britain, but also around the world. Prime Minister Harold Wilson visited his dying predecessor. Wilson, who led the new Labor government, had only been in office for a few months, but wanted to demonstrate good political instincts and respect at the crucial moment.

Violet Bonham Carter, an old friend, came by, but she could only tolerate the scene briefly, becoming emotional and very uncomfortable. She and Winston had been close friends for sixty years. Violet had helped his career along when in 1908 she persuaded her father—H. H. Asquith, then the Prime Minister—to bring Churchill into the cabinet. She had never understood, or even accepted, Winston's choice of Clementine

Hozier for his bride. But on this day, such a thought was far from her mind. She stood at the foot of his bed and simply said, "Goodbye, Winston," before making a quick exit.

Day after day, the vigil continued. One elderly couple almost tiptoed down Hyde Park Gate with a bunch of tulips. They approached a policeman and whispered hesitantly, "Excuse us, Constable, but we'd like to leave these flowers for him."

"Of course. I'll see to it."

"I was in London during the bloody Blitz," the lady told the officer. "And me husband here was in the First War and then that awful mess at Dunkirk. We came because we felt we just had to. We're so grateful for what he done for us."

One young man who had been just a boy back during the war, turned to his friend and said: "Ya know, if it wasn't for Winnie, God bless 'im, we'd have Germans jack-booting up and down these streets with swastikas on their lapels. My pop says that he saved everybody's life."

*

David Ormsby-Gore, the British Ambassador to the United States sat at his desk in the study in the embassy residence in Washington, DC. A fire crackled in the nearby hearth, giving off the only light in the room. Though it was morning and the sun was shining in a cloudless sky, the drapes had been closed to reflect the mood of the room's only occupant. He was making preparations to step down from his role and return to England—but fate seemed to be dealing him one more hand to play before he could do so.

He had, of course, been following the news from home about the final decline of Winston Churchill. But it was more than a professional or patriotic sense of things that occupied his mind, though they were part of what he was feeling. What preoccupied him at this moment, as the world awaited the passing of a giant, was a crisis of conscience that had been plaguing him for over a year.

David Ormsby-Gore had been ambassador since 1961. In an unprecedented move, President John F. Kennedy had personally recommended David to Prime Minister Macmillan during a meeting at Key West, Florida. Macmillan had appeared taken aback by the bold request, but in truth he had been expecting it. He knew of the close friendship between Kennedy and Ormsby-Gore. In fact, Macmillan had been present back in 1938 in Scotland the weekend the two young men met for the first time. And, in a strange twist of history and genetics, Macmillan was distantly related to both Kennedy and Ormsby-Gore.

The 1938 occasion was a typically British late summer gathering hosted by Lord Harlech—David's father—in Oban, Scotland. That particular weekend was unforgettable in large part because of how it ended, with Harlech and most of the others in attendance scrambling to travel back to London. Prime Minister Neville Chamberlain had just announced that he was flying to Munich to meet personally with Hitler about Czechoslovakia. It was history in the making.

In attendance that long-ago weekend, though hardly noticed by anyone, was twenty-one-year-old John Fitzgerald Kennedy, though he much preferred to be called "Jack." He and his older brother Joe were sons of the United States Ambassador to Great Britain, Joseph P. Kennedy. Jack usually found himself in the shadow of his popular and extroverted brother.

Possibly this is what drew him to the son of Lord Harlech, who, like Jack, was the second son of a powerful man. In David's case though, the older brother had died tragically in an automobile accident three years earlier. It was now left to the bookish and boyish younger brother, with none of the charisma possessed by the elder, to carry the mantle for the fallen sibling.

The two of them were sometimes referred to as "slacker second sons," but both were quickly developing skills to enable them to surprise all who made the mistake of underestimating them. The two young men formed an instant bond that weekend around conversations about world affairs, not to mention the ever-present ladies. It was fast-friendship at first sight. Of course, there was a war in their future, one that Jack's older brother would not survive. This would serve to further cement the friendship between Jack and David for years to come.

That was then.

In 1961, when David took up his duties in Washington, following his appointment by Macmillan, it quickly became clear that this to be was much more than a diplomatic relationship. In addition to the many official interactions between the British Embassy and the White House, there were too many "off-the-record" moments with Jack to count. Late night meetings in the Oval Office, travel aboard Air Force One, and winter weekends at the Kennedy compound in Palm Beach. Jack shared secrets with David. They talked about Cuba, the Soviets, and the world.

But David didn't share all *his* secrets with Jack. Especially the big one about how he had been working with a small group of young and well-born British students who had been recruited by Soviet Intelligence since a short while before Jack and he had met. That work continued into his days as the British Ambassador to Camelot. And what was eating at David, and would continue to do so, was that he had known his friend's life—that friend being the President of the United States—had been in jeopardy. While he didn't know all the details, he had known enough that he could have warned Jack not to go to Dallas.

Now David had come upon some new information from the same Soviet source. It was about yet another plot involving yet another President of the United States. But even more than that, it was also a threat to dozens of world leaders and peace on the planet. He had been asked to discover Lyndon Johnson's plans with regard to Churchill's soon-to-come funeral. And the ambassador experienced a chill at the thought of what such a request meant.

So in the darkness of his study, Ambassador David Ormsby-Gore made a decision born of the bitterness that overwhelmed his soul. He would betray again. Only this time, he would find a way to betray the people for whom he had secretly been working for nearly thirty years. *Maybe it would bring redemption*, he thought.

He picked up the telephone on his desk.

"Yes, Mr. Ambassador. How may I help you?" a voice said.

"Please contact a man named William Moyers at the White House. He's a Special Assistant to President Johnson. I need to meet privately with the president as soon as possible. But this needs to be private and 'unofficial.' Do you understand?"

"Yes, Mr. Ambassador. I'll make contact and let you know when it is set."

"Thank you. And no one else around here, other than you and my driver—absolutely no one—is to know anything about this visit."

"Of course, sir. Yes."

CHAPTER ONE

JANUARY 16, 1965

THE DOOR WAS OPEN and the President of the United States
was on the toilet reading that morning's *Washington Post*. Special
Assistant Bill Moyers was about to call out to him when he
heard, "Moyers, you see this thing about Churchill?"

"Um...yes, Mr. President. Saw it. It's item one on your
briefing today."

"Think the old dinosaur is down for the count?"

"Certainly looks that way."

"Well, when it happens, it will be the biggest news since
VE Day," Johnson barked. Moyers thought that the murder of
Kennedy might fit that bill, but recognized his boss's blind spot
in that area.

"I imagine every leader in the world is making preliminary
plans to travel to London for what will likely be a funeral of

epic proportions. You want me to start those wheels turning?" Moyers asked.

"I suppose. But it's not really what I want to be doing in the first days of my term. Hell, the old man could die right on the twentieth."

Moyers headed off his boss's train of thought. "Mr. President, even if that's the case, nothing will get in the way of a great day of national celebration. It's going to be the biggest and best inauguration since Andrew Jackson."

"I'd rather be compared to FDR, boy," Johnson snapped. Moyers took it in stride. He was used to his boss's outbursts. When a friend asked him how he could work for such a mercurial man, Moyers replied, "I work for him despite his faults and he lets me work for him despite my deficiencies."

The young White House aide's pathway to the president's right hand was unusual, to say the least. He had been interested in journalism since his youth in Oklahoma. While in college at the University of Texas in Austin, he worked at a local radio station owned by Lady Bird Johnson, and he met her husband, then Senator Johnson. But journalism and politics soon took a back seat to a call to Christian ministry and a divinity degree from a seminary in Fort Worth. For a time, Reverend Bill Moyers worked as a Baptist pastor, leading a congregation in a small town near Austin.

By 1960, however, he left the pulpit behind and was drawn into the orbit of Mr. Johnson. He rose quickly in the ranks of staff members and sycophants and served as the liaison between the presidential and vice presidential campaigns in 1960. That was followed by service as a deputy director in JFK's Peace Corp.

Everything changed on November 22, 1963. Moyers was in Austin when the news broke about the shooting in Dallas.

He chartered a plane and landed at Love Field in Dallas just minutes before Lyndon Johnson was sworn in as the thirty-sixth president. When the young aide reached Air Force One, he was not allowed on the plane, so he persuaded someone to get a note to LBJ: "If you need me, I am here." Johnson needed him and Moyers was quickly moved into the cramped cabin of the famous Boeing 707 just in time to witness the historic moment. He had been at President Johnson's side, for better or worse, ever since. So he had developed his own coping mechanism when it came to his boss's temper.

"Of course, Mr. President," Moyers replied. "But if I may, sir —"

Johnson looked at his young assistant and then nodded slightly up and down.

"Well, the passing of a giant like Churchill will give you a chance to be front and center on the world stage. You know your history; that means political capital here at home. Everyone who's anyone will be there and you'll be able to work your magic on them one at a time."

Johnson smiled, both at the thought and that his young assistant was so good at kissing ass. Job security. "Well, get busy, but I don't want to be gone a minute longer than I have to. Didn't we just make a big deal about Churchill's birthday?"

"Yes sir, his ninetieth. You sent a message and gifts. It was well reported in the British press."

"Yeah, but not much over here. The editors probably think Kennedy would've done better," LBJ said, with a sigh. Then the toilet flushed, much to the relief of Bill Moyers.

*

Around the same time, although five thousand miles away in a different time zone, a solitary man consulted his time piece, determining that the day had progressed far enough into the afternoon to warrant the first libation of what would surely be many. He walked the short distance from the living room in the small and sparsely furnished apartment to the kitchen area and reached into a cabinet for a bottle of vodka. He looked at it carefully and with a frown. He preferred Scotch.

He muttered out loud, though no one was around to hear it, "Better than nothing, I suppose."

He poured about an inch of vodka into a simple water glass and drank it in one practiced swallow. Then he poured another and made his way over to the only comfortable piece of furniture in the entire flat, a large chair with an ottoman.

He sat down and took another sip of vodka, picking up a copy of a newspaper. It was the *Times of London*, the Sunday edition. This copy had arrived much earlier than previous ones. It was only Tuesday; usually the Sunday newspaper from back home made its way to him no sooner than Thursday.

Harold Adrian Russell Philby, known to friends and former friends as "Kim," missed England. But only in the playground of his mind—he never talked about it. He had recently celebrated his fifty-third birthday—alone. Some of his "friends" had arranged for a bottle of single-malt scotch as a gift. Kim had tried to make it last, he really had. But the bottle was empty by the end of its second day. He had kept the bottle for sentimental reasons.

Kim Philby was good with secrets and had been addicted to the drug of deceit for most of his adult life. He had started spying for the Soviet Union back during his college days at

Cambridge. He was recruited along with three other men: Guy Burgess, Donald MacLean, and Anthony Blunt. Blunt had confessed his treachery to MI-5 in 1964 in exchange for a promise of immunity and anonymity, but Burgess and MacLean had been in Moscow since 1951. Working in London, Philby had helped them get there. From that point on, he was under suspicion himself as the so-called "third man" in the Cambridge spy ring. Kim had managed to deflect and deny the accusations effectively for more than a decade.

By early 1963, he was under scrutiny again. He was living in Beirut, Lebanon at that time, and working as a journalist for a London-based publication. He was married and had two children. But when it became clear that he was about to be exposed as a traitor, he fled—leaving his wife and children, not to mention queen and crown, behind. Now he lived in lonely anonymity in Moscow. There was not even any contact with his old friends Burgess and MacLean. The Soviets loved compartmentalization.

Philby's dream was to live out his final years as a hero in Russia. He wanted to become a full-fledged officer in the KGB. However, his first two years in Moscow had been filled with disappointment. He had not been received warmly by the people he risked everything for. In fact, he quickly found himself feeling like a prisoner in exile. He had always thought that if he did make it to Russia one day, it would be as a hero. But this was far from the case. His new life was built around alcohol and tedium.

That all began to change one day in late 1964 when an official car showed up at his apartment building. Philby was whisked off to a clandestine meeting with a small group of powerful men at a large estate on the outskirts of the city. That day, Kim Philby was briefed on something big. He was excited to finally be involved. But weeks had gone by since that first meeting, and he had heard nothing from the group.

Until today.

As he turned the pages of his precious newspaper and sipped his vodka—by now on his fourth glass—he came across a personal note that had been inserted between pages six and seven of the main section. It simply said, in English: *"Comrade Philby: Be ready at eight o'clock tomorrow morning. A car will pick you up in front of your building. Please pack a bag for several days. Destroy this note immediately after reading."*

CHAPTER TWO

EVERYONE STOOD as the prime minister came through the door. Harold Wilson had been the anointed occupant of 10 Downing Street, complete with its storied Cabinet Room, for just three months. He was still finding his way around the place—not to mention the job—and was determined that very soon, when the eyes of the entire world rested on London after Churchill passed to his reward, he would gain political capital for playing host to world leaders on the global stage.

The prime minister took the center seat nearest the door at the large conference table that filled most of the famous room. A pipe was there. He picked it up, methodically stuffed it with tobacco, and lit it. Then he addressed the group.

"Thank you all for coming. We're on the threshold of an extraordinary moment in the history of our nation. I've called this special meeting because you'll play a vital role in what's ahead. It's clear that Mr. Churchill's days are numbered. His death will mark the end of an age, but also an important moment for the nation and our government. We are determined to give the great man the farewell he deserves, regardless of political affiliation or personal feelings."

At this, they all slapped the massive table with open palms and said in unison, "Hear, hear!"

Wilson continued, "Thank you, gentlemen. Much appreciated. Now, I've asked two men who aren't usually in this room for Cabinet meetings to join us today. First, the Director General of the Security Service, Roger Hollis, will discuss measures being taken to protect the honored guests and world leaders who are certain to be here. Also, please welcome Stuart Palmer. He's the chief assistant to Mr. Fitzalan-Howard, the Earl Marshall who will oversee funeral events and the plans that have been in place for many years. Mr. Palmer, please begin."

"Thank you, Prime Minister," Palmer replied nervously. He wore a conservative suit and a bowtie. He put on a pair of half-frame reading glasses, which rested more than halfway down his rather large nose. "If I might, Sir, with your permission, I'd like to first give some background to let you know how all of this has developed."

"That's a grand idea, Palmer. Proceed," Wilson replied between puffs on his pipe.

"Again, thank you—Prime Minister. The plans for Mr. Churchill's funeral date back to just after our Queen's glorious coronation in 1953. You all know that Her Majesty dubbed Mr. Churchill a Knight of the Garter, but what you may not know is that Sir Winston suffered a stroke a few days later. This news was never released to the public."

"That's an outrage!" thundered a voice. It came from James Callaghan, the Chancellor of the Exchequer—regarded by most as the second most powerful office in the government.

"I was in the Shadow Cabinet then, and we never heard a word about such a thing!"

There were animated whispers around the table, and several men were clearly upset. Prime Minister Wilson raised his hand and brought them back to order. "Gentlemen, I understand your anger, but I do not think any good purpose will be served at this time by second-guessing Mr. Churchill's service and career. He has always been a crafty sort of fellow; I think we can all agree. Please, Mr. Palmer, continue."

"Thank you, Prime Minister. As I said, the illness was not made public at the time, but those closest to him thought Mr. Churchill might very well have to resign. He confounded them, however, with a speedy and full recovery. The queen was well aware of the prime minister's health challenges and was very concerned. By all accounts, she has always had great respect, even affection, for Mr. Churchill. Regards him almost as a beloved uncle."

"This is a vital point to bear in mind, Gentlemen. If any of you find any part of this distasteful because of political and personal disagreements with Sir Winston, I suggest you remember Her Majesty's feelings and wishes," Wilson said.

"Hear, hear!" they all replied.

Wilson looked around the table and said, "Again, Mr. Palmer, please go on. There will be no more interruptions."

"Yes, thank you again, Prime Minister. Well, Her Majesty had witnessed first-hand many of Mr. Churchill's interactions with her father during the difficult days of the London Blitz and the World War. She knew he was a national hero. She also had fresh and painful memories of the passing of her own father, the king. Again, you may recall those circumstances."

Everyone in the room remembered the very sad time. That was when she was *Princess* Elizabeth. She and Prince Philip were in Kenya, when the words "Hyde Park Corner"—the code to be used in the event of the king's death—were dispatched on February 6, 1952. The new reigning monarch of the realm, dealing with shock and grief at the loss of her beloved father, as well as the very idea of becoming queen, was deeply moved a few hours later when Churchill delivered predictably eloquent remarks to the nation: "During these last days, the king walked with death, as if death were a companion, an acquaintance whom he recognized and did not fear. I, whose youth was passed in the august, unchallenged and tranquil glories of the Victorian era, may well feel a thrill in invoking, once more, the prayer and the anthem: God Save the Queen."

Palmer added, "As a point of interest, one which I'm sure you all know, Winston Churchill is the only person to be elected as a Member of Parliament under the reigns of both Victoria and Elizabeth. And his remarks that day, as well as his body language during the period of national mourning, bore witness to his own sense of mortality. But Mr. Churchill has always been guarded when asked about his relationship with Her Majesty. We all remember when he was once asked what he and the queen talked about for so long on so many occasions, he said, 'Mostly horse racing.'"

Many smiled at this reference. "At the time of Churchill's secret illness, Queen Elizabeth was planning her first official royal excursion abroad as the reigning monarch. So it is hardly surprising that she had a discreet discussion beforehand about what should happen in the event of the death of Sir Winston, instructing her staff that if he should pass during her absence from England, he should be given a public funeral on a scale befitting his position in history."

"May I ask a question, Mr. Palmer?" said George Brown, the Secretary of State for Economic Affairs. All eyes went to the prime minister, who frowned slightly. He really didn't know what to do with Brown. No one did. Brown had the tendency to put both feet in his mouth, usually because of his excessive drinking. In fact, though this was a late morning meeting, Brown's demeanor hinted that he had already started on his substantial daily alcohol consumption.

George Brown's worst moment was still painfully fresh in everyone's memory. In the aftermath of the assassination of John F. Kennedy nearly fourteen months earlier, Brown—who often exaggerated his personal closeness to the Kennedy family—appeared on national television as part of a tribute to the fallen leader. He had been drinking most of the day, and his remarks were slurred and incoherent. A day or so later, he apologized. Before than moment his political star had been on the rise. Everyone in the room, including Prime Minister Wilson, knew were it not for his drinking and the public humiliation, Brown might well be living at Number Ten.

Wilson nodded at George Brown, indicating that he could raise his question.

"Thank you, Harold, er, I'm sorry—I mean, Prime Minister." Several men at the table rolled their eyes.

Brown forged ahead. "Wouldn't a full state funeral require a request from the Queen to the House of Commons after Old Winnie's death and an affirmative vote? Has Her Majesty indicated that she plans to do this?" The others glanced at each other, convinced by the informal reference to Mr. Churchill and his slightly slurred delivery that that he had indeed been drinking.

"Yes she has. I expect that such a motion will be made in the House within a few hours of Mr. Churchill's passing and it will be, of course, approved," Palmer replied.

"Thank you, Mr. Palmer," Brown replied. He seemed amused and proud of himself for surprising his colleagues with the short and surprisingly lucid exchange.

Stuart Palmer then summed up his briefing. "So the wheels were set in motion for Winston Churchill's grand farewell a dozen years before his death. The queen's initial directive was soon enhanced, and over time, it was formalized into a working plan. Over the years, ideas were discussed, mostly out of Churchill's view, and by the late 1950s a detailed blueprint was in place. The plan is called, appropriately, *Operation Hope Not*."

"Thank you, Mr. Palmer," Wilson said. Then he addressed the rest of the men around the table. "Each of you will receive a numbered and bound copy of this plan as you leave Number Ten today. You are to keep this in your sole possession and guard it carefully. Are we agreed?"

In unison, they said, "Yes, Prime Minister."

*

The son of an Anglican Bishop, Sir Roger Hollis was an unassuming and easygoing type of man. Everything about him spoke of conservatism, an affectation he deliberately cultivated. Throughout the meeting, he, in his role as Director General of the Security Service, informally known as MI5, took detailed notes. He had only been asked one minor security question about St Paul's Cathedral. That was fine—Hollis preferred to work in the shadows. Not just because of the nature of his job and the agency he oversaw, but because he was a man with secrets beyond the "official" ones he was sworn to keep.

Mr. Hollis was a Soviet agent. He had been recruited in the late 1920s, while working as a journalist in Shanghai, China.

Now as the head of the British version of America's FBI, he was uniquely positioned to alert the Soviets about British affairs and plans, as well as to influence the British government on behalf of the system to which he owed his first loyalty.

The notes Hollis was taking that day in the Cabinet Room at 10 Downing Street would serve a dual purpose, as did most everything else in his life.

*

Several hours later, Hollis dined by himself at The Savoy Grill. He had three vodka martinis along with his usual grilled Chateaubriand with pommes soufflés. After ordering dessert, he made his way to the men's room. The attendant on duty was a man named Alex. No one had made the connection that Alex was on duty anytime the director dined at the Savoy. Not that they were close, mind you. Hollis didn't even know Alex's last name—or real name, for that matter. Alex was simply Hollis's connection to his Soviet friends.

The director entered a stall and pulled an envelope from the inside pocket of his Savile Row suit jacket. He wedged it in behind the toilet tank, knowing that Alex would be retrieving it before anyone else used the stall. His business done, Hollis flushed the toilet, exited the stall, and washed his hands. Alex handed him a towel.

Before leaving the men's room, the Director handed Alex a crisp new five-pound note and said, "Don't spend it all in one place, my good chap." Those words confirmed to Alex that something had been left in the stall for him, and he was to pass it along as soon as possible.

Alex replied, "Very kind, sir, but please allow me to give you some change." Alex then handed Hollis a one-pound note.

This was also code, meaning that Alex had something for him as well. Per the protocol, Hollis removed a piece of paper tucked beneath a stack of towels and left the room. He returned to his table, where a dish of iced peach Melba was waiting for him.

But the head of MI5 skipped the dessert and quickly left the restaurant. He found a phone booth in the hotel's elegant and expansive lobby. He entered and sat down, closing its door behind him. He picked up the telephone and placed a call.

CHAPTER THREE

NINETEEN YEARS EARLIER

"IT'S NOT THE WHITE HOUSE, but it'll do in a pinch," Winston Churchill said. He and his wife surveyed the elegant suite of rooms at the British Embassy in Washington, DC. He lit a long cigar, while Clemmie poured them both a drink.

"Well, President Truman doesn't know you as well as Franklin did," she replied.

"Of course, I understand that. But you weren't with me back in '41, just after the Japanese attacked Pearl Harbor and dragged the Americans into a war we had been fighting for more than two years. He was such a gracious host. Did I tell you that he saw me in all my glory once?"

"He *what?*"

"Oh yes, he wheeled around a corner as I was walking from my bath back to the bedroom."

She smiled tolerantly, "Oh Winston, you and your childish fascination with being naked."

"I told him that Her Majesty's Prime Minister has nothing to hide from the President of the United States."

"Of course you did. Always quick with a quip."

"That was, of course, before my heart episode. It's simply remarkable that the news of the attack during that Christmas visit never got out. That would've ended at least my part of the Grand Alliance."

"Well, it's obvious God had a plan for you, Winston, and He wasn't quite ready to meet you yet," she said. Then she walked across the room and kissed her husband on the forehead as she gave him his glass of whisky.

Winston Churchill looked for a long moment at Clementine. It was like he was looking over the top of eyeglasses he wasn't wearing. He smiled. Then he took in the room once more. "Actually, I think this will be more comfortable for you while I'm away in Missouri with the president," he said.

"And Randolph will be here tomorrow to help me see you off. I don't think it would be fair to unleash your unpredictable son on the White House help," she replied.

They both laughed.

"You're right, indeed, my love. But I do wish you'd consider going with me. This speech may create quite a stir."

"Yes, Winston, I've read it. Iron Curtain, and all that. But aren't you taking a tiger by the tail? Mr. Stalin may not be amused. And you may be putting President Truman in a tight spot. You'll likely get your stir."

"Well, that, I think, is the point, isn't it?"

Clemmie rolled her eyes. "Yes, of course, there must always be a point."

"I was thinking the other day about how I have now lived twenty-five years longer than my father did. I'm an old man—but I'm not dead yet. I know this one speech in a small American town may seem an unlikely platform to mount yet another political comeback, but I'm determined to try."

"Of course you'll come back, Winston. You always do. Never surrender, remember that? But before you get on that train to the middle of nowhere, we need to reply to the cable about the house on Hyde Park Gate in Kensington."

"I know, Clemmie, but I'm finding it hard to make such a decision. It's a lot of money. Chartwell has been our home for nearly a quarter of a century. I labored over that bloody wall—brick by brick—for nearly a decade. Maybe we should just save the money."

"We've gone over this so many times. Your good friends have once again shown themselves to be true."

"I know, my dear. I often think of how our lives would have been so different if I had, in fact, been forced to sell that grand home back before the war, when I had once again squandered what little reserves we had in the markets."

"Lord Camrose and his friends gave us enough funds to make us whole, because they believed you to be a great man—the only man who could be called on to save the nation at a time when the world was becoming increasingly dark. Now they have come to the rescue again. Can't you see this?"

"Of course, yes—you are quite right. But you must admit that the Hyde Park property will cost the proverbial arm and leg."

"Winston! You exasperate me. Since when has money, especially spending it, been any sort of problem for you? Our entire marriage has been one long spending spree without abandon. How many times have I had to meet with our money man only to hear about the butcher bill going unpaid and that he had your word that you would economize by limiting us to only *one* bottle of champagne at dinner? I swear, this awful depression you sink to—the black dog, as you describe it— makes you even more unbearable than is generally the case."

He stood there in rare silence with the countenance of a sad and chastened child on his face.

Clemmie continued, "Lord Camrose and his friends have made us financially comfortable for the first time in our lives, and the money you'll earn for your book about the war will actually make us wealthy."

After a pause, Winston finally spoke with a sigh of resignation. "You are so right, my dear. And the fact that we can still stay at Chartwell as part of the trust's agreement, and that for just 350 pounds annually—well, that was a wonderful act of generosity."

"And it pleases me that after we are gone that beautiful home will belong to the nation as a way for generations to come to remember all you have done to make their lives even possible."

Churchill looked at his wife and smiled broadly. "You're right, of course. No more worries about the butcher bill and whether or not the help is drinking my whisky. I am indeed beginning to climb out of the pit, Clemmie. The voyage across was refreshing, as were the days in Miami and Cuba. But I still very much feel the black dog lurking nearby. That is why I've worked so hard on this speech. Dealing with a great issue is always the best therapy for my mind when it is troubled."

"I know, Dear. I know you're getting better. But we do need to act soon if we want the house."

"All right, send the cable. Make the offer. But make sure we'll be able to annex the section next door. We'll need more space there. Of that fact, I am certain."

"We're going to love the home, Winston. I hated Chartwell for many years, but I've grown to love it. I know you're going to grow to love our new home in London."

Winston smiled at her, and they clinked glasses.

∗

Now, as the great man lingered between life and death at Hyde Park Gate, his epic life was undergoing global eulogistic review. Winston Leonard Spencer-Churchill was born on November 30, 1874 at Blenheim, a palatial country house—one of the largest in the country—long associated with his ancestors. His mother, Jennie, was from America. His father, Randolph, was a sometimes-successful politician whose career and life were abbreviated, in part, because of mental deterioration brought on by syphilis.

Winston had grown up with all the benefits the world of British aristocracy could afford him. He was pampered and spoiled by members of the household staff who functioned as surrogate parents. Most accounts describe him at times as unhappy due to parental neglect. But what he seemed to miss in paternal happiness as a child he made up for with an active imagination fueled by voracious reading habits and a propensity for great dreams.

Following an active and eventful, though brief, military service, he was elected to Parliament in 1900. During the First World War, he served famously as First Lord of the Admiralty, afterward reinventing himself politically and forsaking the

Liberal Party for the Tories. Churchill spent much of the 1930s in the political wilderness, viewed as someone like his own father, who also once had a promising career, but missing the ultimate mark and falling sadly short.

Then a man named Hitler came to power in Germany.

Churchill's countrymen, and certainly members of Parliament, had no stomach for another massive conflict, the memories of the last war fresh in their minds. Winston was therefore often a lone voice as he warned about Germany's potential for aggression. Events and history proved him to be right and eventually he answered the call of King and Country, becoming Prime Minister of Great Britain on May 10, 1940, just as the Nazi war machine trampled Belgium and France.

As the clouds of war gathered over Europe for the second time in a generation, the Ministry of Information in the United Kingdom developed some slogans for morale building— mantras that leaders felt would help people cope with what was believed to be coming. The words were carefully designed for billboards, the walls of buildings, and other venues for public notice. The first of these said, simply: *"Freedom Is in Peril. Defend It with All Your Might."* The next one was a little more to the point: *"Your Courage, Your Cheerfulness, Your Resolution Will Bring Us Victory."*

The third poster in the series was never actually released. It was designed to be part of the public information plastered everywhere if the Germans actually invaded, a big concern at the time. It would say, *"Keep Calm and Carry On."* The Nazis were fast advancing and the threat to the United Kingdom seemed imminent and inevitable. But then, Winston Churchill replaced the ever-wobbly Neville Chamberlain as prime minister. This change at the top rendered the need for mere paper posters obsolete. They now had all the best slogans in the flesh. The new Prime Minister's face quickly became the most famous image of the era and his voice became its soundtrack. Churchill's passionate eloquence tapped into the dormant but indomitable spirit of a battered population. His wartime leadership became the stuff of legend, though it was very real. Legendary newsman Edward R. Murrow was famous for his broadcasts from the Blitz and the trademark phrase, "This is London." He reported from rooftops all over the city as bombs fell from the sky. And in many ways, his words helped prepare Americans for battles yet to come. After the war, Murrow remarked that Churchill had "mobilized the English language and sent it into battle."

When the war in Europe ended in May 1945, he was at what seemed to be a political pinnacle. But several weeks later, his party lost the national elections, and Churchill was suddenly out of office.

In the political wilderness once more, Churchill still had one major comeback in him. It began in the homeland of his mother, the United States of America, in a little town called Fulton, Missouri. There in March 1946, in a gymnasium packed to the rafters, following President Harry Truman's introduction, Churchill shared a speech that shook the world. It was officially titled, "The Sinews of Peace." But that identifier was quickly overshadowed by two resonant words.

Iron Curtain.

In a moment, with a simple turn of a phrase, the concept became an enduring metaphor to characterize the decades-long conflict known as the Cold War. Eventually, British voters returned to the Tories in sufficient numbers to put Winston Churchill back at 10 Downing Street in 1951. By this time, however, the man who guided the realm through its darkest hour was clearly in decline. He often worked from his bed and by 1955, he had to resign due to poor health.

He remained in the House of Commons, however, until he chose not to stand for reelection in October 1964.

Winston Churchill was a man of large habits. He drank alcohol, rarely to excess, but his intake of champagne, brandy, beer, and his beloved Johnny Walker Scotch Whisky, was indeed substantial. Daily, he smoked several of the cigars that eventually became part of his public persona. He fared sumptuously when it came to food, and one friend famously said of him, "He is a man of simple tastes; he is quite easily satisfied with the best of everything!"

Winston loved caviar and in retirement he received regular deliveries of the delicacy from the young Shah of Iran. When hearing of this, Anastas Mikoyan, who served briefly as Chairman of the Presidium in the Soviet Union following the ouster of Nikita Khrushchev in 1964, wrote a note to Churchill saying, "Russian caviar is best." Winston wrote back: "Thank you. All caviar is good."

A gifted and prolific writer, Churchill earned critical praise and a personal fortune through the power of the pen. He wrote for newspapers, periodicals, and authored forty-three books (several of them multi-volume endeavors). He was awarded the Nobel Prize for Literature in 1953, "for his mastery of historical and biographical description as well as for brilliant oratory in defending exalted human values." Ernest Hemingway, a runner-up for that year's honor, suggested that Churchill was a better speaker than writer. But Churchill was used to such snarky retorts and could give as well as receive. At any rate, he wrote to Clementine, "£12,100 free of tax. Not so bad!"

When addressing both Houses of Parliament on his eightieth birthday, in November of 1954, he summed up his philosophy: "If I found the right words you must remember that I have always earned my living by my pen and by my tongue."

Down through the years, Winston Churchill inspired young politicians. Jack Kennedy was one such example. In the late 1930s, when JFK's father, Joseph P. Kennedy, was US Ambassador to Great Britain (the Court of St. James), appeasement was all the rage and Joe Kennedy was a big fan of anything that would keep his sons from going to war with Hitler. The ambassador's eldest son, Joe Jr., agreed with his father, but younger brother Jack saw things differently. He admired Churchill, who at that time was doing his best to awaken his sleeping nation.

That admiration continued over the years, and in 1963 Mr. Kennedy oversaw the unique process of having Sir Winston Leonard Spencer-Churchill declared an honorary citizen of the United States. The only other foreigner ever so honored was the Marquis De Lafayette, who had helped George Washington during the American Revolution. However, by the time of the White House ceremony on April 9, 1963, Mr. Churchill's health precluded his travel to America. Instead, he was represented by his son Randolph. Also in attendance were numerous luminaries, including the sons of Franklin Delano Roosevelt, Bernard Baruch, and Ambassador Joe Kennedy, who by that time was confined to a wheelchair by the devastating effects of his own massive stroke.

Winston and Clementine watched the ceremony live on television at 28 Hyde Park Gate via satellite hookup, one more sign of how much the world had changed since Churchill's Victorian childhood.

Late the next morning, there was a knock on the door at Hyde Park Gate. The caller was David Bruce, the US Ambassador to Great Britain. He was there on official business.

"Mr. Ambassador, so kind of you to call on me today."

"It is my pleasure, Mr. Churchill. I bring greetings from President and Mrs. Kennedy."

A tear developed in Churchill's eyes and he replied, "Mr. Bruce, please convey my deep appreciation to the president and his lovely and charming wife. I am honored by his greeting and your visit."

Ambassador Bruce then presented Churchill with his official United States passport.

Later, and while still grieving the death of their own daughter, Diana (by her own hand), Winston and Clementine watched the same small television, via the same satellite hook-up, as the story of the assassination of John F. Kennedy was told. Roy Howells observed the scene that sad night as the great man who had accomplished so much sat staring into the fire, clearly pondering the magnitude of Kennedy's death.

No doubt, he—with his health challenges and entrenched emotional propensity for depression—was pondering his own mortality as well. He likely also grieved about how the world had passed him by and changed since he was a boy. Back then Britannia ruled the waves, and the sun never set on the empire. Now there was no British Empire and his nation was in the midst of a revolution of manners and morals. It was around this time that he told one of his secretaries, "I have worked very hard all my life, and I have achieved a great deal, in the end to achieve nothing." He emphasized that final word: *"Nothing."*

CHAPTER FOUR

NOVEMBER 1964

ON THE OCCASION of his ninetieth birthday, Winston Churchill experienced a foretaste of the kind of adulation that would mark his ultimate passing. Actually, the celebration had begun the day before. On the twenty-ninth of November 1964, a crowd began to pack the cul-de-sac at the Hyde Park Gate house. They wanted to see Churchill and share birthday greetings.

It was not a completely spontaneous gathering. There had been a notice in several of the London newspapers indicating Churchill would likely be at his front window around one o'clock that afternoon. The cheering up would do him good, thought some on the household staff—thus the notice. And because it was a Sunday, it would be more conducive to drawing a crowd than on his actual birthday, which was on Monday.

Clementine picked one of her husband's eight tailor-made "siren suits," the kind of full-body zipper outfit he wore so often during the war. Several months earlier, when Churchill was told rumors were circulating about his health suggesting he was close to death, his response was predictably defiant and characteristically grand. He ordered three new siren suits in maroon, navy blue, and black velvet, and told the tailor: "You can tell people around you, I intend to wear them out!"

For what would become his final public appearance, however, Mrs. Churchill chose her favorite, the green one. It matched her dress. After he was dressed, she returned to his room and saw her husband of more than fifty-six years standing with the assistance of his cane.

"You look striking, my love," she said. "Just like back in those glorious years when you were in charge." She moved toward him and fiddled with his polka-dot bowtie and then smiled and said, "It's time. Your public awaits, Sir Winston!" Mr. Churchill smiled back, though nervously as he cautiously made his way out of his room and through the house. It was good all of this navigation involved only the main floor. After falling and breaking his hip at the Hotel de Paris in Monte Carlo a couple of years earlier, the home had been retrofitted and all of Winston's needs now required nary a stair.

The members of the household staff made sure the curtains in the drawing room window were closed until the right moment. They didn't want the public to see Mr. Churchill having any difficulty getting into place. So, with appropriate dramatic timing, and just a few long minutes after the published hour, the curtains were quickly opened and those gathered outside the home saw Winston and Clementine Churchill. At first, the old man had a slightly bewildered look on his face, but almost immediately that visage gave way to an obvious smile.

He beamed as the crowd cried with one voice, "Happy birthday, Sir!" Then came the strains of "For He's a Jolly Good Fellow," followed closely by, "Happy Birthday, Dear Winston. Happy Birthday to You!"

Out of view, Roy Howells had hold of Churchill's right arm to steady him, while Clementine supported his left side.

"Who is that, Mummy?" one little girl asked her mother. "Who are those old people in the window?"

"Sweetheart, that is Sir Winston Churchill and his wife, Lady Churchill."

"Is he a Knight or something?"

"In a way, yes. Our queen made him a knight many years ago. He's a great and brave man who has done many great things for our country."

But all of it was lost on the little girl at the time. Years later, she would remember the day fondly, especially after learning all about the great man's role in history. After a while, Churchill, his eyes full of tears, turned from the window and the curtains were closed. Then a few minutes later, the curtains were reopened and the great man appeared again, this time flashing his famous V for victory sign. Like any great actor, he knew how to milk a curtain call.

The crowd lingered for quite a while and repeated best wishes and songs several times. Eventually, Mrs. Churchill came to the door and addressed the crowd, "Sir Winston would like to come to the window again, but he cannot. He heard you all singing and thanks you very much."

She then smiled, and finished with a firm but gentle instruction: "Quiet now, please." They gladly obeyed.

By that time, Winston Churchill was back in the drawing room watching one of his favorite American television shows on the BBC, *Sea Hunt*, starring Lloyd Bridges. Later, it was time for an early dinner. Usually, dinner was served in their home precisely at eight fifteen, but this evening they dined at seven o'clock. This was so the family could watch the very special television tribute to Churchill on the BBC called *Ninety Years On*, scheduled for eight o'clock.

The program had been advertised for several weeks. It was promised as a ninety-five-minute variety show, featuring the biggest names in entertainment. Churchill smiled from the first scene as the famous British playwright, Noel Coward, introduced the program. The honoree hoped Coward would reprise a song that Winston once made him sing over and over again, "Don't Let's Be Beastly to the Germans," a satirical, yet patriotic, number he wrote in 1943 to make the point that some Britons took a far too tolerant view of the enemy. The not-too-subtle sarcasm of the song was missed by much of the public. Some were even outraged and registered complaints with the BBC. They took the words literally and thought it was designed to be pro-German.

"Don't let's be beastly to the Germans, for you can't deprive a gangster of his gun!

Though they've been a little naughty, to the Czechs and Poles and Dutch, I don't suppose those countries really minded very much."

The tune—complete with tongue-in-cheek lyrics—was eventually banned by the BBC. Churchill loved it, nonetheless. And as far as his relationship with Noel Coward was concerned, when Winston was prime minister he persuaded the playwright to do a little espionage work.

Noel Coward began the lavish broadcast that evening by looking directly into the camera and sharing a personal tribute and greeting to Mr. Churchill. It included a special "Churchill Verse" to the song familiar to those who attended Harrow School in their youth. Winston was, by far, that institution's most famous graduate. The school song, "Forty Years On,"—meant to reflect on life when school days were a faint memory—was amended in his honor. Coward did not sing, but he quoted the words:

> *"Blazoned in honour! For each generation you kindled courage to stand and to stay; You led our fathers to fight for the nation, called 'Follow up' and yourself showed the way. We who were born in the calm after thunder, cherish our freedom to think and to do. If in our turn we forgetfully wonder, yet we'll remember we owe it to you. Seventy years on—though in time growing older, younger at heart you return to the Hill. You, who in days of defeat ever bolder, led us to Victory, serve Britain still. Still there are bases to guard or beleaguer. Still must the battle for Freedom be won. Long may you fight, sir, who fearless and eager look back today more than seventy years on."*

It is likely that Noel Coward was unaware of the fact that twenty years earlier Churchill had blocked the famous playwright's knighthood by King George VI, possibly because of Coward's homosexuality (Coward was eventually knighted by Queen Elizabeth II in 1969). Just the thought of that back-channel blackball turned Winston's smile into a guilt-driven frown as he listened to the man's very touching tribute. But that only lasted for a moment. The show on the telly was a tonic to the old man.

Joined by their once-divorced and twice-widowed daughter, Sarah, a lady of the stage herself, Sir Winston and Lady Clementine watched the program from the dining room table, as they enjoyed their after-dinner coffee. The exhilarating events of the day and the ongoing broadcast tribute temporarily neutralized the recent tension between forty-year-old Sarah and her elderly parents. Her ongoing romance with the African-American jazz singer, Lobo Nocho, did not please father or mother.

*

As he was readying for bed about half past ten o'clock that evening, Mrs. Churchill presented her birthday gift to him—a small gold heart bearing the number 90. It was for his watch chain, where it would complement the other gold heart adorning the chain. She gave *that* one to him on the occasion of their engagement back in the summer of 1908, when she was still Miss Clementine Hozier.

As Roy Howells prepared to wake Churchill at ten thirty the next morning, his actual birthday, he was unsure about exactly what to say. Several years earlier, on another such day, he greeted Churchill with the familiar, "many happy returns," phrase, only to receive the disconsolate reply: "Many happy returns? At eighty-four, I shouldn't think there will be many more." So Howells had avoided the customary birthday greeting since.

But today, he chose to use it and hoped the inspiriting effects of the previous day's celebration and evening television tribute would still be in evidence. So, entering the room and drawing back the drapes, Howells, bringing the first greeting to Winston Churchill on his birthday, watched the old man stir in his bed and nervously uttered what he hoped were the right words, "May I wish you many happy returns, sir?" There was a pause and a stare as Churchill garnered his wits and focus. Then came a drowsy smiling yawn and the reply, "Thank you, Howes." Howells had long since ceased to be bothered by that chronic mispronunciation.

Winston Churchill had preferred breakfast in bed for decades, even during his years at 10 Downing Street. He would awaken earlier in those days, usually before eight o'clock, but other than the time, his routine varied little over the years. He would read newspapers and work on his writing—he preferred to dictate, sometimes using the services of four secretaries at a time. While Prime Minister, he had something he called his "gimme box," containing papers and telegrams, things requiring his approval or direction.

But the box and its demanding contents were part of a distant past that morning— as was the writing—as Churchill sat in bed in a blue bed jacket. His butler, a man named Enrique, placed a large tray on the old man's lap. It was apricot jam for the toast instead of the usual blackberry spread. He drank his first cup of coffee and began to peruse the newspapers. However, before he could read all that far into his copy of *The Times*, Clementine came in singing "Happy Birthday to You," followed by a tender kiss.

"That was lovely," he said.

"I'll see you later," she replied, and with that made her way toward the door, while making eye contact with Roy Howells and motioning for him to join her outside.

"Ma'am?"

"Mr. Howells, would you help me with the flowers sent over from Buckingham Palace? I've already had them removed from the wrapping and they've been put in that lovely large white vase."

"Of course, yes, let me see to it." With that, the valet went to the drawing room and returned momentarily with the floral arrangement. "They are lovely flowers, Ma'am, quite exotic looking. What are they?"

Clementine shrugged slightly and said, "I'm sure I don't know. Did you make sure to get the card?"

"Yes, it's right there near the top of the vase."

With that, they both reentered the bedroom and presented the flowers to Winston, who smiled broadly and remarked, "Who sent the lovely Birds of Paradise?" The question provoked a quick meeting of the eyes between Mr. Howells and Lady Churchill.

"These were just delivered from your admirer at Buckingham," Clementine said. "Here's the card."

Winston Churchill's eyes moistened with tears for a moment as he read: "To Sir Winston, with my sincere good wishes and congratulations on your ninetieth birthday, from Elizabeth R," the initial "R" being an abbreviation for the Latin word for queen, "Regina." The queen's flowers were just the first hint of what would become a flood of gifts and tributes. Ultimately, three hundred thousand cards were routed to 28 Hyde Park Gate, keeping several secretaries busy for many days.

President Lyndon Johnson asked his countryman to mark the thirtieth day of November as "Sir Winston Churchill Day." A man with great political instincts, LBJ knew how to exploit a good thing. However, the tall Texan's political reputation would very soon suffer a blow in connection with Churchill.

Also in the States, *Readers Digest* ran a lengthy feature story about Churchill to mark the occasion. Orson Welles narrated the release, via his *Mercury Records,* of the original soundtrack to the movie based on Churchill's war memoirs called, *The Finest Hour.* That evening, Sir Alec Guinness appeared in living rooms throughout the United States and shared a special edition of *The Hallmark Hall of Fame*—this one featuring the paintings of Winston Churchill.

Official greetings made their way to Hyde Park Gate from the leaders of Canada, New Zealand, the Vatican, and South Africa. Marshall Tito sent wishes, as did Charles De Gaulle and Konrad Adenaur.

Next to the flowers from the queen and the warm expressions from his own family, Churchill was most moved by the birthday wishes from former US President, Dwight D. Eisenhower, who had worked closely and sometimes tensely with Churchill during another era as Supreme Commander of the Allied forces in Europe. Ike wrote: "He came to typify for me Britain's courage and perseverance in adversity, its conservatism in success, its valid pride in the glories of the past, its vision of future leadership responsibilities in the family of nations. He was an authentic spokesman for Britain's greatness of spirit. I cherish the warm friendship I enjoy with him. Americans prize his ancestral association with them. With all my heart I wish him a happy birthday."

Likely the oddest gift Winston received that day was from a group of admirers in Ireland, some potatoes, carrots, and tomatoes, packed in peat. Or maybe it was the Turkish cigarettes with filter tips sent by one American tobacco company to a man whose trademark was a cigar; though he did get a beautiful box of fifty cigars from the Swedish Cigar Club.

Randolph gave his father a couple of solid gold ashtrays that featured engravings of the Churchill family crest and Sarah gave him one of her paintings. Winston's daughter Mary and her husband gave him cigars and cologne. By the end of the day, there were nearly five hundred gifts in the house.

A mid-afternoon visit from Prime Minister Harold Wilson was a highlight of Churchill's day, their differences in political philosophy and affiliation notwithstanding. "I bring you the good wishes of the Cabinet," Wilson remarked. Churchill grinned and thanked him.

The birthday cake placed in the dining room for dinner was appropriately grand weighing in at one hundred twenty pounds and lathered with white icing. Accompanying the cake, were thirty pounds of fruit and fifty pounds of eggs. But the part of the massive dessert offering that stood out the most was the scroll adorning the front of the cake. It bore Churchill's words from the first volume of his international bestseller, *The Second World War*. "In war: resolution. In defeat: defiance. In victory: magnanimity. In peace: goodwill."

But the grand moment was fleeting. Within a few days the thrill had passed and Winston Churchill retreated into the familiar world of black dog.

CHAPTER FIVE

LYNDON JOHNSON DRESSED AS BILL MOYERS went through the talking points he had prepared for the morning briefing. There was a report about Vietnam from CIA Director John McCone. Johnson had been escalating America's involvement in Southeast Asia, primarily through McCone's agency and other "under-the-radar" means. Even in the aftermath of the incident in the Gulf of Tonkin the previous summer, Johnson still insisted on not letting the public, or even Congress, know much about what was really going on. Johnson knew that this unsettled McCone, but the president didn't know that the director had already made the decision to leave the job Kennedy appointed him to within the next few months.

En route to the Oval Office, Moyers went over some of the details for the upcoming inauguration. "Weather should be good, certainly better than four years ago." Lyndon frowned at the reference. While he often obsessed in his own mind about how he compared with his predecessor, he hated it when anyone else made even the most benign or indirect reference to Kennedy. "About forty degrees and cloudy, but no more snow, just the inch or so on the ground now."

"Uh-huh, what about the crowd? Anybody got the balls to predict that?"

"Well, sir, all indications are that you'll be making your speech before the largest inauguration crowd ever assembled."

"Well, we'll see. Got my speech?"

"Yes, Mr. President, the latest draft is already on your desk."

"Good—you get Bob Hardesty involved? I like how that fellow writes. Save that egghead Dick Goodwin for the heavy lifting, all that policy stuff, like that Great Society speech last May in Ann Arbor. I want Hardesty all over this one."

"Yes, he's has been a great addition to the team. He went over it and made some recommendations."

"Well, Billy boy, I want your fingerprints on it too. And like I told Hardesty, I want a short speech. Short and to the point. Four letter words, four word sentences, and four sentence paragraphs. None of that flowery Ted Sorenson shit, either. Real words for real people. Stand up. Speak up. Shut up. That's what my pappy always said to the preacher. You've got to write it so that the woman who cleans the building across the street can understand it."

"I agree, sir, and I think you're gonna like what you see."

"You'd better hope so, Moyers. Time's a-running out."

They entered the president's office. When LBJ was seated at his desk, Moyers said, "There's one other thing I want to bring to your attention, sir."

"Fire away, and then get out so I can get some work done. And send in Reedy."

"I will, sir. Now, that one thing is this: the British ambassador is asking for a private meeting with you this morning. Very short notice. It's not really an official request, but something he wants to talk with you about personally."

"Ormsby-Gore, right?"

"Yes, David Ormsby-Gore. He was appointed by MacMillan back in '61."

"I remember. He's a Kennedy pal. He and Jack went way back to when old Joe Kennedy was over there before the war. Kennedy lobbied for his appointment. Odd thing, I thought at the time."

"Yes, the ambassador spent a lot of time with Jack; they traveled together some. Word has it that he's not been the same since Dallas. Depressed, grieving, and such."

"What does he want to talk about?"

"No clue, sir. But he's insistent that it's very important that he speak to you, and he emphasizes that it needs to be a personal and private meeting."

"Okay, give him ten minutes this morning, but stay close. Now get out. I want to read this masterpiece of a speech you and your egghead friends have written for me."

∗

It was early afternoon in London, and Harold Wilson also had a very important speech to prepare. He had cleared his schedule, dedicating the rest of the day to work on it in his private study. He did not know exactly when the address needed to be completely finished, but he knew soon after Sir Winston passed on, there would be a moment of great significance in the House of Commons. He would deliver a message from Her Majesty the Queen, and he would then be expected to speak in favor of her motion. He was determined that this important political moment would not be squandered.

Wilson's father was an industrial chemist in the Yorkshire town of Huddersfield, where young Harold grew up. The new prime minister was now forty-eight years-old, but years earlier he had boasted a brilliant academic career, including a scholarship to Oxford University. He became a lecturer in economics at Oxford at the tender age of twenty-one. He also had a reputation for socialist sympathies, which made the Labor Party a natural fit for him.

When Winston Churchill was leading the war effort in the 1940s, Wilson served as the statistical director at the Ministry of Fuel and Power. He ran for a seat in Parliament in 1945—and won as part of the Labor victory that ousted Churchill. A couple of years later, Prime Minister Clement Attlee tapped Wilson to become president of the Board of Trade, a role similar to that of the US Secretary of Commerce. In fact, at that time Wilson was the youngest man to serve in a British Cabinet in the twentieth century. Younger even—as he never tired of mentioning—than Winston Churchill himself was at the dawn of his own storied career.

Over the next decade, Wilson often found himself to be the odd man out when it came to going along with the Labor Party leadership. But with the sudden—some said mysterious—death of Labor Party leader and presumed one-day Prime Minister Hugh Gaitskell in January 1963, right about the time Mr. Kim Philby was on a slow boat to Russia, Harold Wilson emerged as the leader of the Labor Party. And when Harold MacMillan retired, Wilson was the newly anointed occupant 10 Downing Street.

Wilson was a consummate politician and knew how to make a speech, but this was different. He would be eulogizing one of the most eloquent men who had ever uttered a word in the English language. Add to that the fact that he would not only be speaking to a House Chamber filled beyond capacity, but the BBC would broadcast his speech live to households throughout the United Kingdom and much of the rest of the world. Wilson was determined to create memorable words about an unforgettable man.

He was also determined to write it himself—just as Churchill had written all of his own speeches. His speeches always felt extemporaneous, but in fact, Winston labored over every word, every time.

Wilson sat at his desk and stared at the half-written page. He puffed on his pipe and then put it on an ashtray, picked up his pen, and resumed writing: *"We meet today in this moment of tribute, of spontaneous sympathy this House feels for Lady Churchill and all the members of his family—"*

Shortly after ten a.m., David Ormsby-Gore, the British Ambassador to the United States, was ushered into the Oval Office. Lyndon Johnson was seated at his desk, apparently immersed in something he was reading. Juanita Roberts, the president's personal secretary, waited an awkward moment and then said, "Mr. President? Sir?"

Johnson looked up and looked surprised. "What is it, Juanita?"

"Your appointment's here. The British Ambassador, sir."

Ormsby-Gore stood by in silence and reflected on how things had changed. There was a time when he needed no appointment for an Oval Office meeting. He could just pop over. But that was then. Now there was a new sheriff in town. A cowboy from Texas, not a gentleman from New England. On the ride over to the White House from the embassy, Ormsby-Gore had gotten lost in his memory bank. It was filled with moments involving the man who, just fourteen months earlier, had lived in the famous house on Pennsylvania Avenue. He recalled how they had become friends at first sight. Back then, they were both second sons to famous men, never seeming to measure up to their older siblings or paternal expectations.

But history had other plans. They would reach the pinnacle of power, one as a great leader, and the other as a great manipulator.

Ormsby-Gore came back to himself as Juanita went back to her desk in the outer office and Johnson stood up, removed his glasses, and furiously rubbed his eyes. "Mr. Ambassador," he said, "so great to see you. What can I do for you today?" He motioned for his guest to sit in a chair across from his desk, yet another sign as to how things had changed. No longer was the Oval Office a welcoming place, one where two friends had gossipy bull sessions. Now it was a formal place and all about the business at hand. Even the desk was new, the ambassador noted with a measure of sadness. Gone was JFK's ornate *Resolute Desk*, a gift from Queen Victoria to President Rutherford B. Hayes. Jackie Kennedy found it languishing in a White House storage area and ordered its restoration for her husband. Johnson replaced it with his own desk, the one he had used when he was majority leader of the Senate.

"Mr. President, I'm very grateful for this meeting. Thank you for your time, which I know is precious."

Johnson nodded at him and crossed his arms. "I know you loved President Kennedy like a brother, and I continue to grieve with you over his loss. Every time I come into this office, I have a sense of duty inspired by that great man." Lyndon had a way of pouring it on. His real feelings certainly fell short of this statement, but he was a master at using the weaponry of words.

Truth was, while there was a small part of Johnson that admired Kennedy's grace and charisma, he was filled for the most part with negative feelings, from envy, to contempt, to frustration. The frustration was due to the fact that he knew that the whole Camelot myth about the Kennedy years that was becoming chiseled in cultural stone was all bullshit. Johnson understood the give and take of hard-ball politics, something that JFK was very uncomfortable with. The new president had accomplished more when it came to legislation and policy than Kennedy ever did—or could. And it pissed the president off to no end that most Americans were still so filled with shock and grief about Kennedy's death that Lyndon was hardly noticed. At least to his thinking.

It was like that little runt—as he preferred to think of him—Bobby Kennedy had said at the Democratic convention the previous summer when he quoted those sappy lines from *Romeo and Juliet,* "When he shall die, cut him into little stars, and he shall make the face of heaven so fond, that all the world will fall in love with night and pay no worship to the garish sun." Johnson knew Bobby meant for people to understand that Johnson was the garish sun and JFK was all the pretty little stars. But he also knew how to turn on the humility and charm when it served his interests.

"I am touched by your words, Mr. President. And I know you are already a great president and will lead this country with vision and strength for many years to come. One of the greatest contributions my late friend made to this country was when he chose you to run with him in 1960."

"Thank you, Mr. Ambassador," Johnson said, finding himself surprisingly moved by the sentiment.

"Mr. President, I am sure you know that Mr. Churchill is near death. The information I have is that he will, indeed, pass on to his reward sometime in the next few days. We are, of course, following a plan—a very detailed plan—that has been in place for many years. The old great man has scared us a few times. Sir Winston is a man of history, and his passing will end an era."

"I agree. He's a great man."

"Indeed. But I did not ask for this time to rehearse all of Mr. Churchill's exploits. Rather, I wanted to talk with you personally about something that has come to my attention."

"Okay, fine. I'm listening."

"Well, Mr. President, first off, you need to know what I am about to share did not come my way through, shall we say, official channels. Nor am I really here in my official role as Ambassador. I know this sounds rather odd, but I need you to know this."

Johnson just nodded affirmatively, while his eyes grew narrow, almost as if he was squinting. He said nothing.

Ormsby-Gore continued, "Thank you, sir, for understanding. Here's what I know: I've picked up on some talk—what those in your intelligence service might call chatter—emanating from certain quarters, that if and when the great man passes, his funeral might become the stage or backdrop for a major international incident."

"Incident?"

"Yes, well, I know I am being awfully cryptic, but please bear with me."

Bearing with anyone was not Lyndon Johnson's best trait, but he indicated again that he was listening.

"Because of my position, I have to distance myself from reacting to mere gossip or partial information. Our embassy is a breeding ground for such things. It's just that because of what we have seen in the past, there are some things worth taking with much more than the proverbial grain of salt. And my information on this comes from a similar place as some of the things I was hearing in the aftermath of President Kennedy's tragic death," he said. He paused to garner control of his emotional mix of grief and guilt. In reality, he knew deep down that he had been hearing things even *before* Jack was killed. But that was to remain the Ambassador's sad and dark secret for several decades.

Johnson just stared at his guest.

Ormsby-Gore resumed by saying, "It's the Soviet Union. It seems that there may be hardliners in the Kremlin who have designs on Western Europe and would love any opportunity to take action."

"Opportunity? What the hell are you talking about, Mr. Ambassador? Break it down to the nut gut."

Ormsby-Gore was not familiar with that particular expression, one that Johnson was fond of using, but he discerned the essence. The president wanted the bottom line.

"Of course, well, what I'm talking about, the nut gut as you call it, is the fact that while leaders from around the world are in London to pay respects to Mr. Churchill, it would be a great time for some dramatic incident, even attack, that would instantly serve to create the kind of chaos that could become a smokescreen—or cover, as you might say here in America—for aggressive action."

"You mean a military move?"

"That is certainly one possible scenario."

"You think they actually have such a plan?"

"Mr. President, I don't know if you know much about my background, but I have dealt with the Soviets for many years." Johnson and the world had no idea just how closely. "They want the world, but they don't want to fight a world war. If they can move swiftly to effectively neutralize any opposition, they would love to turn all of Europe into their playground."

"Khrushchev was ousted last summer, and we don't have all that much solid information about what is happening in the Kremlin," Johnson countered. He had personally been grateful for the timing of the odd and surprising news out of Moscow the previous October. It had helped to bury a potentially embarrassing news item that had just broken, having to do with one of Johnson's trusted aides being arrested on a "morals" charge in the middle of a political campaign.

"I may be able to help you there, Mr. President. My sense is those in charge are more hardline than Khrushchev. These are the men who wanted to go to war over Cuba, a war they were confident they could win."

"Even nuclear war?"

"Yes, at least a tactical nuclear war. They were ready to annihilate American troops on the beaches had there been an invasion in 1962."

"Yes, I've read reports about that from our people."

"I believe they are waiting for a moment to bring their global vision to pass. And the gathering of more than one hundred heads of state in one room, well, such an opportunity may prove too hard to resist."

"Yes, but there'd be international outrage—certainly the United Nations would oppose them."

"Of course they would, if—that's the key word—*if* their fingerprints were clearly on whatever sparked such a scenario."

"What do you mean?" Lyndon Johnson sat up in his swivel chair and leaned forward. He was completely engaged in what he now saw as much more than some kind of perfunctory or ceremonial meeting with a high-level diplomat. David Ormsby-Gore was giving him valuable information, even more than his own intelligence advisors.

"A *false flag* operation. Suppose something catastrophic should happen, something that, say, killed seventy-five world leaders. And what if such an event were made to look like the work of one of many possible terrorist groups, for example— and just an example here, mind you—the IRA?"

"False flag? You saying they'd make it look like an Irish terrorist job?"

"What I'm suggesting, Mr. President, is that they are quite good at misdirection and are more than capable of using the IRA without the IRA never knowing why they were doing it. I have it on good authority that they have had agents inside the IRA for many years."

"This is very serious, Mr. Ambassador. I need to look into this."

"Of course. But, sir, please leave me and my government out of it. Prime Minister Wilson is not someone to talk to about this. He is unschooled in such things and also not trustworthy with information." The ambassador also had good reason to believe that Wilson was a diehard sympathizer with Soviet Russia, though not publicly.

Johnson was struck by how his guest spoke of the new British Prime Minister, but he decided not to pursue this line with Ormsby-Gore. "Okay, David—may I call you David?"

"By all means, Mr. President."

"How about over here, our intelligence services—what about them? You were around President Kennedy a lot and have a sense about this, I'd imagine."

"Indeed, sir, I do. Frankly, I wouldn't take this through the official channels, but rather find a way to look into it behind the scenes. Maybe someone who knows how the intelligence world works, but isn't working these days for the government. Maybe someone like Allen Dulles. I've always held him in high esteem, even when President Kennedy fired him."

"Well, you know I put him on that Warren Commission. That's a great idea. I think I'll run all this by him. And I promise, I'll leave your name out of it."

"I'd be ever so grateful, sir. I'm going to be resigning soon and going home, and I'd rather do so quietly. I just felt like I needed to step up and share what I know, or at least think I know, with you, Mr. President."

As soon as David Ormsby-Gore left, President Johnson picked up his phone, almost violently, and shouted, "Moyers, get me Allen Dulles!"

"I'll have him on the line in a minute or so, sir."

"Not on the phone, you jackass! Get him *here* within the hour."

"Yes sir!"

CHAPTER SIX

MICHAEL WHEELAN FINISHED HIS PINT of Guinness and thought for a long moment about having a second drink. He was due back at work for another quarter-hour. He had devoured his lunch, consisting of two scotch eggs, but found himself still hungry. Maybe it was the boredom. Things were slow at work—Newman Brothers Coffin Works around the corner from the pub, on Fleet Street. Nothing much going on there, so he smiled at the young lady behind the bar and said, "Might I have one more, Maggie?"

"My pleasure," she said, with a smile of her own. It was a mild flirtation that had been going on during the lunch hour most days over the past few years. "Here you go." She handed him the glass, though the head had far from settled.

"Thank you, my dear."

"Two glasses today, is it Mr. Wheelan? You in a celebratin' mood?"

"Nothing of the kind. Just a bit bored. That's all."

"Well, you work on boxes for dead bodies all day, I would say one would get tired of that grind. How long you been at Newman's?"

"Going on eight years now, I guess," he said, with a look of surprise on his face.

"It's honest work. And I guess you never run out of customers," she laughed.

"Right you are, Maggie dear."

"Been a while since I saw that handsome son of yours around here. Does he still live with you?"

"No, he moved to London last year. Got himself a fine job with the government."

"Are you proud or pissed? After all, I've heard you go on about the crown and such. You being an Irish patriot and all."

"One day things will change. In the meantime, I'm just glad the lad is moving up in the world. Molly and I may need him to care for us one day."

"Ah yes, Molly. You need to bring her in again soon," she said. Then she looked up at the clock and said, "Haven't you better finish that drink and be on your way?"

He looked up and saw the time and grabbed his glass, draining it. "Ah, delicious. Until tomorrow, my dear." He raced out the door, pulling his coat on as he pushed the heavy door and walked into the cold air. Just before he turned the corner and walked back toward Newman Brothers, he saw a familiar face on the opposite corner. The two men made eye contact, and Michael made his way across the road toward the other man.

"Looks like the rain has stopped for a bit," the man on the corner said.

"Indeed. I did not expect to see you today."

"When have I ever announced my arrival?"

"True."

"I have something for you, my friend."

"You do? Well, I should say it is about time. I've been here forever and nothing. Beginning to wonder."

"Ah, Michael my boy, as I told you when I arranged for your job through my contacts in the local labor union, one day you would be called on to help in a matter. Today is that day."

"I guess I was celebrating, after all," Michael smiled.

"I'm sorry?"

"Oh, nothing. Just a thought. How can I help you today?"

The man Michael knew only by the name "Yuri" handed him a small envelope. He then said, "Note inside will explain. Best of luck to you, Michael." And "Yuri" walked up the block the other way.

Michael walked back to work, and a when he found a private moment, he opened the envelope. It contained a key and a two sentences type-written note: "Go straight home with the key after work. Destroy this envelope and page."

＊

Michael and Molly Wheelan had worked for Soviet intelligence for nearly thirty years. Their twenty-four-year-old son, Sean, had also joined the effort, though he was living and working these days in London. Michael was a graduate of the University of Oxford, and it was there, in the years before World War II, that he was exposed to the ideas behind communism. Though the recruitment of spies at Cambridge University was more pronounced and fruitful, the Soviet influence at Oxford was significant.

Wheelan had been told several times that he was one of the most promising recruits, seen as someone who could effectively be buried deep in the movement to "liberate" Northern Ireland from British rule, a cause ready-made for exploitation by the Soviets. The combination of Marxist ideology and the burning desire to see Northern Ireland free from British control made him vulnerable to recruitment by the NKVD, the forerunner to the KGB.

His Soviet handler, a man he only knew as "Viktor," introduced Michael to Molly McNally, the daughter of a Belfast newspaperman, someone also sympathetic to communist ideas. The Soviets were always on the lookout for ways to exploit the Irish struggle, just as they did with other struggles around the globe in their quest to destroy capitalism. Dissatisfaction, anger, and oppression were all kindling used to fuel the fires of revolution. But the Russians had to be careful not to tip their hand. The IRA wanted Northern Ireland to be free from the crown for political, as well as religious reasons. So their Irish Catholic faith made any actual alliance with the godless communists—as the Soviets were so often called—unlikely, if not impossible.

The Wheelans lived in Birmingham, a city of industry, and home of a strong labor movement. Michael, though proudly Irish, had actually lived there all of his life, other than his Oxford days. His parents had moved there in the 1920s from Port Stewart, a small town in Londonderry County on the coast of Northern Ireland. Michael's father, now deceased, had earned his doctorate at Queens University in Belfast, and joined the faculty at the University of Birmingham a few years later, teaching history and philosophy.

Michael grew up in a comfortable, quiet, and loving home, which was odd considering the turn his life had taken. Most spies had an ax to grind, one which began with family. But the years before World War II were unique, as a global economic crisis paved the way for the rise of fascism. It was the battle against fascism, in places like Germany, Italy, and Spain, which attracted so many naive young people to the leftist "Popular Front," which was, in fact, a movement orchestrated and manipulated by the "Comintern"—the Communist International. It was the brain-child of Josef Stalin and company as a vehicle for the advancement of global communism.

The non-aggression pact the Soviet Union signed with the Nazis in 1939 was an eye-opener to a great number of students in Britain who had flirted with communism. The unlikely alliance was confusing and disillusioning, and for many their flirtation with the works of Marx and Engels ended then and there.

But not everyone.

That turned out to be the moment which separated the merely curious from the fully devoted. Michael Wheelan was in the latter group. During the war, and then after, he served in various roles in the secretive Irish Republican Army (IRA), but his real allegiance was always to Moscow.

It was all part of a long laid plan to have someone in the right place at the right time. Or so they hoped. When it came to intelligence work, the Russians were willing to sit on a potential operation and wait for years, even decades, for the right moment, if need be. And some of their intelligence operatives in Great Britain had informed the Russians early on, that part of the detailed plan for the eventual funeral for Winston Churchill would include having a large and ornate casket outfitted at Newman Brothers in Birmingham, where Michael "happened" to be employed.

A large casket had already been built. All that was needed were some finishing touches—a Newman Brothers specialty. Michael's job was simple. When the time approached, he was to make sure some specific materials were hidden in the coffin. He was not sure what the materials were (though he had a good idea). He had been told by his handler that they would be supplied when they were needed. So he waited and worked. He also read all the news out of London about the great man's final drift toward death.

∗

The afternoon seemed to crawl by as Michael attended to his duties at Newman Brothers. He overheard one of his bosses talking to a secretary about Churchill's condition and how he expected a call any day for the special coffin to be sent to London. But there was no update on that yet.

Michael got home shortly after seven p.m., smiling when he smelled corned beef and cabbage. Molly served it on special occasions. And this evening—the one they'd been waiting for—was going to be special indeed.

But dinner would have to wait a few minutes. Molly took Michael into their bedroom. "I had a visitor a bit ago," she said, with a slightly wicked smile.

"Oh?" he replied, deciding to hear what she had to say before he told her *his* news.

"Yes, a woman came to see me. She did not look familiar. But there was something about her. She was carrying a satchel. And she called me by name and asked if she could come in. I was a bit uneasy, but I let her in."

"I see," Michael said.

She continued, "She told me that she had something for you—the satchel. It was locked, but she told me that you would know what to do. Odd, isn't it?"

Michael smiled at her and then took her into his arms and kissed her passionately.

"Why Mr. Wheelan, why are we being so fresh?"

"Is that a complaint?"

She smiled and said, "Not at all. I like fresh."

"Now, before we get back to that business, we have other business, my sweet Molly. You see, I had a visitor of my own today. Actually, we talked on a street corner after my lunch."

"The Pub?"

"Yes, of course."

"And how was that Maggie girl today?"

"I am sure she was fine, but you are missing my point."

"Just wanting to be sure that some other filly isn't lighting the fire that you brought home with you."

"Not a chance, Molly. Now, let me finish my story. This man...you know him. It was 'Yuri'—the man who set up my employment at Newman Brothers."

Molly thought for a moment and then nodded that she remembered him. "What did he say?"

"Not much, but he gave me an envelope. It contained a key, which I imagine is how to unlock that satchel. The question is, do we unlock it first, or do we unlock your knickers first?"

Molly blushed, something that came easy to the red-haired girl. "That can wait, my love—let's open the curious bag."

With that, Michael opened the satchel. He and Molly looked at its contents for a long moment and then looked at each other, confusion on their faces. "I suppose I should read the note," he said.

The note was actually a three-page set of instructions. First, a description of the materials. "Semtex, plastic explosive, 18 ounces" was the main item. Then there were two items that resembled cameras, or radios—one larger, one smaller. The instructions were straightforward. Michael had read about the fairly new development in explosives—particularly the creation of a pliable and stable plastic material out of Czechoslovakia, and he assumed this was what he had received from his Soviet masters.

"So what is it you're to do with all this, Michael?"

"Simple, my beautiful flower. I'm to hide explosives and a detonator in the casket reserved for Mr. Churchill. Then we're to travel to London and deliver the remote detonator to someone. Yuri will make sure we know who and when. Then we'll watch what happens when his coffin explodes in the church as his funeral service is underway," Michael said. He was overwhelmed with emotion at the thought that he and Molly were going to fulfill their purpose for moving to Birmingham.

Molly gasped and covered her mouth with her hand. She had no love for Churchill or anything he stood for. He had long been the enemy of everything she held dear. But such an act would not only destroy his remains, it would kill many, many others in the church.

"But so many will die," she said.

"Apparently, that's the plan. Our people know that the room will be filled with world leaders and it's clear that they have a grand plan to change the course of history."

"My—oh, my," Molly said. "I need a whiskey."

"Let's have a glass of Tullamore Dew and toast the success of our operation."

"Yes to the whiskey, but I was thinking more of steadying me nerves," she said with a faltering smile.

"I agree about the whiskey, and I have a great way to steady your nerves," he said. He poured two large glasses of whiskey. After handing one of the glasses to his wife, he led her by the hand toward their small bedroom.

A short while later, they ate the wonderful supper Molly had prepared. Then Michael Wheelan spent much of the evening thinking about how to accomplish his assigned task. He decided to go back to *Newman Brothers* in the middle of the night to get everything done. He had a key to the place, although the owner never knew it. His handler had obtained it for him. He had never used it—never had the occasion to. But on this night it would come in handy.

Shortly before two a.m., he entered the building on Fleet Street and went to the room where the casket designated for Mr. Churchill was being stored. He needed to hide the materials in a way so that they would be difficult to discover—that part was obvious to him—and he had a plan, something he had devised during his post-supper meditations.

Michael opened the casket and, using a torch he had brought with him, examined it from head to foot. He hoped the batteries in his light held out. He felt around the area at the foot of the rectangular box, thinking it would be best to conceal something at that end rather than the head. *No one looks at a dead man's feet*, he thought.

He carefully pulled the fabric away from the floor of the box, revealing some foam cushion customary in casket lining. It was much more pliable than the plastic explosive he was working with, but he was sure he could make it work. He continued to pull on the fabric, surprised at how easily it came loose, until he had exposed nearly half the box—the half that would remain closed even if the head of the casket remained open for viewing.

Then he saw something that surprised him. There was metal where wood would normally be. This was an expensive oak casket. One fit for royalty or a man who has held high office. He quickly realized the casket was lined with lead. Michael was familiar with the idea, of course. Many people believed the lining protected the loved one's remains from the elements, or at least significantly delayed the impact of water, bugs, and such. Michael was fairly sure the people he worked for had not anticipated the presence of the metal. He wondered how it would factor in when it came to the power of an explosion.

Before he got too anxious, he noticed the lead had been applied in sections. There were clear seams. He wondered if he could somehow pull up a couple of the sections, but he didn't want to do any noticeable damage. He found a spot at the intersection of the casket wall and floor. Using a tool from a nearby workbench, he probed the seam and then pulled at it a bit. He rolled the lining back about an inch. It peeled almost like tin foil, only somewhat thicker.

Then it hit him—the perfect solution.

Michael spent the better part of the next thirty minutes carefully—very carefully—removing two sections of the metal lining from the floor of the casket. He then went to the satchel provided by his handlers and cleared off a section on the top of the workbench. He removed some of the plastic explosive from its wrapping and began to mold it. After a few minutes, he had created a flat pie-crust-like section, which he then spread on the casket floor.

He repeated this several times, and removed two more sections of the lead lining to make all the materials fit, with little residue left over. It was a big casket, for a big man, and that worked to Wheelan's advantage. There was plenty of available floor space in the box.

Then he pondered where to put the small receiver—one tied to another device. The idea was that the explosive could only be detonated remotely, but the person pushing the button had to be within one hundred feet of the materials. The receiver would start a clock, which would count down toward detonation. Michael assumed this was so the person activating the device would have time to move a safe distance away.

Michael decided to put the receiver in the left corner of the casket, and he inserted four wires directly into the plastic explosive. He wasn't worried about it detonating, since the companion device was a few miles away back at his house. He smiled with satisfaction as he replaced the foam and fabric and made sure the inside of the casket was once again in pristine condition. Then he gathered the scraps around him, put the purloined lead sheets in the satchel, and policed the area so there would be no hint anyone had disturbed anything.

Michael was back home a little after five o'clock that morning. He put the satchel on the floor near the bed and quietly crawled under the covers next to Molly. She rolled over and smiled at him.

"Everything is all set," he told her.

Their part was over—but for the trip to London and passing off of the detonator. They were both relieved. They made love again and then drifted back to sleep.

CHAPTER SEVEN

As ALLEN DULLES HURRIED to answer the summons from President Johnson, he was lost in thought. This was the second time Kennedy's successor had reached out to him. It was nice to be back on the inside, he thought, after having experienced the Kennedy-treatment following the Bay of Pigs debacle. Dulles had assumed Kennedy would never let such an operation fail, and gambled that all protestations aside, American military might would support the fledgling and failing Cubans who were dying on that awful beach back in '61.

Being fired by a man who hadn't even been born when Dulles began his diplomatic career was humiliating. Allen smiled a bit at the thought of the irony having been asked by President Johnson to be part of the small team conducting the "official" investigation into Kennedy's assassination. He also found it hard to resist a trip down memory lane as he drove toward a parking area after entering a White House gate. It was still hard for him to believe that his older brother John Foster

Dulles had been gone nearly six years. He fought a long battle with colon cancer, yet managed to continue to serve as Secretary of State under President Eisenhower. Those were heady days. Allen running the CIA and John running the State Department. They owned the city. Not too bad for a couple of preacher's kids from way up in Watertown, New York. Not anymore. But then again, maybe Johnson had something big for him. He parked and walked into the West Wing.

Bill Moyers was thrilled that he had managed to produce Allen Dulles within the hour, as Johnson had angrily insisted. In fact, when Dulles walked into the Oval Office, Moyers noted he had two minutes to spare. But he didn't mention it to the president.

The former CIA director had a ruddy complexion, and his hair was both receding and graying significantly. He sported a small mustache and rimless glasses, which seemed to accent the keenness of his blue eyes. He had graduated from Princeton in 1916 and entered government service as a diplomat that same year. He was stationed in Bern, Switzerland as America entered the Great War in 1917. He was assigned to the American delegation to the Paris Peace Conference following the war, and few years later he enrolled in law school at George Washington University. After graduation in 1926, he went to work for his older brother's law firm in New York. He was recruited by the Office of Strategic Services (O.S.S.) shortly after the attack on Pearl Harbor and moved back to Bern, where he oversaw vast espionage operations. Dulles went to work for the Central Intelligence Agency in 1947, and became its director in 1953—a position he held until Kennedy sacked him in '61.

On this day, as he entered the Oval Office, he was wearing a gray herringbone jacket and black slacks. He walked briskly toward the president's desk and said, "Good morning, Mr. President. I'm at your service, sir."

"Allen, welcome. Thanks for stopping by on such short notice."

"My pleasure, Mr. President, always glad to be of help— but I'm curious as to what this is about?"

"We'll get there, my friend. What's your poison?"

Dulles looked at his watch. It was seven minutes past eleven o'clock in the morning. He said, "Well, it's five o'clock somewhere, I suppose. I'm fine with what you're having."

"Great," Johnson said as he grabbed his phone. "Bring two glasses of Cutty, two fingers each, for me and the director, and add some water and ice." That was code. It meant to make his own drink weak—more water than scotch, a game LBJ liked to play, always looking for an edge. In less than a minute a steward brought the drinks and quickly left.

"Allen, you and the boys did a great job on the Kennedy thing. I know some have been critical, but you were thorough and fair. Most of all, you helped to put the whole thing behind us, and I know that helped me in the election."

"Thank you, sir. I feel that we did the job we were asked to do," Dulles replied, lighting his ever-present pipe. It was a mark of his self-confidence that he didn't bother to ask the president's permission to smoke. As far as the just-completed "Kennedy thing" was concerned, he knew the Warren Commission was more about political theater than real fact-finding. He also knew his role was primarily to protect his former agency, as well as the one watched over by Mr. Hoover, so there were many details deliberately left out of the voluminous Warren Commission record. Details such as the existence of past attempts by the CIA to assassinate Fidel

Castro and agency's tortured strange-bedfellows' relationship with the Mafia.

"You up for another assignment?" Johnson asked, shifting gears from small talk.

"Always honored to serve my country and my president."

"Well, this one is more up your alley, Allen. But it's one that you're gonna to have to handle pretty much on your own—at least at first."

"All right…what can I do for you, sir?"

Lyndon Johnson then briefed Allen Dulles on what the British ambassador had told him. He admonished his guest that he didn't want a word of it to see the light of day. Dulles was simply to find out—and fast—whether there might be anything to what Ormsby-Gore had warned.

"You don't seem surprised by what I'm telling you here," the president noted. The veteran spy took it all in stride.

"I wish I could tell you what you're telling me is surprising, but I can't. I've caught wind of something like this a few times—back when I was the director, and even since," Dulles told Johnson.

"You mean lately, Allen?"

Dulles puffed on his pipe, blew some smoke, and said, "Has McCone ever briefed you about the Soviet defector we've been working with since late '61? His name is Golitsyn, Anatoly Golitsyn."

Johnson replied, "Not that I recall. Who the hell is he? What's his story?"

"Well, sir, it's a long and complicated one. He came out through Helsinki, brought his wife and daughter too. High-up KGB official. Now, mind you, this all happened after my watch ended, after Mr. Kennedy let me go. But I've maintained close contact with many in the agency, as you might imagine."

"And as I hope. Allen, we need you in the loop, just like I needed to keep Hoover over at the FBI. You men know where the bodies are buried, or should be buried," the president said, with a slight smile.

Dulles nodded stoically and continued, "Well, some of my former associates set up a meeting between me and this Golitsyn fellow. They brought him to my house once, and then we met a couple of other times after that. Something he said made me think that our 'friends' in the Kremlin have some pretty grand plans."

"What kind of plans?"

"For one thing, Golitsyn believes that Harold Wilson, the British Prime Minister, is a Soviet agent."

"What the hell?" Johnson barked.

"I know, I know, it sounds far-fetched, but this defector says he was in a position to know about plans. He told us there were plans to make sure those sympathetic to Soviet aims would rise to power. So when that British Labor leader Hugh Gaitskell died, it was really murder made to look like natural causes, to pave the way for Wilson to become prime minister. And you may recall, the reason Labor was elected in the first place had to do with that spy scandal back in '63—the Profumo thing."

"Yeah, I think Jack Kennedy was watching that one pretty close, sweating it out. There were some connections over here. I think one of his girlfriends was connected."

"Indeed, that's why his brother had that East German girl, Ellen Rometsch, deported so quickly."

"I remember," Johnson said. Of course, he also remembered how close he had personally gotten to being burned by that same flame. He thought. He drifted for a moment thinking about how his old protégé Bobby Baker was up to his balls in that scandalous world—a time bomb waiting to explode and spray shrapnel all over Johnson's career. When he became the president, one of the first things Johnson had done was to reach out to J. Edgar Hoover, promising the man job security in exchange for the director's help with his Baker problem.

Dulles looked across the desk and waited, as Johnson seemed to be lost in thought. Then he continued, "Well, we have no real way to confirm any of this, but this defector has given us much good information in other areas. Angleton—you know him?"

"Who?"

"James Jesus Angleton, head of counterintelligence at Langley."

"I've heard of him, never met him, though."

"Well, he thinks this Golitsyn is a real defector, and he's even tried to warn his counterparts over at MI5 and MI6 in England. But I'm not sure where any of it's gone. Angleton also thinks, and this is from Golitsyn as well, the Brits have a problem with a highly-placed Soviet mole."

"You mean another guy like that man Philby?"

"Yes. And what's more, there's some indication we may have a similar problem over here."

"Shit, Allen. You tellin' me our own CIA has been infiltrated?"

"I'm not saying that, for sure, Mr. President, but I know the Soviets have been aggressively heading toward that goal for years. Problem is, another Russian approached us a few months ago, named Nosenko."

"What's his story?" Johnson asked.

"That's just the thing. His story is that Golitsyn is a double agent still working for the Soviets. Nosenko's information undercuts everything Golitsyn has told us."

Johnson sighed and took a long sip of his scotch. The ice had melted away. "Well, damn it all to hell, Allen. Which son-of-a-bitch is telling the truth?"

"Depends on who you ask, sir."

"I'm asking you, Allen," Johnson responded, angrily.

"I understand, Mr. President," Dulles countered, respectfully. "My instincts tell me that Golitsyn is the real thing and Nosenko has been sent to undermine him. But I must tell you, there are many at Langley who take a different view."

"Well, I trust your instincts, Allen. You just help me figure out what's going on. And be mighty careful who you talk to about any of what I just told you."

"I'll do my best, Mr. President. Give me twenty-four hours, and I'll report back to you. I'll be beyond discreet; you can count on that."

*

The former Director of the CIA had a long memory. And what Johnson had to say prompted it. He recalled in nearly perfect detail the development of a plan by the Pentagon war back in '57. It was called *DROPSHOT*—what NATO would do if the Soviets ever moved on Western Europe. Such a scenario wasn't as incredible as many would think. He assumed the basics of the plan were in place, or at least not far from being activated and mobilized. The first thing Dulles needed to do was check on the readiness of the plan. Then he had to somehow get word to a few key players that the upcoming convergence of world leaders on London would require not only intense security on-site, but also complete readiness on the part of American and NATO forces.

One person who might have a perspective was Air Force General Curtis LeMay. The well-known and colorful LeMay had advocated aggressive military action in Cuba in October 1962, and was doing the same these days about Vietnam. He talked about the need to bomb the North Vietnamese "back to the stone age," but such counsel fell on deaf ears in the Johnson White House. In fact, Dulles had heard rumors that LeMay was soon to retire, largely out of frustration with Johnson and his inherited Secretary of Defense, Robert McNamara. Maybe, Dulles thought, LeMay would help him. They had never been close, but they were both veterans of the days of the Cold War.

Dulles met LeMay at an apartment the former director maintained in Georgetown. After exchanging pleasantries, they talked through what Dulles had learned from the president.

"Can't say I'm surprised. Shit, the commies are evil bastards, and they'll only be stopped by one thing—brute force."

"I'm well aware of your feelings on the subject, General. But I don't see how any use of overt military might applies to the current situation. We have other tools than a hammer in our box."

LeMay didn't trust the Russians one bit. He saw Kennedy's handling of the Cuban Missile Crisis as appeasement. He was a "ready-fire-aim" kind of guy and also had his ear to the ground when it came to rumblings, rumors, and various kinds of chatter. So he took the rebuke from Dulles in stride and shifted gears.

LeMay suggested, "Find someone to send to London. Someone who can keep his trap shut, who knows how the cloak and dagger game is played."

At that moment Dulles thought of the perfect man for the job, but he didn't mention the name to LeMay.

"You're right, General. Absolutely right.

After meeting with Dulles, LeMay reached out to Edward Landsdale, another Air Force General, one who had a background with the old O.S.S. Luckily, Landsdale was in Washington for a few days, before heading back to Vietnam.

Dulles, LeMay, and Landsdale were all men of experience and discretion. They picked up the scent and followed a trail of clues they hoped would lead to hard evidence about the Soviets. They wanted it to be true. They felt that confrontation with the Soviets was inevitable and were committed to do all in their power to see America and its NATO allies kick their Bolshevik asses back to Russia and out of every inch of territory they had stolen in the aftermath of World War II.

And once Dulles briefed them about the man he wanted to send to London—they agreed unanimously.

CHAPTER EIGHT

DULLES WAS BACK at his office in less than twenty minutes. After taking off his coat and hat and attaching them to the appropriate hooks near the door, he walked directly over to a painting hanging on the wall to his left. It was a beautiful portrait of Bern, Switzerland's Old City.

The veteran spy always smiled a bit when he took a moment to look at the Bern scene. Fond memories usually followed—memories of his "cloak and dagger" days when he was "Wild Bill" Donovan's man there during the war, representing the OSS. Those days he lived at 23 Herrengasse and kept a close eye on the Nazis. But his favorite memory of Bern was from his days as part of America's delegation in the Swiss city during the earlier war—back in 1917. It was also one of his most painful recollections. It was a Sunday in April, and he had been alone in the office. He'd answered a telephone, and the caller was insistent about meeting with someone official. The man's English was poor and the accent thick.

"I'm sorry, but there's no one here to help you right now," Dulles told the caller that day.

"But I have a matter of historical significance to discuss," the caller replied.

"Let me take your name, and I'll have someone call you tomorrow."

"This is Lenin. Pity. Tomorrow will be too late."

And so, for years Dulles had been teaching young would-be spies the value of taking time to talk to a source, no matter how unpromising it seemed. Because at the moment of that telephone call, Vladimir Lenin was en route from Germany to St. Petersburg, Russia to start a revolution, courtesy of the Germans, who wanted Russia out of the war. They had made a deal with the man who would become the dictator of Russia. Dulles always wondered if Lenin might have been calling because he was interested in making a deal with the Americans, who were not quite yet in The Great War.

Now Dulles, though out of office "officially," was being tasked by the president of the United States to investigate a possible plot of gargantuan proportions.

He moved the portrait and began to work the dial on the safe hidden behind it. Moments later, he opened the door and rummaged through papers and other items until he found what he was hunting for. "There you are, old friend. Now let's see if you can help me." It was a small blue notebook, containing, among other things, contact information for old contacts still working for the agency he once ran. He flipped through the pages and quickly came to the name he needed.

*

The sun was fading in the western sky and beginning to slip into the shadows behind the beauty of the city. But as for Harvey Elton King, who enjoyed a walk and some fresh air in the late afternoon, he hated Rome. Not so much the city itself—all the history was fine enough. The fountains and all were beautiful. Though not a Catholic, he had no problem with the religion. No, he hated the place because of why he was there. The city on seven hills was his Siberia—a place of humiliating exile. He pulled a flask from his suit coat pocket and took a swig. He gritted his teeth as the booze went down. Then he turned a corner and headed back to his spartan office.

At one time, King had been thought of as a living legend in intelligence circles. Some still thought so. But not those whose opinions mattered. People like John McCone, the director of the CIA, appointed by President Kennedy after the unceremonious firing of Allen Dulles in the wake of what was quickly being referred to as the Bay of Pigs fiasco.

King had survived the house cleaning when Dulles was swept out. But he hadn't survived the wrath of Robert F. Kennedy after another famous Caribbean episode involving Soviet missiles in Cuba—that one working out somewhat better for the good guys. While the world applauded President Kennedy as a peacemaker who had brought the world back from the brink of thermo-nuclear catastrophe, big changes had to be made far out of plain sight. America's policy toward Cuba changed with the promise Kennedy made to his Soviet counterpart. He had assured Mr. Khrushchev that, among other concessions, America would not invade Cuba.

Problem was, Harvey King and a whole cast of characters, from CIA agents and operatives, to Cubans exiled in Miami, to members of the Mafia, were united in a common and compelling mission to kill Fidel Castro and make Cuba like it was before the infamous revolution.

Free and profitable.

Harvey was mad as hell when Bobby Kennedy told him to close up shop. They argued. King was half-drunk in one key meeting and had some choice words for the attorney general. His tirade ended with, "And you and your glamour boy brother can go straight to hell."

Next stop: Siberia near the Mediterranean.

*

Harvey King was back at his desk and finishing his fifth belt of scotch of the day. He was also trying to focus on some papers he kept shuffling. It was approaching six o'clock in the evening local time. As the CIA Chief of Station, King seldom went home before seven o'clock, or his seventh drink—whichever came first. His telephone buzzed and he reached for it, punching the button for line two. He succeeded the second time he tried.

"Mr. King, there's a call from Washington," the professional sounding female voice said from the speaker tethered to the desk phone by a single wire.

"Who is it?"

"The caller wouldn't say, just insisted he be put through."

"Fine. I'll take it."

"Yes, sir. Just stay on the line, and I'll connect you," she said.

He heard the customary click and nearly shouted, "King here. Who's calling?"

"Relax, Harvey. It's Allen."

"Allen who?" King asked. Then he let out a loud laugh and barked, "Ha! 'Course I know who it is. Been a long time, sport. To what do I owe a phone call from the world's most famous spook?"

"Cut the shit, King. I'm sure you've been hitting the sauce all day, but I need you sober as a judge, right now. I've got something serious for you. Can you get your ass on a plane back to Washington tonight? I need you here as soon as possible."

"What the hell you talking about, Dulles? What's so important that I need to drop everything and wing it home? Lyndon putting you back in charge of The Company because you did such a good job whitewashing the Kennedy thing in that Warren Report?"

Ignoring the dig, Dulles continued, "Now, Harvey, I know you have a tough time listening to anyone. But you'd better listen to me right now. This may be your big break out of the shit-house. Bobby Kennedy's in the Senate now, and the president has confidence in my judgment. He's given me an assignment. A big one. One that may save the world as we know it. *That* big. And I need you for it. So stop bellyaching. Put the cork in the bottle. Take a shower. Pack a clean shirt or two. There's a TWA flight from Rome to Idlewild that leaves in two hours. Make sure you're on it. Then take a train to Union Station here in DC. I'll send someone to pick you up and bring you over."

"Over where? Gotta give me at least that, Allen."

"The White House," Dulles replied. Then he hung up.

Harvey King moved the telephone from his ear, staring at it.

"Son of a bitch!"

∗

Immediately after talking to Harvey King in Rome, Dulles drove the short distance to Arlington, to the home of a man he regarded as a friend but had never quite understood. He was a quirky soul. Their meeting took place, as was usually the case when he came calling, in the greenhouse behind a spacious house located on a little less than five acres. That was where the orchids were.

James Jesus Angleton loved his orchids. He also loved the Central Intelligence Agency that he had served since its inception. These days, he was the agency's Chief of Counterintelligence.

Angleton was a thin, even frail-looking, man. He wore thick horn-rimmed glasses and chain-smoked cigarettes. He was also depressed, had been so for more than a year. The defection of Kim Philby, a man he had once regarded as a close friend, in January 1963 had devastated Angleton and further fueled his near-obsession with the idea of moles in the American intelligence community.

"Good to see you, as always, Allen," Angleton said when he saw his former boss walk into the greenhouse.

"You're looking good, Jim. Beautiful flowers. You have a gift."

"They're a gift to me, Allen. They comfort my mind." He paused. "What can I do for you? You're not one to make social calls."

"Guilty as charged, Jim. We have a situation. The president called me in. Off the record. McCone's not to know."

Angleton looked up and away from the flowers for the first time. He put the small gardening tool on a nearby table. "Understood, Allen. How can I help?"

"Well, I want your read on our cousins across the pond. Who can we trust over there?"

Angleton thought for a moment, measuring his words. "As far as I'm concerned, that fish stinks from the head. I've tried to warn my sources over there about Harold Wilson," he said. "I'm convinced that he's a KGB plant."

"I'm aware of your thoughts on that, Jim. I'm also aware that you're convinced that Anatoly Golitsyn is the real defector and that Yuri Nosenko is the double agent, even though most in the agency think differently."

"What do you want from me, Allen?" Angleton asked, with a note of irritation.

"I want your read on MI5. Who can we trust there if we need something?"

"Roger Hollis is also a KGB agent," Angleton replied firmly.

"Jim, surely you don't think everyone over there works for Moscow?"

"Of course not, Allen. But MI5 is compromised from the top down."

"The president's convinced there may be a terrorist attack on the horizon in conjunction with Churchill's funeral, when all the world leaders will be in London. In fact, he's so persuaded of this, I'm guessing he'll be staying home and skipping the big event."

Angleton looked surprised. "From where has Lyndon obtained this information?"

"I'm not at liberty—"

"Allen, you know me better than that. I need to know this."

Dulles sighed. "It comes from the British ambassador, but Johnson swore me to secrecy about this."

"Understood," Angleton said. He looked away for a moment and was quiet. Finally, he said, "And I believe the ambassador has unusually good contacts in Moscow."

Dulles, unsure what to make of that comment, continued on. "Harvey King is flying over from Rome. He'll be meeting with the president. I wanted Johnson to meet him face to face, but off the books. Then I'm sending King over to sniff around. Tiernan Brogan will go with him."

"They're good men, Allen. Anything I can do?"

"Yes, Jim. When the time comes, I may need you to contact someone you trust at MI5 with an important message."

"I'll be ready and waiting, my friend."

The two men looked at each other and broke into slight smiles. They had both been part of the great game for a long time.

"Could you pass me those shears?" Angleton asked, interrupting the moment.

*

Harvey King got to the airplane in Rome just as the doors were closing, but he made the flight. A while later, putting a twirl of pasta in his mouth, he was struck by a thought. The next day was January twentieth, the day Lyndon Johnson's inauguration was to take place. This fact made him even more curious. "Why am I going to the White House on such a day?" he wondered.

Just then, an attractive stewardess came by. "Would you care for a drink after dinner? Cognac, maybe?"

"Thanks, gorgeous, but I think I'll pass," he replied. She ignored his crude attempt at flirtation. He smiled at the absurdity of him—Harvey King—passing up anything having to do with alcohol. He reached for the newspaper he had been handed by someone just before takeoff. It was the European edition of the *New York Herald Tribune*.

Almost every story from page one to about halfway through had something to do with the impending demise of Winston Churchill. On the front page, only a couple of paragraphs were dedicated to the other big story of the day, the plans for Lyndon Johnson's big day.

CHAPTER NINE

LYNDON JOHNSON'S SPEECH was one of the shortest inaugural addresses on record. It took him just twenty-two minutes to share fifteen hundred words. Applause slowed him down a bit—he counted eleven sustained interruptions, and he mentioned that fact to friends throughout the day. And there was indeed a record-breaking crowd on hand. It was a Texas-sized affair from start to finish. Among the things he told his fellow Americans were these words: *"Our enemies have always made the same mistake. In my lifetime—in depression and in war—they have awaited our defeat. Each time, from the secret places of the American heart, came forth the faith they could not see or that they could not even imagine. It brought us victory. And it will again."*

They were words with a deeper meaning, as only he and a few other men knew at the time. As he spoke, he hoped the investigation he had set in motion was bearing fruit. These thoughts preoccupied Mr. Johnson as he watched the parade that day and attended several Inaugural Balls that evening.

Lyndon Johnson knew that at a little after midnight he would be meeting with Allen Dulles and another man unknown to him. All under the radar and off the record, of course. Few would ever know about the meeting, but it would be one of the most important of the tall Texan's presidency.

Shortly before one a.m., the President of the United States sat in an oversized chair in the Oval Office, while two men occupied the sofa across from him. One was Allen Dulles. Johnson had never met the other man, but he had certainly heard about him. Johnson was familiar with Harvey King's reputation. He was colorful, mysterious, and there were stories about how he had been one of the inspirations for Ian Fleming's fictional creation—James Bond. So LBJ was very interested. He was also amused by the idea that he was somehow rescuing the intelligence operative from his Kennedy-imposed exile.

While Harvey King might have inspired Ian Fleming, he sure didn't look, act, or speak anything like Sean Connery. Not a bit. King was overweight, balding, and dressed in an unkempt manner. He tended to look like he had been on an overnight flight even after he showered and dressed the first thing in the morning. He was hard-drinking, hard-charging, and hardheaded man—the proverbial bull in a china shop. And he took his own china shop with him wherever he went.

He had also been involved in some of the CIA's most important covert operations over the previous decade, from a coup in Guatemala, to a tunnel beneath the Soviet sector in Berlin (nicknamed, "Harvey's Hole"), to being the point man for the Kennedy brothers in their near obsession to see Cuban leader Fidel Castro not only toppled, but banished from the face of the earth. King was even one of the first American intelligence experts to mark the British diplomat Harold Adrian

Russell Philby, better known by his familiar nickname, "Kim," as a Soviet agent.

That was in 1951. It took nearly twelve more years for the rest of the American and British intelligence establishment to catch on to Philby's nefarious activities, and that only after the traitor's defection one rainy night from Lebanon to a freighter bound for the Ukrainian port of Odessa in January 1963. His ultimate destination was Moscow, Russia.

During the Kennedy days, King worked closely with Robert Kennedy, who was in charge of the anti-Castro initiative dubbed Operation Mongoose, but one day, he was summoned to the Oval Office. JFK, a big fan of James Bond novels, wanted to meet the real-life spy. Legend had it that Mr. King had to leave two guns at the door, but actually had another on him for the late night "meet-and-greet," to the chagrin of the Secret Service agent on duty.

Harvey King and Bobby Kennedy did not get along at all. The president's younger brother tended to be arrogant, condescending, and abrupt when dealing with subordinates. King resented and had little respect for the attorney general. And when Operation Mongoose was unceremoniously shut down after the resolution of the Cuban Missile Crisis, Harvey King—who up till then had gone from rising star to living legend in the intelligence world—was suddenly in the dog house and exiled to a watching-paint-dry boring post in Rome.

*

So when the out-of-favor spy got a message from his old boss Allen Dulles, he caught the next available flight to the States. He flew into Idlewild in New York, then took the train to DC's

Union Station the night of the inauguration. King was tired, and though he hadn't had any alcohol on the *flight*, he gave in and had nursed a series of J&B scotches with water and ice on the train. *So much for sobriety,* he thought. But then again, by the time of their meeting, President Johnson had himself put away a significant amount of his preferred Cutty Sark. Neither man was drunk, but they were loose, and their conversation quickly became animated about a point of agreement—the Kennedy brothers—particularly Bobby.

Not usually one to kiss ass, Harvey King had determined to get out of the doghouse and decided to use his hatred of Bobby Kennedy to ingratiate himself with LBJ, whose loathing of the newly installed New York senator was well known. Allen Dulles was as sober as a judge and was amused as he witnessed the back and forth between Johnson and King.

"Well, I'll tell you, Harvey—okay if I call you Harvey?" The president asked.

"Of course. Okay if I call you, Mr. President?"

They laughed. "Fine by me."

"Any enemy of Bobby Kennedy is a friend of mine. That little piss-ant runt treated me like shit, even though I was vice president of these United States! His brother always treated me with respect, at least in public and face to face, but that Bobby is just as mean as a rabid raccoon."

"I know, sir. But things are different now."

"Indeed, Harvey. Freshen your drink?"

"Yes, thank you, sir. One more for me."

Johnson mashed a buzzer on his desk and shouted a command for two more scotches.

Meanwhile, Dulles just took it all in. He was fascinated that on this day of all days—one of great triumph for the president—the man could be capable of what could only be described as pettiness beneath the dignity of his office. But he just relit his pipe a few times while the two men aired it out.

Finally, they all got around to the point of the meeting, rapport having been established. "Allen, I assume you briefed our friend about what we might be dealing with," Johnson said.

Dulles replied, "Yes, Mr. President. Harvey's up to speed and ready to head over to London later today."

"Great! We need to get to the bottom of this. How do you propose to proceed?" Both men looked at Harvey for his response.

"Well, I have a few friends who are former MI6, sir. They are still tied in there, as I am with Langley. Once a spook, always a spook," King said, smiling. "If there's something to this, there must be some chatter. I'll find out if anything is on their radar. Allen mentioned your source talked about the possibility of some kind of operation made to look like the IRA. Bombs are their signature. I'd like to get the plans for Churchill's funeral even before the old man buys the farm. That way, I can try to figure out the weak spots, just where someone might blow things up."

"The key, Mr. President," Dulles interrupted, "is in the details, as we know. We need to get ahold of the official state plans for the funeral. Do you think your source—and we respect that you are guarding his identity—is in a position to get his hands on that information?"

President Johnson replied, "I wouldn't be a bit surprised. I'll see what I can do before you leave today."

"One more thing, Mr. President," Dulles added. "We need to get Harvey into Great Britain without leaving a trail. Just want you to know we are going to bend some rules along the way."

"Hell, break the damn things. I couldn't care less. Just make sure nothing traces back to this office."

"We understand, sir. I have access to a private aircraft owned by one of the companies I work with, and we're going to send Harvey to England along with another man I trust, someone who can help him along."

"Fine," Johnson said, holding out his hands with the palms facing out. "Just don't give me too many details. I don't need 'em. I just need you men to help us avoid World War III."

Dulles hesitated.

"Mr. President...there's one more thing."

"Uh huh," Johnson said.

"I'm hoping you're not going to Mr. Churchill's funeral when the time comes. It could be very dangerous, and if the unthinkable happens, we need a leader who can lead. Frankly, I don't think our new vice president is up to the job."

"Damn straight. Hubert doesn't know his ass from a hole in the ground. I hated putting him on the ticket. The guy talks too much and says nothing. I guess I could send him to England, but the idiot would probably embarrass us."

Dulles smiled. "Well, sir, you'll have many options when the time comes. Right now, we'll leave you to get some rest. Harvey will be ready to fly out this evening."

"Thank you, Gentlemen, and I'll see what I can do on those funeral plans. I guess I could make an official request or something from their embassy," Johnson said.

After Dulles and King left, Johnson picked up his phone. An operator's voice came on the line, "Yes, Mr. President?"

"Good, glad to see someone is at work down there. I need you to call Moyers at home and get him over here right away."

Moyers had just arrived at his small apartment and was getting ready for bed—he knew he would get only a few hours of sleep that night. Johnson had already told him to be in his office by six a.m., but when the call came from the White House switchboard, he quickly dressed, and raced through now near-empty DC streets to the White House. He parked and entered the West Wing, noticing a clock on the wall showing the time was almost half-past two a.m.

Johnson was barking his order as Moyers closed the door of the Oval Office behind him. "Now you get ahold of Dean Rusk over at State and have him contact the British Embassy and see if they have any advance details about a funeral for Mr. Churchill."

"Certainly, sir. Should I wake him?"

"Hell, yes. I need it on my desk five minutes ago. Now you get this done. Bird wants me up in bed, so I'm heading over there. But you make sure to wake me when you get the report. I don't care what time it is. You tell that guard outside our door that he is to let you into the room."

Bill Moyers resisted a suicidal urge to ask his boss why the request was so urgent. Instead, he did as ordered. He called Rusk. The secretary of state drowsily answered on the third ring. Rusk called the British Embassy.

Shortly before five a.m., the materials were delivered to the White House and Moyers went to the White House residence, knowing that Johnson was asleep. He entered the room. Johnson was snoring, and then he coughed himself awake, just as Moyers was walking toward the bed. He saw him and held up a hand, motioning him back out, pointing at Ladybird, who was asleep next to him.

In the hallway, just outside the president's bedroom, Moyers handed the report to Johnson, who at that moment realized he had left his glasses on the night table next to his bed. He squinted as his eyes adjusted to the light and tried to read. "Hell, I can't read this thing. How'd you get it here so fast? You got a girlfriend over there, Billy boy?" Johnson smiled, knowing that his aide was a devout Baptist.

"Um, no sir," Moyers replied. "But I think the ambassador himself facilitated the delivery of this material. That's what Rusk said. Might it have had anything to do with his visit the other day?"

The president ignored the reference and leafed through the report. It was a spiral bound document, complete with a hard cover bearing the title: *Operation Hope Not—Preparations for the Funeral of Sir Winston Leonard Spencer-Churchill.* "Did you go through it?" the president asked.

"No sir, Mr. President," Moyers replied with a slight tone of protest.

"Fine by me if you do. I'm gonna take a dump and a shower. I'll meet you in my office in twenty minutes. I want you to make some copies with that magic machine in the office."

"It's called a *Xerox* machine, sir."

Johnson looked at Moyers. "What the hell do I care what it's called, do I look like some dip shit clerk?"

Moyer deflected the dig. Barbed words were just Johnson's way. "How many copies, sir?"

"Make four or five, and keep one for yourself. I want you to go over this thing with a fine-toothed comb. But keep it between us. Give me the other copies. Don't task some pretty girl for this. You know how to work that machine?"

Moyers almost smiled at the reference to having a pretty girl make the copies, seeing as it was so early. Johnson's presidency ran on its own time. "Yes I can work it. I'll be there in twenty."

Johnson was at his desk when Moyers entered the Oval Office, several copies of the British report in hand. He handed them to the president, who immediately began to read it. Moyers also read a copy. It was an impressive and thorough plan. The funeral details for Churchill had apparently been in development for more than a decade. It was planned down to the last detail. All indications were that it was certainly going to be an epic event—one for the history books.

"The old man's funeral is gonna make Kennedy's look like a small country buryin'," Johnson said, breaking the silence.

The presidential aide did not know how to respond to his boss's comment, one that was over the top, even for Johnson. "Yes, sir," he replied with the only words he could manage.

"Now, you get two copies of this to Allen Dulles, right away. He'll be waiting for it. Don't send a courier or some flunky. You get in that car of yours and drive it over to his place in Georgetown yourself. You hear?"

"Absolutely, sir."

*

Moyers was on the doorstep of Dulles's townhome forty-five minutes later. The former CIA director devoured the material. Meanwhile, Harvey King was upstairs in a spare bedroom sound asleep. Dulles had pulled every string he had to find a short-notice hotel room for his guest, but the inauguration ensured everything in the DC are was booked solid—and expensive, too. So, Dulles brought King home with him. It was also a good way to keep an eye on the sometimes-erratic operative.

King woke up around eleven a.m. He walked downstairs and poured himself a cup of coffee. "Got any Irish?" he asked his host, who was sitting in an easy chair in his study and making notes on a copy of the Churchill funeral plan.

"Knock it off, Harvey. You need to lay off the sauce for the next few days. This is a big operation, and it's your chance to turn your career around."

"Aw hell, sport—I was joking about the whiskey. Of course, I know the drill. I won't let you down."

"Well, you'll need to read this thing," Dulles said, holdup up the document. "Then read it again and again. I'm sure the bad guys know this material inside and out. Make sure Brogan reads it, too."

*

Dulles arranged for an aircraft and crew for King's flight to England. It was a brand-new Learjet 23, one of the first of its kind. The aircraft was owned by a company with secret ties to the United Fruit Company, the large conglomerate with holdings throughout South and Central America. The Dulles brothers, Allen and the late John (the Dulles of Dulles International Airport) had a longstanding relationship with UFC. One that involved money, power, intrigue—and the great game of espionage.

King was wide awake for the duration of the flight. He followed Dulles's advice and read through the *Operation Hope Not* plan several times, making copious notes in a notebook.

Tiernan Brogan was also on board, and he read through the report, as well. A short, stocky, round-faced and red-haired man, Brogan had infiltrated the IRA for British intelligence during the Border Campaign, a guerrilla effort against conspirators in Northern Ireland. The campaign had ended a few years earlier, but Brogan still had a number of contacts from those days. He and King hoped those connections would come in handy. After being seriously wounded in Belfast, Brogan "retired" and settled in America, where he cultivated a consulting role with the CIA. He also became an unofficial conduit for information flowing back and forth between elements of the American and British intelligence services. Brogan was divorced—a marriage that lasted less than a year. He was married to his work, he rationalized. And it was true.

As for Harvey King, he spent some time reflecting at the swift change in his prospects. He was back in the game and grateful to Allen Dulles—and Lyndon Johnson.

CHAPTER TEN

As THE WORLD WAITED for the now-inevitable passing of Winston Churchill, the ever-present crowd near his Hyde Park Gate home now included Harvey King and Tiernan Brogan. Both men chased away the chill as they stood in the London cold with sips from King's ever-present flask. They were there to pick up any scent of a plot—if there was one. They looked the crowd over, trying to find clues in the faces. King was particularly drawn to a couple of men who seemed out of place.

"Okay, sport," King spoke softly to Brogan, "I'll stay here and keep an eye on things. You should hit the bricks and check out the places where some of your old crowd might hang out."

"You mean pubs," Brogan said with a smile.

"Smart man. We don't want Allen to get reports about me hanging around such establishments, now do we?"

"Leave it to me. I'll visit every pub in London for a great cause," Brogan teased.

Brogan left the Churchill home and began visiting places known to be favorites of men and women fond of the IRA and who hated the British crown.

*

King kept his eye on the two men in the crowd. They wore raincoats that seemed a little bulkier than the typical Londoner wore. But it was the look on their faces that struck him. They just stared at the house in a way that was different from others in the crowd. They didn't seem curious or sentimental. The way they watched reminded him of how some of his friends in the Secret Service looked when on duty. They were watching, King thought, for some reason beyond just respect for a great man in decline.

After about an hour, two other men—similarly dressed— joined them. Then a few minutes later, the first two men left. King decided to follow them. His gut was starting to suggest to him that they were KGB. His years of intelligence work, particularly in Berlin, taught him to trust that ample gut.

He was a little surprised at where they went—or at least at how they got there. The two men took a cab to the Soviet Embassy, seemingly with no concern about anyone possibly watching them. In fact, King noticed that there seemed to be no British agents around at all. He found it curious, but chalked it up to what he considered to be typical laxity on the part of British intelligence. So much for tradecraft. King had taken a dim view of MI6 since the days of Philby. Even after he had warned them back in 1951 that Kim was a spy, they had kept the man in the loop until he defected for Moscow in January 1963. His gut had been right, and the Brits had been wrong.

Watching the Russians move about without surveillance that day in London simply reinforced King's belief that when it came to the Soviets, the British had a monumental blind spot. *Hell,* he thought, *maybe Harold Wilson is a commie, after all.* One thing was for sure, the Soviets, for whatever reason, were interested in the health and impending death of Winston Churchill. And it was likely for other than compassionate or humanitarian reasons.

The men Harvey King had followed were indeed members of the KGB, the Soviet intelligence service. Even more than that, they were operatives who worked in the KGB's mysterious Department Thirteen in the organization's First Directorate. This group was responsible for an assortment of nefarious deeds, ranging from sabotage to kidnapping, and more.

The agents were obviously reporting the latest from 28 Hyde Park Gate to people in the Soviet Embassy. King surmised that the embassy was also relaying reports to Moscow. He wondered if the Presidium was monitoring the details of Churchill's decline.

*

In fact, the Presidium was doing just that—and more. They were assembled around a large table in an ornate room deep inside the Kremlin. This powerful cadre had recently disposed of unpleasant business when they deposed Nikita Khrushchev from his chairmanship. The former strongman had been exiled to his dacha in the country.

It was a delegation from Department Thirteen in the KGB's First Directorate that had invited Kim Philby in as a consultant a few months earlier. Weeks later, the British spy was once again meeting with the group, now as an official member of the KGB, with the rank of colonel. Though they had to work much of the time through a translator when communicating with Philby, he was picking up the language—at the least the parts of it related to his work with the powerful men. Philby was handling questions from the group about his knowledge of security in Great Britain. The men in the room were convinced war with the West was inevitable and were determined to fight such a war on their terms, even if that meant taking the "initiative." Therefore, they had signed off on an ambitious plan, one crafted in Department Thirteen in the First Directorate of the KGB.

And they needed Kim Philby's assistance.

"Comrade Philby, your report on British intelligence and security is most helpful. As you well know, we have our assets positioned in London when the moment for action comes," said Leonid Brezhnev, the chairman of the group.

"It was my p-p-privilege, Chairman Brezhnev. I'm aware of those very assets and I'm certainly w-w-willing to help with them in any way you and the c-c-committee see fit," Philby stammered.

Another man spoke up. "One vital question we have is about the Americans. You did not deal with this in your report." This comment came from Alexei Kosygin, who held the title of premier.

Philby was momentarily flustered. Up to this moment, all of his interactions with the group had been cordial, even friendly. He had never been pushed or challenged. But he quickly gathered his thoughts and tried to fight off his stutter—which became more pronounced when he was under stress—and ventured a careful reply. "My ap-p-ologies, Premier Kosygin. My instructions about the report I was to p-prepare did not include anything about the Americ-c-cans. I can prepare something on that for you."

Brezhnev interrupted, "Comrade Philby, there is no need to prepare a written report. Please, just tell us your opinions, if you have them, about President Johnson. We know it has been many years since you lived in the United States, and we do not expect you to be able to provide significant intelligence there. We also know your proud journey to our great nation has created a very tense situation between British security and the American CIA."

"Yes, I s-s-suppose it has," Philby replied, with a smile.

Brezhnev looked directly across the table. "Comrade Semichastny, do you have any questions on this matter for our friend?" Vladimir Semichastny had been the Chairman of the KGB for the past few years, though he had no previous intelligence experience. He was in his position purely because he was Brezhnev's political ally.

"Yes, Comrade Chairman," Semichastny replied, and then he picked up a paper and seemed to read from it as he addressed Philby. "Comrade Philby, we have reports that this man Angleton from the American CIA has been trying to convince some in British Intelligence there is a highly placed Soviet agent in what they call MI5. Are you aware of this?"

"Yes, Comrade Semichastny, I'm aware of this, and I know Mr. Ang-g-gleton, very well. We were once very close friends. I believe Jim has been influenced by this m-m-an Golitsyn."

"That is correct," Semichastny replied. "We have sent our own man Nosenko to try to convince the Americans that he is in fact the real defector and this mudak Golitsyn is a double agent. Early indications are that there is now much confusion about this inside the American intelligence community. My question to you is, will this man Angleton be convinced? Or will he be a problem?"

Philby reflected for a pregnant moment. Then he replied, "I wish I c-c-ould assure you that Angleton will be no problem, but I know him too well. He will continue his mole hunt and should not be underestimated."

*

The plan was called "KOBA," after the early name used by their late leader, Josef Stalin. KOBA was designed to fulfill the vision of Lenin and Stalin: complete Soviet dominance of Europe—the continent, and even Great Britain. The plan was fiendishly simple. First, they would incapacitate the nations of Europe and the world through an unprecedented act of political terror.

In the immediate aftermath of the loss of dozens of world leaders, agents provocateur—men and women who had been in place for many years—would initiate a series of targeted bombings and assassinations. Collaborators would instigate political demonstrations against the governments of Western Europe—the same governments that would presumably be reeling from the catastrophe. This would create a unmatched chaotic window of vulnerability and opportunity. Through that window the Red Army would march swiftly. They had ninety motor rifle divisions deployed and ready. These were augmented by fifty tank divisions. Seven airborne divisions completed the picture.

The plan called for a swift air attack on NATO forces followed by the massive insertion of airborne forces behind NATO lines. Then the tanks would roll, followed by millions of men. The goal would be to control every part of Continental Europe within thirty days. The tactical part was the brainchild of Defense Minister Andrei Grechko. But the spark that would begin the Soviet Union's great victory had been imagined elsewhere.

Years earlier, a young and ambitious strategist working for the KGB, a man named Yuri Andropov, had conceived a plan to exploit the inevitable death of Winston Churchill, a man whose hatred for the Soviet System had been a thorn in their side since the days of the October Revolution. Though Churchill and Stalin had been allies during The Great Patriotic War, as the Soviets referred to World War II, the Soviet leader had never trusted his British counterpart. He even tried to have him assassinated after the war, at one of Churchill's speaking events at a small college in America. If he had had his way, the words "Iron Curtain" would never have seen the light of day. That attempt never got off the ground, but Stalin's dream never died—not even after he did.

As part of the plan, they had planted agents in the Irish Republican Army, which at the time was somewhat sympathetic to Marxist-Leninist ideas. These people—a man, his wife, and their now-grown son—had been tasked with key roles in KOBA. They waited for the death of Stalin's old nemesis, knowing that a plan was in place that would change the world.

It was almost time.

*

"Your car will be ready in a few minutes, comrade," said Chairman Leonid Brezhnev. "While we wait, I'd like a private word with you." He led Kim Philby to a small office. Vladimir Semichastny joined them.

"We have a job for you connected with the plan codename KOBA," Brezhnev said.

"A job for me?" Philby asked.

"Yes, comrade. With your experience in the British Security Services, you are a valuable asset to us. We're sending you to London tonight."

Kim Philby was shocked. "London? Tonight? You can't be serious!" he protested. The idea of going back to London seemed ludicrous. He was a wanted man. He would be most certainly be captured and prosecuted. Fear gripped him.

The chairman stared coldly at Philby. "I'm very serious. You must know that I'm not one for tricks or jokes."

Philby summoned all his will power to control his anxiety and asked, "How? What will I do?"

With a nod from Brezhnev, the KGB Chairman produced a large envelope and emptied its contents on a nearby table. Semichastny said, "You'll be disguised with a full beard and hair piece that will significantly alter your appearance. Your cover name is William Henderson. You are a British citizen originally from Oxford, but you currently live in Copenhagen, Denmark, where you work as a rare book dealer. You own a company called *Bibliophile Limited.* We have a shop rented there and one of our friends is in place there. You are visiting London on business. Further details are in this dossier we've prepared for you. Please study it and memorize the key details. You travel frequently, so your British passport is well-worn. You'll be flying to London from Copenhagen. We will take you to Denmark on a private aircraft and land well away from the city at a remote site. You'll be driven from there to the airport in Copenhagen, where you will board a British airliner. We've booked a room in that name at The Savoy. We'll furnish you currency in pounds, and you'll have a contact at the hotel. You'll know him as 'Alex.'"

"How l-long have you been planning this?"

"Since well before your extraction from Beirut," Semichastny said with a smile. "Our plan is for you to monitor MI6, as well as the American CIA during KOBA."

"But surely MI5 will discover me. I'm certain they monitor all visitors and movements at the Soviet Embassy."

"Indeed they do. In fact, the head of MI5 *knows* you're coming."

Philby grimaced. "That doesn't sound very inviting."

"Nothing to be bothered about. You and Mr. Roger Hollis have much in common," Brezhnev said with a sinister smile.

Then it dawned on Philby and cracked a nervous smile. Brezhnev smiled back, and all three men laughed for a moment at the sheer sinister nature of what they were doing.

After the initial shock and fear began to wane, Kim Philby found himself increasingly excited at the thought that he would soon be going home. And he was even more delighted with the idea of a suite with all the amenities at The Savoy.

CHAPTER ELEVEN

TIERNAN BROGAN'S TOUR of London's Irish pubs had yielded nothing but mild hangovers after two nights. He decided to visit the Tipperary on Fleet Street again, one of the more well-known IRA-frequented establishments. He had spent some time there on occasion back when he was working undercover for MI5, and hoped to see a few characters from the old days, which hadn't really been all that long ago.

He ordered a Smithwick's and planted himself at a table in a corner to wait and watch. An attractive lady a few tables away caught his eye, and he had the feeling that he had already caught hers. His first instinct was to look away and avoid encouraging her. But then, something about her felt familiar. *Do I know her?* he wondered.

It took him about ten minutes, but it finally hit him. Her name still escaped him, but he was sure she had been involved in a couple of the operations during The Border Campaign.

She was not on the front line, but worked as part of the support team.

What was she doing in London?

Before he could approach her, she came his way, bearing two fresh glasses of Smithwick's. She was stunning and seemed to carry a general excitement buzzing about her. Her red hair was a shade or two brighter than his own.

"Fancy another drink, love?"

"Why, yes, thank you."

"You don't remember me, darlin', do ya?"

"Sure I do, but I just can't place it."

"Belfast. You're Sean Walsh. I'm Kaitlyn Dorcey," she said, followed by a wink. She called him the name Brogan had used when working undercover in the IRA.

The wink rattled him a bit. Was it flirtation, or was it something else? Did she know that Walsh wasn't his real name? He chose to go with the flirtation theory. "Of course, now I remember. May I say, you're looking splendid, Miss Dorcey?"

"Why, thank you, Sean. You're not so bad yourself. What has you in London?"

Thinking fast, he replied, "Just waiting for something exciting to come my way. Looks like I picked the right place to wait."

"That you, did, Sean. That you did."

Tiernan doubted that he'd learn much from Miss Dorcey that night, but he was pleasantly surprised with the contact, for professional and personal reasons. They stayed at the Tipperary for several hours, eventually switching from the brew to Jameson whiskey. He was glad that he had learned how to hold his liquor, because Miss Dorcey could certainly hold hers. At one point, he wondered if he was being played, instead of the other way around, but he dismissed the notion. She seemed to be off the clock and just having fun.

Then abruptly, she said, "Well, Mr. Walsh, 'tis been a lovely evening, but I must go. I may be back here tomorrow evening, though—if you're lucky." She smiled and then kissed him passionately before walking away, leaving him stunned and wanting more time with her. After she left, he followed her, keeping a safe distance. She walked two blocks then up some stairs to a flat. He saw the lights come on in a window, and then a few minutes later the window went dark again. He thought about hanging around, but decided that Miss Dorcey was in for the night. He went directly to The Dorchester Hotel on Park Lane, where he was sharing a rather small room with Harvey King, who was already proving to be an unpleasant roommate.

King was on one of the beds with a glass of something in his hand. A half-empty bottle was on the nightstand next to his bed. His shirt and pants—and socks—were strewn on the floor. A small television that sat on table was on, and a newsman was giving the latest report about Mr. Churchill. "Hey, sport. Where you been? Any luck finding the bad guys?"

"Actually, I may be on to something. I ran into a contact from years back. Not sure if she knows anything, but I have a feeling there's something there."

"She? You been hanging out all night with a dame?" Harvey asked.

"Her name is Kaitlyn Dorcey. We were part of an IRA operation several years ago," Brogan said. "Met her at the Tipperary and we had a few drinks. I'm sure I'll regret that in the morning," he said, while rubbing his temples.

"Well, while you were flirting with some gal in a pub, I was working the shoe leather."

"It wasn't like that, King. It was all business."

"I see. And what does this Miss Dorcey look like—she easy on the old eyes?"

At that, Brogan smiled sheepishly.

King continued, "Do I see you turning even more red that you already are, Mr. Brogan?"

Ignoring the question, Tiernan probed, "Tell me about your four friends. Are they still watching things in shifts and reporting back to the embassy?"

"Yeah. Like clockwork. But there was something new today. I followed a couple of them to another location, in an area called Paddington."

"What were they doing there?"

"They were visiting a funeral home."

"The devil you say? Do you recall the name of this establishment?"

"Sure, sport. I'm a pro, right? The joint is called *J. H. Kenyon.*"

"It's a famous place."

"Famous funeral home?"

"Indeed. They are the official funeral directors for the Royals," Brogan said.

*

The next morning, while it was still dark, Brogan went back to Kaitlyn's flat. By this time, his head—though aching—was clear enough for him to survey his memories of Miss Dorcey. She was indeed involved back then with the IRA and probably still was. He watched her window from half a block away. Soon a light came on. About 45 minutes later, Kaitlyn walked out her door. It was just before 8:00 AM. She walked a few blocks to a nondescript building that looked like it had recently housed a business that had gone broke. She knocked at a side door and it was opened by a woman. Kaitlyn disappeared inside.

Within ten minutes, five others entered the building, all men. It was a meeting of some kind. *Were they all IRA operatives,* he wondered? As Brogan pondered his next move, he saw another two men approach the building. They were dressed in suits, while the previous subjects were dressed in casual, even workman's, clothes. As the latest arrivals entered the building, Brogan saw yet another figure walking slowly toward the building. He was less than a block away. This man stopped when the men he was apparently following were inside.

After a moment, Brogan realized he was looking at Harvey King.

Harvey King and Tiernan Brogan were now together watching the building where nine people—seven men, Kaitlyn Dorcey, and one other woman—were having a meeting of some kind. They knew that at least two of the men in the meeting were Soviet agents who had visited a funeral home, possibly the one to be used for Churchill.

But inside the building, the Russians told a different tale. To Kaitlyn and company, they were members of the Polish Underground press involved in publishing *Samizdat* materials— prohibited pamphlets, newspapers, and other such things seen by Soviet leaders as subversive material. The two KGB agents had connected with the IRA members purportedly to work in common cause, something they would never agree to with anyone officially connected to the Soviet Union.

The Russians had persuaded their IRA friends to plan a joint venture—one designed to reflect badly on the Soviet Union and global Communism. But the real attraction for the Irish operatives wasn't just bad press for the Kremlin, though that was appealing. The IRA relished the idea of striking at the heart of the British establishment at a moment when the nation would be remembering and glorifying its ugly imperialist past. A past embodied by Churchill himself.

The Irish operatives, however, were being duped. The real Soviet agenda was to affix blame for whatever was about to happen on the IRA itself in a classic case of misdirection. An event of monumental importance would shake the world, and while the dust was settling, and before any fires could be completely extinguished, a leadership vacuum would be created by the simultaneous death of dozens of world leaders. And no one, not even the Americans, would be able to do anything about it.

Kaitlyn and her IRA friends were unaware of the scope and subversion of this monumental scheme. They just wanted to be part of something to strike at the heart of British life. And the potential disruption of Churchill's funeral fit the bill. It would be poetic symbolism. They were repulsed by all the attention from around the world for the dying former prime minister. He had done nothing for them, and it was good to be finally rid of the old sot, as far as they were concerned.

✳

Inside the building being watched by King and Brogan, Michael Wheelan, there with his wife Molly, opened his satchel, retrieved a small device, and placed it on a table. "A push of this button when one is near enough to the casket will start the clock. There is a five-minute timer. That's as far as I can take you. I imagine one of you will be handling this part of the operation."

They looked around at each other. Then one of the Soviet agents spoke up. "Yes, yes. This is already taken care of. We have someone who will be well positioned to take care of this."

＊

Later that night, the flight carrying Kim Philby from Copenhagen landed at London Airport. He was now sporting a beard, wig, and new glasses. He was filled with joy to be back. He had missed home, but he didn't really know how deeply he felt until back on British soil. William Henderson—aka, Kim Philby—cleared immigration and customs quickly and took a cab to the Savoy Hotel. A bellman carrying Philby's luggage, followed him into his room.

"Can I help you with anything else, Mr. Henderson?" the bellman asked.

"No, just put the bags anywhere. What's this?" Philby asked, walking over toward a large basket of provisions on a desk.

"I brought that up for you a bit ago, sir. Someone brought it to the hotel for you," the bellman said. He was waiting for a tip.

After a moment, Philby said, "Oh my, where are my manners." He reached into his pocket and pulled out money for a modest tip. "Here you go, my boy. Thanks ever so much."

After the bellman left, Philby further examined the basket. It contained fruit, cheeses, crackers, and several kinds of nuts. There was a card. It read: "Welcome to London, Mr. Henderson. Enjoy your stay." It was signed, simply: "Alex."

CHAPTER TWELVE

THE CHURCHILL WATCH LASTED A WEEK. During that time, the crowd near his home seldom dipped below two hundred fifty people, even in the middle of the night, and no matter what kind of weather London in January had to offer. Beyond that, newspapers around the world had the story of Winston Churchill's life-threatening illness on page one. Lyndon Johnson sent a message: "We are all very sorry for your illness and we are praying for a rapid and complete recovery. All of us continue to look to you for wise counsel and judgment."

Meanwhile, the other Churchill news coming out of Washington, DC was that the proposed statue of Churchill, which was to stand astride the dividing line between the British Embassy and American soil, would indeed include a cigar. There had been strong opposition to this from some members of Washington, DC branch of the English-Speaking Union, but ultimately eighty percent of them voted in favor of the familiar Churchillian appendage.

Former President Eisenhower sent word from his farm in Gettysburg: "Mrs. Eisenhower and I are deeply distressed to learn that our old friend has been stricken with another illness." Charles De Gaulle's message described his own "feeling of shock" at Churchill's decline. And world leaders began to instruct their aides to begin making travel and logistical plans in the event of a funeral to come.

While the headlines each day tried to communicate the same news in different ways—"Sir Winston Losing Ground," "Condition of Sir Winston Worsens," "Churchill Clinging to Life,"—it seemed as if the world had stopped, or at least slowed down spinning on its axis. Likely Churchill never knew he had stopped a strike from his sickbed, but such was the case. Schoolteachers in Great Britain had been prepared to walk off the job over a pay dispute, but cited the great man's illness as the key to their decision to stage the protest "at a more suitable time." Certainly, this move by labor would have amused the longtime Tory leader.

The expressions coming out of the Soviet Union were predictably colder. Radio reports in Moscow tended to be terse and limited. For its part, the official newspaper for Soviet defense, *Krasnaya Zvezda*, included language calling Churchill the godfather of the Cold War, indicating that the Briton had not been forgiven for his 1946 reference to that pesky iron curtain.

＊

By Thursday, January 21, Dr. Moran was reporting that his famous patient was at a low point. Archbishop of Canterbury, Michael Ramsey, told an interviewer the great man was approaching death. By this time, however, the crowds were gone, at Lady Churchill's request. Fresh fallen snow marked the area recently clogged by people on the narrow dead-end street. Edmund Murray and the other three officers stood guard, nonetheless, now more as an act of honor than protection.

Even the press had been moved back a block or so, something Mrs. Churchill deeply appreciated. Anthony Montague Brown, one of Churchill's secretaries and who had been the bearer of Lady Churchill's request that everyone move away from the area around the house, walked over to where the reporters were now gathered and read an appreciative message: "I would like to thank you for the speed with which you complied with Lady Churchill's request. She was very touched. She has been feeling the strain." The journalists nodded affirmatively, almost bowing in respect. The Friday news was more of the same, though there was a stir of sorts when the home directly behind 28 Hyde Park Gate caught fire. However, even the three fire engines responding to the blaze did their part to respect the need for quiet—they arrived at the scene without sounding sirens or bells.

Later that Friday, Lady Churchill was summoned to the telephone for a call from her grandson, Winston. Her face broke into a broad smile—the first for her in a long time—as she learned of the birth of their third great-grandchild, a boy, born at Westminster Hospital. The child was premature but doing quite well, the proud father reported, adding that his wife, Minnie, was fine, as well. Clementine shared the joyous news with everyone and then went into her husband's room and whispered it in his ear. But the great man, though breathing, was likely never aware of the blessed event. And soon Clementine's smile was again absent from her face.

Also around this time, the casket from Newman Brothers in Birmingham was well on its way to London, being driven to town in a Rolls Royce hearse. It was delivered to the J. H. Kenyon Ltd funeral home in Paddington. The proprietors were known famously as "Funeral Directors for the Royal Household." They had handled every funeral connected to the royals since 1929.

The next day was Saturday and someone noted the Sunday coming would be the anniversary of the death of Winston's father. A dozen years earlier, while he was shaving one January morning, he reflected on the significance of that date to his valet. "My father passed away on this date many years ago. I believe I shall also die on the twenty-fourth day of January in a year to come." The valet shared the comment with the household staff. Now many of them wondered if the great man was somehow mustering all the courage and fortitude he had to make it until the page of the calendar and hands of the clock moved to the point of his personal prophecy?

Long after the household went to bed that night, Clementine visited Winston's room around one a.m. She held his hand and sat silent next to him for a bit before heading back to bed. By the time she returned to his room about six hours later, it was clear that there had been a change for the worse. The family was summoned. Less than thirty minutes later, Randolph arrived with his son, Winston, joining Mary, Sarah, and Clementine in the drawing room. A few minutes later Lords Moran and Brian came in. One of the nurses put out a tray of coffee. Everyone stood by in somber silence.

A little before eight a.m., Roy Howells appeared and cleared his throat, saying, "I think you had all better come in." They formed a line and, one by one, went to his bed; some knelt immediately, some whispered to him. Eventually, all those in the room knelt prayerfully. And just as a clock down the hallway finished pealing eight times marking the morning hour on Sunday, January 24, 1965, Winston Leonard Spencer-Churchill drew his last breath and was gathered unto his fathers.

CHAPTER THIRTEEN

AN HOUR OR SO AFTER SUNSET on the day Churchill died, Lyndon Johnson summoned several reporters to his private bedroom in the White House residence. It was all part of an elaborate ruse. A day or so earlier, the president had disappeared from sight in the White House, not going near the Oval Office. Meanwhile a story was making its way around the rumor mill that Johnson wasn't feeling well. This was quite a contrast to the vibrant picture LBJ had presented to the nation a few days earlier at his inauguration.

The day before—Saturday, the twenty-third—the president had a lengthy conversation with his personal physician, Rear Admiral George G. Burkley, who was then tasked with bringing the other White House medical officers on board.

"Now, can't go into detail, Doc, but it's important that I have a good reason to avoid traveling to the big funeral over in England, when the time comes."

"I've been watching the news, sir, and it looks like he doesn't have long. I imagine maybe another twenty-four hours at the most," Burkley replied. He was surprised at Johnson's request, but did his best not to let on.

"I'm sure you're right. So how are we gonna play this? It can't be anything serious—just enough to keep me off that airplane. Don't give me the plague or a heart problem. Don't want people to start paying attention to Hubert."

"Understood. Well, we could say you have a very bad cold and cough, sir. Your predecessor pulled that one off pretty successfully during the Cuban crisis in '62. The cover story was that he had a cold when he had to return to Washington from Chicago to deal with Soviet missiles in Cuba."

Johnson was annoyed at the Kennedy reference: a reminder that he had inherited the good doctor from JFK, along with so many other things. But then as he paused and stared at the physician, he remembered this man had protected Kennedy's medical secrets, including the big one about the man's Addison's Disease. That one had always irked LBJ. He had suspected for years that Jack Kennedy was not as robust as his public image. So in the run up to the 1960 campaign, when Johnson was seeking the presidential nomination for himself, he sent investigators to dig up the truth about Kennedy's health. A doctor who had treated Kennedy confirmed the Addison's diagnosis.

Somehow Kennedy's denials were enough for the press, and the issue had gone away. But Johnson was one of few people present who was not at all surprised that sad day at Parkland Hospital in Dallas when Dr. Burkley advised emergency room personnel who were trying to save Kennedy's life that they should administer steroids because he had Addison's Disease.

LBJ also knew this was the real reason the Kennedy people had been so adamant about no autopsy being performed in Dallas. That secret, along with so many others, including the use of amphetamines, and his chronic experience with venereal disease, had gone to that Arlington Cemetery grave with John F. Kennedy. Johnson knew the doctor was good with secrets and understood the concept of absolute discretion—not to mention doctor-patient privilege.

He barked, "Well, you just look out for me like you did for him and we'll be fine, Doc, okay?"

"Yes, sir. Then what I recommend is that we use a bad cold as your cover. It's fairly non-specific. But it'll be up to you to sell it, Mr. President."

"You give me the cold and I'll sell it, you can count on it. I'll put on a show that'd make John Wayne proud. Do you have any of that Vicks stuff? The salve? Let's smear it on me all over. Nothing says cold better than that God-awful smell."

"Great idea. I'll fetch some right away."

Burkley was the only medical officer privy to the ruse, though his assistant, Navy Captain James Young, and a New York throat specialist by the name of W. J. Gould, would be brought into the "case" soon. In fact, all three physicians were on hand when those seven reporters entered the president's bedroom that Sunday evening. They saw Johnson in bed, his hair uncombed and coughing a great deal. The fragrance of menthol filled the room.

The president spoke barely above a whisper. "Fellas, my medical people are advising against a trip to London for Mr. Churchill's funeral, and I want you to know I've fought 'em on it, but Lady Bird agrees, and she's the boss."

"How do you feel, Mr. President?" one of the reporters asked.

"Well, not good. I guess I don't have the bouncy feeling I usually have," the president replied, blowing his nose.

A couple of reporters made eye contact with each other, trying to suppress smiles about LBJ's strange characterization.

Just then, Dr. Burkley spoke up—he and his colleagues were standing over near a corner of the room. "Um, gentlemen, the president is suffering from a very bad cold, and it's gone down into his chest, so we have to watch it. A lengthy airplane trip at this time would likely aggravate his condition."

Johnson looked over at Burkley and nodded. It was his way of thanking him for the save.

"Who will you send in your stead, sir?" another reporter asked.

"Well, I'm gonna send Dean Rusk and Earl Warren over there."

"And Vice President Humphrey?" a reporter asked the obvious question.

"No, the vice president won't be going either," was his surprising reply.

When the bedside press conference was over, the reporters made their way out of LBJ's room and soon exited the White House. Three of them climbed into one car, and when they were out of sight and earshot, they did what they had wanted to do since they heard the president's strange phrase. They broke into a version of a recent number one song in the United States by the Righteous Brothers, only the words were changed: *"He's lost that bouncy feeling, whoa oh, that bouncy feeling..."*

Lyndon Johnson was a savvy politician and knew his reason for skipping the big funeral would be viewed with suspicion, even ridicule. But it was the price he had to pay for security. It wasn't a decision made out of fear. He was determined not only to avoid a potential catastrophe, but to be positioned to deal with the damage should the unthinkable happen. He didn't know if the Soviets would be able to pull off such an ambitious plan, but by staying home he would already give them something to ponder—would they want to blow up the world if the United States wouldn't be impacted?

✳

Back in 1938, during a debate about defense, Churchill was demanding increased appropriations for air defense, arguing that the Chamberlain government hadn't appropriated enough to meet the threat of an expanding Luftwaffe. An irate MP shouted out, "How much is enough?" The future prime minister said the questioner reminded him of the man who received a cable from Brazil informing him of the death of his mother-in-law and requesting instructions. "Embalm, cremate, bury at sea," the man wired back. "Take no chances."

When it came to the treatment of the earthly remains of the great man, nothing was left to chance. A few hours after Churchill breathed his last, a distinguished gentleman showed up at the Churchill home. He was the best at his craft. Desmond Henley was an embalmer. He was ushered into the house by Dr. Moran. Henley paid his respects to Clementine and the family members gathered in the sitting room. Moran then led the embalmer through the house to Churchill's room. An assistant followed him, pushing a small cart carrying equipment. By then, Churchill had been dead for nearly four hours. "Please wait here," Henley said as he and Dr. Moran entered the room. "I'll call for you if I need you. And please, no one past this door now, understood?"

"Yes, sir," the assistant replied.

Henley and Moran worked without speaking a word. Churchill's eyes were closed and sealed, as were his lips. They carefully undressed him and then cleaned the body with a sponge and solution. Henley then massaged the arms and legs to undo the stiffening due to rigor mortis. An incision was then made on the neck, beginning the process of draining the blood and replacing it with a formaldehyde-based fluid. Following this, the body was dressed in elegant silk pajamas and robe. He would remain in his bedroom for more than forty-eight hours.

$*$

The announcement about LBJ's curious decision not to travel to London was being discussed in Moscow the very next day. The hardliners had to defend the KOBA plan against nervous questions from a few members of the Presidium. But the questions were soon dismissed, the plan was left intact, and no one thought to ask if the decision by Johnson to skip the funeral meant their plan had been compromised.

They were also informed the "package" had been prepared and was in place. Winston Churchill's lifeless body had been prepared for burial and soon would occupy a large lead-lined oak casket in London. A casket that also contained enough explosive material to change the course of human history.

CHAPTER FOURTEEN

FOURTEEN MONTHS EARLIER, America and the world had paid respects to a fallen president—John F. Kennedy. There were no plans in place for such an event because it was unexpected and unimaginable. Sometime late in the evening on November 22, 1963, the president's widow, Jacqueline Kennedy, with her sense of history and ever-present grace, garnered her thoughts and asked for a quick, but thorough, review of the funeral of Abraham Lincoln that had taken place nearly 100 years earlier. She wanted to use it as a reference for the farewell to her murdered husband.

In a similar way, the model for much of what would transpire during the last week of January 1965 was an earlier, famous funeral in Great Britain. That one was back in 1898, when England said goodbye to William Ewart Gladstone. It was also the first time a funeral had been a global media event. As with Churchill in the twentieth century, Gladstone towered over his times in the nineteenth. He served as prime minister four separate times over four decades. He was sometimes referred to as "GOM," which stood for "Grand Old Man." His contemporary and longtime political rival, Benjamin Disraeli, suggested the initials meant, "God's Only Mistake."

The parallels between Gladstone and Churchill resembled those often drawn between Kennedy and Lincoln, including the way they were laid to final rest. But there was one notable distinction. Queen Victoria detested Mr. Gladstone, who was known around the royal court as the man the queen most loved to hate. She was convinced that Gladstone was a dangerous man. Mr. Disraeli was more her cup of tea. Victoria ignored Gladstone in death as much as she despised him in life. She was silent on the matter of a State Funeral for him and only agreed when it was clear that Parliament overwhelmingly approved. Her son, the Prince of Wales, who would become King Edward VII upon his mother's passing in January 1901, was embarrassed by his mother's behavior, and personally apologized to Gladstone's widow as she was leaving the service at Westminster Abbey.

Of course, things were completely different when Winston Churchill died. Queen Elizabeth II had great affection for him, and her recommendation for a full State Funeral made its way to the House of Commons within hours of his death.

*

While news of Winston Churchill's death was making its way around the realm and world, the long-laid and frequently revised plan called *Operation Hope Not* was coming to life. Details of what was to transpire over the next week were beginning to be made public. He would lie in state in

Westminster Hall from Wednesday through Friday. This 250-foot long hall adjoined the House of Commons, where Churchill spent his political career. When William Gladstone's body lay in state there in 1898, more than a quarter of a million people walked by to pay respects. No one dared to try to estimate the number of people who would course by over the upcoming three days.

On Saturday morning, the casket bearing Churchill's body would be placed on a gun carriage for the journey to St. Paul's Cathedral, the site of the funeral service. Following the service, the body would be taken to a pier near the Tower of London. It would travel by barge to Festival Pier on the south side of the river and in view of the Houses of Parliament. From there the casket would be taken to Waterloo Station and loaded onto a special Funeral Train for the 70-mile journey to Churchill's ancestral home, Blenheim Palace, where a burial would take place in a nearby churchyard. Churchill would be joining his father and mother, who had been buried decades before.

That was the basic plan. But the real drama would be in the details.

In fact, as the world focused its attention on London that week, all the pomp and ceremony would involve a cast of thousands. In a sense, it would be a theater production writ large—very large. And overseeing all of it would be the Earl Marshall—a fifty-six-year-old man named Bernard Fitzalan-Howard, Sixteenth Duke of Norfolk. He was an old hand at big events, having overseen the coronations of George VI in 1936 and Elizabeth II in 1953. His role dated back to medieval times, serving as one of the seven Great Offices of State. And since ceremony was his main job—really his only job—he spent a lot of time waiting and preparing for ultimate moments, like an army general in peacetime. He loved cricket and had recently managed the English team in Australia. Fitzalan-Howard had been watching Churchill's health over the past few years, not in a morbid way, but out of the very real desire to be ready to give the great man the sendoff he and the nation deserved.

The Earl Marshall had been the guardian of *Operation Hope Not* from its inception. Now he was set to produce and direct an unprecedented and unparalleled event. He was also determined that his nation and its long-held and practiced traditions, sometimes scorned and mocked in the modern age, would, through civility and ceremony, impress and even rebuke those who embraced what he saw as degenerative cultural change. And since more than a hundred nations would be sending delegations, including many actual heads of state, he knew it would all be watched and analyzed by several hundred million people.

The eyes of the world would be on his masterpiece.

CHAPTER FIFTEEN

HAROLD HIGGINS STOOD UNCOMFORTABLY in his uniform—bearing the initials h.h.—and watched the pomp and ceremony of yet another rehearsal at St. Paul's Cathedral unfold. Over the past several months, he had been one of the many sextons tasked with caring for the famous church. He was good with his hands and could fix just about anything, so Harry quickly became a popular member of the team. Of course, he couldn't fix what he knew was really wrong with the place. Nor could he tell anyone the real reason he had taken the job.

The hardest part for Harry was putting up with the pomp and ceremony of the Anglican service. It wasn't that he was against ritual, not at all. He just saw how the British did things as woefully inferior to his own religious experience. He was an Irish Catholic, masquerading as a loyal member of the Church of England, under the leadership of Her Majesty the Queen.

But it was his assignment, so as a loyal member of the IRA he took it all in stride. When he was approached months earlier about working at St. Paul's, it wasn't by an official emissary of the church but rather by someone from back home in Belfast. In fact, he and this contact had been altar boys together and had remained fast friends throughout all the years. Now they were in their forties. They were also committed to the great cause of liberating Belfast and all of so-called Northern Ireland from British dominion. Harry had gotten his hands dirty many times and always managed to avoid the authorities. He didn't know why he had been placed at St. Paul's, but it didn't matter to him. He would always do his duty. So he waited.

Then, today, from out of the blue, he had discovered a note from an old friend in the pages of his morning newspaper. He smiled as he read it: *"Harry dear: A few of us are getting together tonight at the Tipperary for a pint or two, please join us. Seven o'clock. There is much to talk about. I miss you. Love, KAITLYN."*

He could think of nothing else throughout the day. He was still in love with the fiery redhead. She popped in and out of his life whenever her whim led her. Yes, she even used him— but he didn't care. Life was always better when she was in the room.

He wondered, though, if her invitation was in any way connected to his work at St. Paul's. It would be hard to make seven o'clock, because everyone was working extra hours due to the big funeral scheduled in a few days. Later that day, and as he tried to figure out how to slip out early enough to meet up with Kaitlyn, a light came on and he realized her invitation, his job at the famous church, and the funeral for Mr. Churchill were likely all connected. He looked forward to learning why and how.

✳

Harry made it to the pub about ten minutes past seven. Kaitlyn was seated at a table with a man and a woman. He walked over to them. They were already working on their second, or maybe third, drinks.

"Harry Higgins! It's been far too long, darlin'. Please meet me friends, Michael and Molly Wheelan. They're in London on holiday for a few days."

"You don't say?" Harry replied, before excusing himself and ordering a pint at the bar. When he came back to the table with his drink, he asked, "Where you from, Michael?"

"Birmingham."

Harry tried to hide his frown—Birmingham was not his favorite place—and hoped he was being successful as he said, "Oh yes, that's a wonderful city."

At that moment Tiernan Brogan came in the door. He had stopped by the Tipperary the past two nights in hopes of seeing Kaitlyn, but she hadn't shown. Tonight he was lucky.

"Over here, Sean," Kaitlyn shouted as their eyes met across the bar. "Grab a pint and join us, why don't you?"

"Don't mind if I do." He was back in a moment with his drink.

"Once around again," said Kaitlyn. "This is my friend from back when. Name's Sean Walsh. And Sean, these fine folks be Michael and Molly Wheelan and Harry Higgins."

Brogan thought Michael looked vaguely familiar and did a subtle double take. Wheelan didn't notice. After a few minutes, it came to him: he remembered the name from an old operation.

After another round of drinks, Kaitlyn announced that she had to leave. The party broke up just like that. Nothing subtle about her. Harry, Michael, and Molly left at the same time, after saying their goodbyes. They went their separate ways. Brogan waited for a moment to put distance between him and Kaitlyn before following. He wound up trailing all four of them because they were going someplace *together*—and in a hurry. After a few turns, Brogan realized their destination was the building he and Harvey King had watched earlier. He watched them enter and waited for a bit.

Then he went back to the hotel and briefed Harvey King.

"What does this Wheelan guy do in Birmingham?" Harvey asked.

"Don't know, but should be easy enough to find out. I've got an old contact at MI5 who keeps files on IRA types. I'm sure this Wheelan is connected."

Brogan called his contact and a few minutes later the phone rang back—the contact was ready with the requested information. As he listened to the voice on the phone, Harvey King watched the blood drain from Tiernan Brogan's face.

"Son of a bitch!" Brogan said.

"What's up?"

"Grab your coat. We need to head to Birmingham right now!"

By the time Tiernan Brogan and Harvey King were on a train making that was its way toward Birmingham that night, Harry Higgins was back at his small flat not far from St. Paul's Cathedral. He removed a small device from his pocket and placed it in a small space beneath a loose floorboard in one corner. Michael Wheelan had given it to him. Higgins now knew why they had wanted him to get the job at the famous Anglican Church. And he was ready to carry out his assignment.

CHAPTER SIXTEEN

THE TRAIN LEFT London's Easton station shortly after nine p.m. It was scheduled to arrive at Birmingham's New Street station about eleven thirty. Harvey King and Tiernan Brogan sat a safe distance away from other passengers in the car that was less than half full. They wanted to be able to talk far away from listening ears.

"Okay, sport," King said. He loved calling men "sport" for reasons only he knew. Brogan wondered if the legendary spy simply couldn't remember his name. Whatever the case, he found it increasingly annoying. "So here's what we have. There's chatter in DC about some potential plot and incident having to do with Winnie's funeral. And now we have some clown who has a background with the IRA who just happens to be in London, though he is from Birmingham and works at the very factory where Churchill's jumbo casket was built?"

"Outfitted, actually."

"What?"

"Outfitted. The casket was built somewhere else—not sure where. This company *Newman Brothers* is famous for decking out caskets for the rich and famous. My contact at Five told me that they are big into brass and shit like that," Brogan said.

"Okay, well, whatever the hell they do, it's too much of a coincidence not to mean something."

"I agree. What's the plan once we get to Birmingham? It'll be almost midnight."

"That's the best time to work in the shadows, sport. The question is do we check out their home or go straight to the casket factory?"

"I say we check out the factory. If something's been fooled with, that's where the clues would be."

Around midnight, the two travelers were on Birmingham's Fleet Street surveying the multi-story brick building of Newman Brothers. The facility was dark and the street was surprisingly desolate.

"Looks pretty straightforward to me. Let's find a side door and go in. It's been a while since I did a covert entry. It'll be fun," King said.

Brogan didn't really know what to make of the legendary spy. But he didn't argue with him. He was beginning to see through King's rough exterior. Sure, the guy looked like an alcoholic has-been, but his mind seemed razor-sharp. King pulled a slender case from his suction pocket and began to work on the lock. "Keep an eye out, Brogan," he whispered. Tiernan smiled at the fact that King remembered his name after all. Working swiftly, they were soon inside the building and looking around with their flashlights.

"Look for anything with Wheelan's name or initials. Or any clue as to where the big man's casket was worked on. Try to find a room or area that looks like where they put stuff together," King said.

They had been in the facility for about twenty minutes, walking about thirty feet apart, when Brogan suddenly called in a whispered shout, "Over here!"

He had found a workstation with Wheelan's name written on a sign nearby. They went through his desk and looked around but found nothing useful.

"Hard to know what you're looking for when you don't know what you're looking for, huh, Harvey?" Brogan said with a frustrated tone.

Harvey didn't respond. Brogan went over to where he was and saw King on his knees, rubbing something between his fingers.

"What is it?" Brogan asked.

"Not sure. But I'll tell you what I think it might be. It feels and looks like a few small pieces of plastic explosive. It's called *Semtex.*"

"Holy hell!"

"Indeed, my Irish friend. This Wheelan fool may have planted some of the stuff in Winston's big box."

"I think it might be time to tell someone and get some help with this thing."

"You're right, sport. But who can we trust? This thing has conspiracy written all over it. Allen Dulles told me to trust no one."

*

At that moment, Harvey King and Tiernan Brogan had no clue just how true Dulles's caveat had been. They did not have even a slight suspicion someone might have followed them to Birmingham. There is no way Tiernan could have known that when he called his trusted contact at MI5 for some background on Michael Wheelan, that one small request would set off silent alarm bells at the highest levels of that agency.

As King and Brogan made their way out of Newman Brothers in the dark of the night, they came face-to-face with three ominous-looking figures in the shadows. Harvey King quickly surmised they were not representing the local constable. He guessed that they weren't even British. He saw them as what they were because he had dealt with the likes of them more times than he could count over the years. They were Russians.

One man spoke up and his accent confirmed King's suspicion said, "We would like to talk with you. Please come with us. We mean you no harm."

But Harvey King sensed the lie. The trio was really there to learn what, if anything, he and Brogan knew. King decided that they meant a whole lot of harm. Thinking quickly, he calculated only two possible outcomes—kill or be killed.

He drew his gun with a quick fluid motion and fired three shots with poise and precision. He dropped all three men in less than two seconds.

Brogan leaped back and fell to the ground for cover. "What the hell, King? You might tell a guy what you're gonna do. Now we'll have the authorities on our case," he protested.

"Not a chance, sport. Let's get the hell out of here."

"How can you be sure they weren't just company security?"

"I have a nose for Commies, Brogan. I know 'em when I see 'em. And when I get the chance, I kill 'em, before they can kill me. I just saved your ass. You're welcome. Now, let's move!"

Within the hour, King and Brogan were on another train back to London, with no idea what to do next. Meanwhile, still in Birmingham, local authorities were arriving on the scene of the shooting. But within an hour, word came down from Scotland Yard that the events that night at Newman Brothers were a matter of national security. It was to be kept out of the newspapers. Once agents arrived from London, all evidence in the case, including the lifeless bodies, was to be turned over to MI5. No questions asked. The order was authoritative and unambiguous. *Official Secrets Act* and all. Under normal conditions, the killing of three men near where Churchill's casket was adorned would be big news, at least one would think.

But it would never see the light of day.

CHAPTER SEVENTEEN

THE TRAIN CARRYING HARVEY KING and Tiernan Brogan was scheduled to arrive back at Easton station in London a few minutes past four o'clock early Monday morning. They read several newspaper articles about Churchill's death and the preparations for his funeral. The great man had been dead less than twenty-four hours. They also discussed their next move. They were essentially on their own and blind. There was no one in England to call or ask for help. It was up to them to figure out what was happening. King had left the full-length report about Churchill's funeral in his satchel back at the hotel. But he had taken a few notes on what he read. They were in a small notebook he kept in his inside jacket pocket. One of the items he had written down had to do with something that struck him as strange at the time—that Churchill's body would be embalmed at his home and not be moved from there until he was taken to Westminster to lie in state.

"But he can't be taken to Westminster until the House of Commons votes on it?" King asked Brogan, who was naturally more familiar with British protocol than the American was.

"Correct. And the paper says that the House will meet in special session Monday, er, later this morning. They'll vote and then adjourn for the week."

"So where's the fancy casket now?"

"Your guess is as good as mine," Brogan replied. "Probably at some London mortuary."

"I didn't see anything in the newspaper about that, did you?"

"No."

"Well, if that casket has been tampered with in any way..."

"You mean if explosive materials have been put in there?"

"Of course I mean that, jackass!" Then Harvey caught himself and checked his anger. "Sorry, sport. I'm tired."

"We both are. But we need to figure out where that box is. You sure you don't remember reading about a mortuary in that report you read on the plane?"

"It has to be that place over in Paddington where I followed those two guys from the Soviet Embassy. What's the name?"

"The name is Kenyon," Brogan said. Then he seemed lost in thought for a moment. "I remember it from when George the Sixth died and then his mother, Queen Mary, a year later, back in the early '50s. I was in college. That's the place. Funeral directors to the royals, and all that."

"Great. When we hit town, we'll check it out. No telling when that casket will leave there and head over to Churchill's home. Once he's tucked away in that big box, we'll never get a peek inside."

After a long silence between them, Brogan asked, "So how do you know about that explosive material? I've never heard of it?"

"There was a memo about it six months or so ago, something circulated to all CIA stations. Don't usually read much, but since there is nothing else to do in Rome but go to church or drink, I read up on the stuff. It's going to become the stuff of choice to bombers in the future. Very stable. Made in Czechoslovakia."

"Does fire trigger it?"

"No. It'll just burn if lit with a match. It takes a real jolt, like something electrical to blow it up. But when it blows up, it's very powerful."

"So how would it be set off?"

"Well, sport, I think there is probably a device attached to it—something that will give it the shock it needs. And I would then guess that there will be someone nearby with another device to send a signal. Then—boom!"

Roger Hollis handpicked Sean Welling as one of his personal assistants less than a year after the young man had joined MI5. An Oxford graduate with a first-class honors degree in early European history, Welling was a tireless worker and someone the director seemed to enjoy talking with very much, at work and even after hours. This raised a few eyebrows and there were rumors that maybe the director and the young assistant were more than just coworkers.

They were, but not in the way some suspected.

In fact, in many ways, Welling had been *created* by Roger Hollis. Or at least, recreated. The file in the official records stored at the headquarters of the Security Service at Leconfield House on Curzon Street in the Mayfair section of London, told quite a story about Mr. Welling. He was born out of wedlock in Hastings. His mother gave him up when he was just four months old. He was passed around from home to home until finding a measure of domestic permanence with a childless couple in Yorkshire, Clive and Elizabeth Welling.

Mr. Welling was a teacher, and Mrs. Welling did domestic work for hire. Young Sean went to live with them when he was just shy of his sixth birthday. He grew into a fine young man. He studied hard and found his way to Oxford, where he distinguished himself as a bit of a scholar. He was then recruited into the Security Service, where he, like cream rising to the top, soon found himself moving in heady circles. But he did so in a way that seemed to bother no one. He was friendly, humble, likable, and dedicated.

And every word of it was *untrue*.

Sean Welling was really Sean Wheelan, only son of Soviet spies Michael and Molly from Birmingham. Long before he left their home in Birmingham to study at Oxford, his new persona was fully developed. He committed his life to follow in his parents' covert footsteps. There was little chance that anyone would have any reason to dig very deep in the records to find out the truth about a teenage boy who was starting university study.

But if anyone had been of a mind to snoop and dig deep enough, they might have learned that the real Clive and Elizabeth Welling, along with their infant son Sean, had died during a German bombing raid back in 1941.

∗

On this first day after the passing of Sir Winston Churchill, Sean Welling was at his post just outside the director's office at Leconfield House at a little before six a.m. There was much work to be done, official and otherwise. It was the latter that was uppermost on his mind as he sipped a cup of heavily creamed, and even more heavily sugared, coffee.

He had spent some time with his parents—his real parents—a few hours earlier. Mike and Molly managed traveled to London a couple of times a month to see Sean. This, though, was more than a familial get together. They did not discuss the complete details, but it was clear to the three of them that they were on the threshold of something extraordinary. A lifetime of waiting and working would soon lead to a great and victorious moment for the cause to which they had been devoted for so long.

Sean was uniquely positioned to monitor the flow of information at Leconfield House and was therefore able to respond quickly when he learned of Tiernan Brogan's query regarding Michael the evening before. The fact that the three men his handler sent to Birmingham were now dead was a problem. But so far, he had been able to keep a lid on things. An authoritative directive from the personal assistant to the director of MI5 carried much weight. Sean had not yet briefed his boss on all of this. That would be job one when Roger Hollis arrived at the office.

The director would not be happy.

∗

King and Brogan grabbed breakfast in the restaurant at their hotel around six thirty. Though the night had been sleepless, except for a few fleeting moments on the train back to London, they were wide awake and fully alert. The latest edition of the *Daily Mail* contained an article confirming the fact that JH. Kenyon Funeral Directors in Westminster were indeed handling most of the funeral arrangements for Churchill, including housing the special casket until it was needed at 28 Hyde Park Gate.

The article also indicated that the casket would be delivered there on Tuesday. This gave the men the rest of that day and night to try to find a way to access it to determine if it contained explosive materials.

They weighed their options. Clearly, Brogan's call to MI5 had put the three now very dead Russians on their trail.

"Still trying to figure out how a call to British Security Service triggered Russian operatives," Brogan asked.

"Moles," King replied to what he considered a very naive question.

"Moles?"

"Yeah, moles. Both the Brits and Americans have that problem. The Russkies have worked on this for decades. You think Philby, MacLean, and Burgess were all of it?"

"Obviously you don't."

"Damn straight, sport. In fact, there are some people in the CIA who think the top man in your government is a KGB plant."

"You don't mean the prime minister?"

"That's exactly what I mean. This fish stinks from the head down. We can't trust anyone official over here."

Brogan thought for a moment as he finished the last bite of the strip of toast he had dipped into a soft-boiled egg. Then he asked, "How about unofficial?"

"Gonna have to give me more than that, sport."

"Well, look at this little tidbit in the paper," he said. Brogan folded the paper a couple of times and handed it to King with a brief article in the center. The headline read: *FORMER BODYGUARD RECALLS CHURCHILL'S COURAGE*. King took a moment to read the short piece.

"Oh yeah, Walter Thompson wrote that book about his time with Churchill. My ex-wife and I watched him on *To Tell the Truth* on television a couple of years ago. He was old Winnie's personal bodyguard back in the war. Saved Churchill's life several times, to hear him tell it. Retired Scotland Yard man. Must be at least seventy-five years old," King said.

"He loved Churchill," Brogan answered. "If he knew what we knew, he'd move heaven and earth, and even hell to get to the bottom of it. And he's absolutely unofficial. But he'd know how to open doors, or even kick 'em in if need."

"So how do we find old Mr. Thompson?"

"Well, the article mentioned a London flat, so it shouldn't be too hard. Besides, it's the only lead we have. We should leg it."

"What?"

"Leg it. You know, run for it."

"Why don't you just speak English, sport?"

CHAPTER EIGHTEEN

MARY BROUGHT ANOTHER CUP of tea to her husband as he watched the telly. Walter Thompson's eyes had been glued to the small screen for hours. He had slept in his living room chair, and he remained dressed in his conservative business suit. The elderly former lawman was grief-stricken. He was hoping there would be more interviews like the one he had given a day earlier in the immediate hours following his former boss's death, but so far no one else had reached out.

Then came the knock on the door of the flat.

"Mary dear, let me head to the back for a moment and wash my face. Let whoever it is in, and tell them that I'll be right out."

"Of course, my love," she replied as she made her way to the door. She opened it and saw two men. "Yes?" she asked.

"Mrs. Thompson, we're sorry to bother you so early, but we'd love to have a word with your husband."

"Certainly, and what newspaper are you with?"

King and Brogan looked at each other. "Newspaper, um, yes, we're with the *Times*."

"The devil you say? Well, please come in. I'll fetch Mr. Thompson. Can I offer a cup of tea?"

Brogan answered for the duo. "Yes, that'd be lovely. Many thanks, Mrs. Thompson."

A few moments later, Walter Thompson, impeccably dressed and looking like he had benefited from a great night's sleep, walked into the room. "Mrs. Thompson says you gentlemen are from the *Times*. Mighty fine. I'm happy to talk to you about Mr. Churchill. And please let me sign copies of my book for you."

"Very kind of you," Brogan replied. "You served Mr. Churchill during the war?"

"Actually, I did two tours of duty with him. Back in the 1920s, then, yes, during the war. He was a demanding boss."

"There are stories that you saved his life."

"Many times. I have written about it all in my book."

"Yes, of course," Brogan said tolerantly.

Harvey King had never been known for his patience. So just about the time Mary Thompson was preparing to serve the tea, he decided to end the charade. "Mr. Thompson, we have great respect for you and your work, but we are not journalists. We've been sent here by the President of the United States."

Mary dropped an empty teacup on the carpet.

Walter Thompson calmly asked, "To what do I owe this kind of visit and honor on this particular day?"

"Well, sir, we've been sent to Great Britain to investigate a possible plot involving Mr. Churchill," Brogan replied.

Thompson smiled. "Well, I suppose you men have heard the news. Churchill is gone. He is now out of any danger from this world. I suppose he is in a summit meeting with his Maker right about now. Here's hoping that his Maker was ready for the meeting." Thompson picked up his cup of tea.

"Of course we know he's dead, Thompson," King replied, curtly. Then he caught himself. "Sorry, sir. My partner and I didn't get much sleep last night."

"I know how you feel. I understand. Please proceed, and tell me how I can help you and President Johnson."

"Recently, someone in the British government told President Johnson that Mr. Churchill's funeral might become the backdrop for exploitation on the part of the Soviet Union," King said.

"How so?"

"We're not at liberty to talk about the details, but our investigation has led us to believe that there's a measure of credibility to this possibility."

"What can you tell me?"

King was doing all the talking. "Just this. I left three Russian thugs dead in a doorway in Birmingham a few hours ago."

"What the devil were you doing all the way over there—and what does it have to do with the late prime minister?"

"We paid a visit to the establishment where Mr. Churchill's casket was prepared, and we found evidence that leads us to believe what President Johnson told us may be very true," King replied.

"And this evidence?"

"Let's just say, that it's possible that the casket in which Mr. Churchill's body is to be placed in a few hours contains explosive materials."

Thompson grew agitated. "This is not possible!"

Brogan finally chimed in. "I know it sounds incredible, Mr. Thompson. But it is very true."

"It's vital that we get access to that casket. Do you know anyone close to the family? Someone who can be discreet and trusted?" King asked the retired lawman.

Thompson reflected for a moment, then said, "Actually, my friends, I think I know just the bloke."

CHAPTER NINETEEN

HARRY HYLTON-FOSTER HAD PRESIDED over the House of Commons in Parliament for nearly five years. Most of his work was routine, punctuated with moments of drama, but he thoroughly enjoyed his role. His support—as with most of the men who had held his post down through the decades and centuries—was bipartisan. And his job was secure despite the vicissitudes of British politics.

The Speaker was just shy of his sixty-fifth birthday. *Churchill was my age when he first became Prime Minister*, he thought. He looked at his reflection in the full-length mirror in his small anteroom adjacent to the House floor. *I am planning to retire in a few months, after a full career. Yet old Winnie reinvented himself at my age and changed the world. What a man!*

He was just about fully dressed and ready to enter the famous room—the House of Commons Chamber. As he surveyed his outfit in the mirror's reflection—white shirt and bands, black coat concealing a black gown underneath, stockings and buckled shoes—he was struck by the quiet in the next room. The chamber was usually a noisy place, and he would most often hear that noise even in his adjacent private room. Any other day and he would have wondered if anyone was there—but not today. He anticipated every Member's seat would be filled, and the galleries overflowing.

The Speaker reached for the final adornment to complete the customary costume identified for so long with his important office—a full-bottomed wig. He placed it on his head and adjusted it for a moment. Then Harry Hylton-Foster took a deep breath and looked over at the clock on the wall. It was now nearly half-past two. He made his way toward his elevated seat.

Everyone stood as the Speaker took his place. As he surveyed the room, he immediately focused on one man.

"Mr. Prime Minister," the Speaker bellowed.

Harold Wilson took a few steps to the podium. "Mr. Speaker, I have a message to the House of Commons from Her Majesty the Queen." Wilson then walked toward the Speaker's elevated chair and handed the document to Hylton-Foster, who read the message to the House:

"From Her Majesty the Queen: I know that it will be the wish of all my people that the loss which we have sustained by the death of the Right Honourable Sir Winston Churchill, K.G., should be met in the most fitting manner and that they should have an opportunity of expressing their sorrow at the loss and their veneration of the memory of that outstanding man who in war and peace served his country unfailingly for more than fifty years and in the hours of our greatest danger was the inspiring leader who strengthened and supported us all. Confident that I can rely upon the support of my faithful Commons and upon their liberality in making suitable provision for the proper discharge of our debt of gratitude and tribute of national sorrow, I have directed that Sir Winston's body shall lie in state in Westminster Hall and that thereafter the Funeral Service shall be held in the Cathedral Church of St. Paul.' – ELIZABETH REGINA."

Prime Minister Wilson stood once again and moved to the podium. He paused and then began to read the words he had so carefully crafted over several days:

"I beg to move, that an humble address be presented to Her Majesty humbly to thank Her Majesty for having given directions for the body of the Rt. Hon. Sir Winston Churchill, K.G., to lie in state in Westminster Hall and for the funeral service to be held in the Cathedral Church of St. Paul and assuring Her Majesty of our cordial aid and concurrence in these measures for expressing the affection and admiration in which the memory of this great man is held by this House and all Her Majesty's faithful subjects. In accepting this Motion, this House, and, by virtue of its representation in this House, the nation, collectively and reverently will be paying its tribute to a great statesman, a great Parliamentarian, a great leader of this country—"

*

The television was on in the background back at the Thompsons' London flat. As Prime Minister Wilson moved through his lengthy address, Mary Thompson filled the teacups yet again as King and Brogan continued their conversation with Churchill's former bodyguard.

"Yes, of course, I know people on his staff. His chief guard is called Ed Murray. He's on loan from Scotland Yard, same as I was all those years ago," Thompson said.

"What we need is to find someone who will get us access to Kenyon's Mortuary. And it has to be under the radar, so to speak. Do you understand?" King asked.

"Yes, of course I understand. I'm old, not daft. You wouldn't even know the word 'RADAR' were it not for Churchill. I was there when we approved that project. It was one more way the great man saved the nation and the world."

"No argument here, Thompson," King replied. "We mean no disrespect."

Thompson put his hands up, palms forward. "I'm also not a sensitive old man. You have a job to do, and I want to help. You want me to try to talk to Detective Sergeant Murray about this?"

Brogan spoke up. "You see, the thing is that we know there is someone at MI5 who has already tried to stop us. I'd imagine that the same people who have people there have people at Scotland Yard."

"Likely," Thompson said. "But not Murray. No one can be around Churchill as long as he has been without practiced loyalty and discretion."

"How would you contact him?" King asked.

"Simple. I'd head over to the home and pay my respects. Mrs. Churchill never liked me that much, but she knows that her husband did. Then I'll find a way to talk with Murray in private and see if we can find a way in to look at the casket. Leave it to me."

160

Back in the House of Commons, Harold Wilson was nearing the end of his speech:

"We meet today in this moment of tribute, of spontaneous sympathy this House feels for Lady Churchill and all the members of his family. We are conscious only that the tempestuous years are over; the years of appraisal are yet to come. It is a moment for the heartfelt tribute that this House, of all places, desires to pay in an atmosphere of quiet.

"For now the noise of hooves thundering across the veldt; the clamour of the hustings in a score of contests; the shots in Sidney Street, the angry guns of Gallipoli, Flanders, Coronel and the Falkland Islands; the sullen feet of marching men in Tony pandy; the urgent warnings of the Nazi threat; the whine of the sirens and the dawn bombardment of the Normandy beaches--all these now are silent. There is a stillness. And in that stillness, echoes and memories. To each whose life has been touched by Winston Churchill, to each his memory. And as those memories are told and retold, as the world pours in its tributes, as world leaders announce their intention, in this jet age, of coming to join in this vast assembly to pay honour and respect to his memory, we in this House treasure one thought, and it was a thought some of us felt it right to express in the Parliamentary tributes on his retirement. Each one of us recalls some little incident--many of us, as in my own case, a kind action, graced with the courtesy of a past generation and going far beyond the normal calls of Parliamentary comradeship. Each of us has his own memory, for in the tumultuous diapason of a world's tributes, all of us here at least know the epitaph he would have chosen for himself: 'He was a good House of Commons man.'"

The room was uncharacteristically silent as Harold Wilson stepped back and took his seat. The House of Commons became a platform for British eloquence for the next hour or so, as several prominent members weighed in about Winston Churchill.

One of the last speakers that day seemed to sum it all up for everyone listening—in the room and via radio worldwide. He was a "back-bencher" named R.H. Turton. Churchill himself, though remembered for so many great deeds, had spent a great deal of time in his political career riding the back benches of the House of Commons. So Turton's words, as well as the fact that it was someone like him sharing them, were powerful:

> "Sir Winston Churchill loved this House. Your freshest memory of him, Mr. Speaker, will be of him rising from that seat below the Gangway, reluctantly accepting the support of two honorable Members, tottering to the Bar of the House and there making his bow to you, Mr. Speaker, and to Parliament, which he loved. As this afternoon we sadly leave this Chamber and pass under the Churchill Arch, we will recollect that that arch was left by him untouched and un-repaired to remind Parliament of the fury the Nazis unleashed against this nation and this Parliament. To many of us in future that battered and chipped relic of the former Chamber will be a permanent memorial to the man who loved democratic freedom, who revered our Parliamentary procedure and who in the judgment of all was the greatest Member that Parliament, in all its 700 years, has ever known."

Soon thereafter, the question was called and agreed to unanimously. What had been assumed was now official. The grand farewell for Sir Winston Leonard Spencer Churchill would be of the highest order—a full state funeral. He was the first commoner to be so honored since William Gladstone.

CHAPTER TWENTY

A LITTLE MORE THAN AN HOUR LATER, Walter Thompson made his way through a small crowd and knocked on the door at 28 Hyde Park gate. He was hoping that a familiar face would greet him, though it had been a few years since he had last visited the Churchill home. He was pleasantly surprised when the door opened.

"Thompson! So nice of you to call. Please come in," said Edmund Murray.

"I thought to call first, but then decided to just pop over this way. Sorry if this is an intrusion."

"Not at all. Would you like to speak to Mrs. Churchill?"

"Oh, well, yes—to pay my respects and that sort of thing. But the real purpose of my visit is to speak with you."

"Me? What the devil for?"

"Well, can we find a quiet spot? I'll fill you in. I think there is information you need to know."

Murray hesitated. "Okay, Thompson. Let's talk first. Then I'll take you to the family," he said, with a hint of suspicion. Murray led Thompson through a couple of hallways and then down some stairs to an area that looked like a small office. "We can talk here. It's my spot."

"Excellent, and thank you so much for this courtesy."

"Well, you have me curious."

"I understand. Let me plunge right into it. I was paid a visit a bit ago by two men who said they had been sent by the American president."

"Lyndon Johnson?"

"I think they only have the one president, so yes, that's the bloke."

"We just got word from Ambassador David Bruce that President Johnson is very ill and will not be able to attend Sir Winston's funeral."

Thompson pondered Murray's words for a brief moment and then said, "Well, that would certainly make sense in light of what his two emissaries told me."

"Why you, Thompson? If they have a message for this family, they should send it through official channels. I'm sorry, but this makes no sense at all."

"I suppose it doesn't. And it's about to get worse."

*

King and Brogan returned to their hotel. They waited for Walter Thompson to come by following his visit to Hyde Park Gate. King headed down to the bar and Brogan felt the need to follow. For all his skills and insight, the legend of Harvey King also included a reputation for significant alcohol consumption.

But on this day, he and Harvey needed to be clear-eyed. Their lack of sleep made this even more important. He was determined to stop Harvey after one drink.

He pulled up a stool a few feet away from King just in time to hear the spy order his drink. "Your finest ginger ale, sport."

"No hard stuff, Harvey?"

"Hey, we're on a case. You can get shit-faced if you want, but as for me, it's soft drinks until we get to the bottom of this thing."

Tiernan Brogan motioned to the bartender. "I'll have what my American friend is having."

*

"I suppose I could find some reason to make a trip over to Kenyon, but I'm sure it would be noticed. It's risky, and it seems to me that this is all a bit on the sketchy side," Murray told Thompson.

"I disagree. I don't think it's, as you say—sketchy. You've already mentioned that Johnson won't be traveling here. How about the Soviets—who are they sending?"

"Not sure."

"You should check. I'll wager that it will be some lower level bloke. You'll likely see no major Politburo members on the list of important people coming to St. Paul's next Saturday," Thompson said.

*

"We've been burned, sport," King said. "Someone, somewhere knows that we are on the trail. Most likely they have eyes either on or *in* that funeral home."

"How will we get in?"

"I don't think *we* are."

"Who, then?"

"How about our new friend, Mr. Thompson?"

"He's old and not all that steady. I'm not sure he's up to it."

"Listen, Brogan. The man spent decades in harm's way to protect good old Mr. Churchill. I think the adrenaline alone will take a quarter-century off the old guy's clock—at least for enough time to get the job done."

"Maybe so. But will he do it?"

"Of course he will. He'll see it as his duty. I know his type."

*

A short while later, Walter Thompson entered the bar at the Dorchester. He sat at a corner table. Harvey—looking at a mirror behind the bar—saw the retired lawman enter and motioned to Brogan, leading him over to Thompson's table.

"Mr. Murray will lend his support to our investigation," Thompson said.

"Have a drink, Mr. Thompson?" Brogan asked.

"Nothing for me, thank you. I'm back on duty," the older man said with a big smile.

"Indeed you are, sir," Brogan replied.

"How shall we proceed?"

Harvey responded. "Well, there is no 'we' on this one."

"I don't understand."

"We're burned, Thompson, at least me and the redhead here. Can't go anywhere near that funeral joint."

Thompson grimaced at the use of the word "joint," but he let it go. "Are you saying this is a solo operation?"

"That's exactly what we're saying, old man," King said.

"Well, you might start by not calling me old. Apparently, I'm the only operative you have."

King and Brogan smiled and raised their glasses. Thompson had no drink, so he picked up his hat from the table, put it on his head, and tipped it to the two men.

"So, you need to square it with this Murray guy. I think the best plan is for you to do your examination of the casket sometime tonight," King said.

"I'll set it up, Mr. King. Let's say about half-past nine. That should be late enough to avoid too much attention, yet give us enough time to figure out what to do if there *is* a bomb in that box."

"Won't look like a bomb, per se. What you'll be looking for is some plastic explosive. It's like putty and can be worked into just about any shape."

"I'm familiar with it."

"Good. Now, it's obviously hidden out of sight. Maybe in the lining?"

Thompson nodded. "My guess is that the casket is lined with lead."

"Lead?"

"Yes. Protects the remains from the elements down through the years."

"Is that lining inside the wood?"

"Not likely. I'd say it was an insert, like veneer."

169

King thought for a moment. "I'll bet you a new hat the funny putty is in between that lead lining and the wood. I'd look there first. You'll need some tools."

"Oh yes. I have some fine tools. They've been in storage. I will get to play with some old toys."

Walter Thompson lingered at the Dorchester hotel bar for another fifteen minutes. Harvey King had gotten to asking him about the old days, when the lawman was still guarding Churchill. Soon Thompson was in the middle of an animated story.

"Just a day or so after Mr. Churchill became Prime Minister—this would be May 1940—he decided, against my advice, to travel to Paris to meet with Paul Reynaud. The French were on the brink of catastrophe and the old man wanted to persuade them to fight on. I remember that the boss turned to me at one point, just as he was about to meet Reynaud, and said, 'Give me your gun, Thompson. You never know what will happen. I do not intend to be taken alive,'" the lawman said with a bit of a chuckle.

"Would he have done it? Would he have taken his own life?" Brogan asked.

"Not bloody likely. He might have taken a bullet from another gun, though. I'm sure, however, if he did die like that, he would've taken quite a few of the enemy with him to the other side."

"Fascinating," Brogan said. Then he saw a wide smile come to Thompson's face. "What?"

"I was just remembering what happened when we did finally meet the French Prime Minister."

"Do tell," King said, now growing slightly bored and regretting having asked about the past.

"Well, Reynaud was in the company of his mistress—some Countess such and such. He had sent his family out of the city and toward the coast for safety. This crazy tart suddenly lunges at Mr. Churchill with a knife in hand. It was Reynaud's mistress and she hated Mr. Churchill. She had ties to Nazis in Germany and Fascists in Italy. Her name was Hélène de Portes and she had hidden a knife in her expensive Christian-Dior dress. I grabbed it as she went for the old man's throat and shoved her away."

"Incredible," Brogan said.

"Indeed. Might have been the shortest British Premiership in history. And we wouldn't be here making our big plans today," Thompson said. He then pulled out his watch and said, "Well, gentlemen, I need to be on my way. Where shall we meet up after I'm finished with the assignment—here?"

King replied, "No. Let's rendezvous at your flat—say about eleven?"

"Splendid. I shall see you both then. Wish me luck."

"God speed, Mr. Thompson," Brogan said.

Thompson gave the duo another tip of the hat and made his way to the exit.

CHAPTER TWENTY-ONE

"ABOUT DONE, HARVEY?" Brogan asked. Then he saw alarm in his colleague's face. "What is it?"

"We have company. Look at the mirror behind the bar to your left. You should be able to see a couple of ugly-ass fellows."

Brogan casually glanced and saw what King saw: two men surveying the room and finally sitting at a table across the room from them. King slid his chair slightly to the left and motioned for Brogan to do the same—thus taking them out of direct view of the visitors.

"I'd bet my left nut that they are friends of the gentlemen we met in Birmingham."

"Well, we can't sit here for long. If we can see them in the mirror, they can see us. We need to move."

"I agree, sport. And it's obvious that we can't go back up to the room—it's probably blown, too."

"I'm listening. You're the boss here, Harvey."

"Gee, thanks." King paused. Finally, he said, "Here's the plan. Whatever happens, meet me at The Criterion in Piccadilly in one hour."

"Okay, got it. But how do we get from here to there?"

"Need a diversion. Then we run like hell."

"What kind of diversion?"

"There are two ways out of here. We'll split up. You go out the side door, I'll head out the front. Now, I want you to get up and walk slowly toward this end of the bar—the toilets are out that door."

"Okay—"

"When you get near the bar, fling that glass of yours down toward the middle of that big mirror. Then hightail it out the door. I'll watch the bad guys and plan my exit accordingly."

"I'm sure they'll be following me."

"Better for me," King said with a broad smile. "After all, you're younger and faster."

Brogan stood up slowly. With his back to the bad guys, he shuffled over toward the bar. He looked at King just before turning and flinging his glass, a fairly sturdy mug. that hit the mirror and shattered it in a split second. There was commotion. The two visitors jumped up and ran toward Brogan, who was out the door in a flash. King disappeared through the main entrance, and was soon out on the street.

Meanwhile, Brogan had entered the lady's privy, which was, fortunately, unoccupied. Three long minutes later, the coast was clear and Brogan made his way out a back exit of the Dorchester and into a narrow alley.

*

Around the time King and Brogan were taking different routes to Piccadilly to meet up at The Criterion, Sean Welling's desk telephone rang, and he answered it.

"H-h-hello," a voice said. "I'm c-calling from The Savoy Hotel to confirm the director's dinner reservation for six thirty this evening."

Welling was puzzled for a brief moment because he knew of no such dinner plans on the director's calendar. Then he realized that this was about something else.

"Oh, er, yes—that is confirmed. The director will be there."

"Wonderful," the voice said. Then the caller rang off.

Welling took a breath and then stood up and walked over to his boss's door. He knocked and heard a reply through the door.

"Very sorry to bother you, Director. But you just got a call from the Savoy confirming your dinner there tonight."

"Tonight? The Dorchester? I don't recall—"

"Yes, Director. You remember—six thirty?" Welling said, a look in his eyes.

"Ah yes," Roger Hollis said, his expression changing with understanding. "Did the caller identify himself?"

"No, Director—he did not. Sounded nervous, though-- almost like he had a stutter."

"A stutter, you say?" Hollis said, as he seemed to drift off in thought.

"Sir?" Welling pressed.

"Well, thank you, Sean. That's all for now."

Sean closed the door, pondering the look on his boss's face and his quick and curious dismissal.

*

A minute or so after three o'clock, Tiernan Brogan entered the beautiful restaurant. He immediately spotted Harvey King at the bar. As he walked over and sat on a stool next to the American, he also saw that the spy had left ginger ale in the dust in favor of something much stronger.

"Gotta keep a clear head, Harvey. Better take it easy on the hard stuff," Brogan said with a small laugh.

"Mind your own damn business. We got plenty of time— nothing but time until eleven. So I figure I can take a break. Join me?"

"Just one, I s'pose. What're you drinking?"

"Irish, in honor of my partner," King said, as he lifted his glass. "Barkeep, please bring my friend a glass of this fine whiskey—what do you call it?"

"Tullamore Dew. Coming right up."

"You had me checked out all the way down to my whiskey—do I have that right?"

"You're quick, sport. Real quick," King said. Then he winked at Brogan as the barkeep set a glass in front of him.

"How are we going to get back into our room at The Dorchester?"

"We're not."

"What about our things?"

"What do you have there that can't be replaced in thirty minutes at Selfridges? We left nothing of value in the room— certainly nothing that would be of any interest to anyone snooping around. That's the beauty of traveling light. I got my gun and my notes. Let's pick up a few things later, and maybe we could persuade our new former Scotland Yard friend to let us flop at his flat."

"Whatever you say, Harvey. Now what?"

"Let's find a way to call Dulles back home. We're long overdue to check in. He's probably pissing blood by now."

"Need a secure line," Brogan warned.

"Hell, we just need to speak in generalities. Dulles knows the drill. We can use any old phone. No matter who listens, they'll never figure out what we're talking about."

*

Kim Philby was thrilled to be back in London. His suite at the Savoy was a reminder of what he had had to leave in service of the Soviet cause. He knew that many people believed he indeed sold his soul in a prolonged act of betrayal, but part of that soul that missed England. His two years in Moscow had been eye opening. He was amused by the idea that his masters would trust him so much.

What Philby didn't know was that the people in Moscow did not trust him at all. Which is why they had assigned two of their best covert agents to keep a close watch over him. Kim had no clue. The master spy who prided himself on his instincts for tradecraft was oblivious to their presence.

His instructions were to stay in his suite, unless he was needed at the embassy. But Kim was determined to make the most of his visit home. He did not know how long he would be in England, and he wanted to savor every last moment.

Shortly after making the call to Sean Welling and getting the message to Roger Hollis, Kim ventured down to the hotel's American Bar. It was off limits—in fact, he had been told explicitly to stay out of public view and away from alcohol. But Kim was not one for rules. So after checking his disguise, complete with beard and glasses, he walked in and took a spot at the far end of the bar.

"What can I get you, guv'nor?"

"Thank you, my g-good m-man. Black Label please. A double."

Kim enjoyed his drink and never noticed the two men at the other end of the bar. If he looked closer, he might have noticed they were drinking Russian vodka.

*

"Yes sir. We've pretty much confirmed things," King said. He was speaking with a fairly loud voice into the receiver in a red telephone box one block from The Criterion.

"As bad as we thought?" Allen Dulles asked.

"It's starting to look that way, sir. But we'll know more later tonight."

"How much later?"

"Eleven o'clock or so here—six your time."

"All right then. Find a way to call me."

"Yes, sir."

CHAPTER TWENTY-TWO

MARY HEARD HER HUSBAND ENTER the flat and called out a hello from the kitchen. But there was no reply. Thompson had disappeared into a small room he used as an office of sorts, when that was needed, which was rarely these days.

By the time Mary came into the living room, her clearly preoccupied husband had exited a small room he used as his office and was now heading back out the front door with a small satchel in his left hand. She watched him turn left to their storage area just outside with curiosity.

Mary returned to her work in the kitchen, but after a few moments curiosity got the best of her. She walked quietly, feeling a twinge of guilt for sneaking up on her husband. When she peeked around a corner near the storage area, she saw that Walter had unlocked a locker-type door and was putting a few things in the small satchel.

"Something for a rainy day, dear?" she said, deciding to speak up.

Walter was momentarily startled, but quickly recovered. "I need some tools for an assignment," he said.

"I'd imagine this has much to do with those two men who visited us."

"Yes. But it's not something I can talk about. All very hush-hush."

"Haven't heard that phrase for years. Used to hear it all the time when you worked for Mr. Churchill."

"When *we* worked for Mr. Churchill."

Mary smiled and said, "Yes, of course. We worked for him. But I just typed his endless letters. You saved his life."

"And I'm about to do it again, my dear Mary."

"The devil you say. And how might one go about saving the life of a dead man?"

"For starters, Mary, we can help make sure this dead man doesn't lead to more dead men."

*

Roger Hollis took his usual table at The Savoy Grill. He sent the wine steward away, insisting on just a simple bowl of chicken soup. While waiting for the soup, he made a trip to the men's room. Alex was on duty again. Hollis washed his hands and then handed the attendant a five-pound note.

"Very kind of you, sir. Please let me give you some change," Alex said, as he handed a one-pound note to Hollis. Hollis then picked up a small stack of towels and retrieved a small slip of paper bearing the instruction: "Room 312."

The director returned to his table and ate about half of his bowl of soup. He summoned the waiter and gave him sufficient funds to pay the bill, including a generous tip. "I forgot an important meeting, sorry to leave so abruptly," he said. "Please keep the change, my good fellow."

Hollis walked out of the restaurant and purchased an evening paper at the newsstand. He looked around to make sure no one was watching. Once he was convinced it was safe, he entered the lift and told the attendant, "Third floor, please. Thank you so much."

Kim Philby, sans fake beard and mustache, greeted Roger Hollis with a big grin. Hollis smiled back at the familiar face. Though Philby had long since been "retired" from the British Security Services, Hollis was actually seven years older than his fellow traitor and conspirator.

"R-Roger, you old son of a bitch, so nice to see you," Philby said.

"Color me surprised, Kim. Never thought I'd see the likes of you again—at least not in London," Hollis replied. The two men laughed.

"I'm drinking Black Label; can I fix you one, old fellow?"

"Please, yes, thank you. But I must ask two things of you."

"Fire away," Kim said as he poured Hollis's drink and another for himself.

"First, what the hell are you doing here? And second, what the hell are you doing here?"

"Simple, Mr. Director. I'm on of-f-ficial business for our mutual friends."

"I gather that. But what is it that requires such risk?"

"Simply the most bold and visionary thing our friends have ever contemplated. It's a vision that Comrade Stalin first had, and one that after his death was kept alive for the right moment."

"And that moment has arrived?"

"I think you already know the answer to that, Roger. Please don't be coy." Philby smiled and took a long pull from his glass. "You're not in the dark. I'm aware that you've been in the loop for a while. This is no time for games. We go back too far."

"Indeed we do, Kim. Indeed we do," Hollis said as he took only a small sip of his drink. "I was thinking today about our old friend Igor Gouzenko."

Philby said, "Ah yes, Canada."

"You sent me on that mission back in '46. He was naming names and causing so much trouble for our friends. That was when you were on track to become the head of MI6," Hollis said.

"Yes. It's t-t-rue. Can you imagine? I should be the head of MI6 now. That was always the plan. And it would have h-h-appened, but for that awful wreck of a man, Guy Burgess."

Likely the most notorious member of the infamous Cambridge Spy Ring, Burgess had a penchant for outrageous behavior, made all the more dangerous as he spiraled down into severe alcoholism. But even as he scorned his former comrade in conspiracy, Philby knew that he had himself to blame for taking Burgess into his home in Washington, DC. And once Burgess bolted for the other side of the Iron Curtain with fellow-traveler Donald McLean in May 1951, suspicion fell on Philby and any chance of a long-term career as a Soviet mole leading MI6 was gone.

Hollis said, "I heard he died a while back. Did you ever get a chance to visit with him in Moscow?"

"Why would I have wanted to do a thing like that? The man ruined my life. He wanted me to visit him when he was dying—it was shortly after I arrived in Moscow, but I refused," Philby replied. He was growing more and more agitated with every word. Then he paused. "It was his liver, you know."

"I'm sorry."

"Yes, it was all very sad. He did leave his library to me. A few weeks after his demise, several boxes appeared at my doorstep. The man had great taste in books, got to give him that. Six collector's edition copies of *Middlemarch*, can you imagine it?"

Changing the subject, Hollis asked, "What's life like in Moscow?"

"Bloody boring," Philby replied reflexively. Then he caught himself. "It's a rem-m-arkable place, though."

"But you miss England, don't you?" Hollis said, sensing the obvious.

"I suppose that's true. But it's all so much water under London Bridge, old fellow."

Hollis conjured a half-smile. "I can't stay all that long, so please tell me what you need to tell me."

"Certainly. Well, it's called KOBA. It's going to change the world."

*

At precisely nine o'clock, Walter Thompson and Edmund Murray approached a side door marked Office. "Thank you so much, Murray, for agreeing to help with this," Thompson said.

"Not at all. We share something in common: a love for the Churchill family. And I'd sure hate to see something so sinister as what you are suggesting happen," Murray replied. Murray had a brief word with two officers standing guard, identifying himself as a fellow officer and indicating his assignment to the Churchill family.

Thompson knocked at the door, but said, "Good that you're here to take the lead since you are active duty and I'm an old has-been."

"Aw hell. You're a living legend and you know it," Murray replied, as a young man opened the door. "Good evening," Murray said. "I'm from Scotland Yard. My partner and I represent the Churchill family."

"Oh yes—please come in. I'm Winston Fleming, and it's pretty much just me and a cleaning crew here right now, but for the officers in the front," he said.

"Winston, huh?" Murray asked.

"Yes, sir. I was born on May 11, 1940, the day after he became prime minister. Now I gets to be a little part of history, I guess."

"Indeed you do, young man. Indeed you do," said Thompson.

Fleming looked at Thompson and a gleam came to his eye. "Hey, I know you. You're the bloke who guarded Churchill all those years. Saw you on the telly. I pretty much watch and read everything about Churchill, seeing as I was named for him, and all."

"Yes, young man. I'm Walter Thompson."

"So the family brought you out of retirement to help with security!"

"Yes, that's it. Now, we need to have access to the casket for about a half hour. Could you direct us to the room?"

Fleming hesitated. "I'm not sure I can do that. I'm under strict orders not to let anyone have access to it."

"I'm sure it's fine. The officers outside know who we are," Murray replied.

"I have no doubt about that," Fleming said. "But they aren't the blokes I'm concerned about. It's the men with the casket right now."

"More men from Scotland Yard?" Thompson asked.

"I think not," Fleming said, almost in a whisper. He drew the men close and continued, "I think they are from something higher up. I think they're from MI-5. All I know is that they told me that my head would roll if I let anyone in."

Murray and Thompson glanced at each other, then Thompson, thinking quickly, said, "Oh, I see. Fine then. We just wanted to make sure the casket was secure. We'll wait for it to come to the residence."

Fleming was clearly relieved. He said, "Yes, that would be best, I think. I'm sorry I couldn't be of more help."

CHAPTER TWENTY-THREE

MEANWHILE, HARVEY KING and Tiernan Brogan, driven by equal measures of boredom and curiosity, were in a good position to observe as Murray and Thompson gained entrance into the Kenyon funeral establishment. Their perch was on the roof of a small building half a block away.

A minute or so after Murray and Thompson entered the funeral home, King and Brogan noticed two men across the block who were also watching the Kenyon building. Harvey used his small binoculars and realized that the two men across the way were the same men who tried to corner them at the Dorchester a few hours earlier.

"Those bastards," he muttered.

"Who?"

King handed the glasses to Brogan. He pointed and said, "Those two across the street."

Brogan adjusted his eyes and then said, "That's them. What the hell are they doing here?"

"Obviously they followed either Murray or Thompson."

"Which one?"

"Your guess is as good as mine. But they're trouble for sure," King said. "We need to make sure they don't follow either man from the funeral home."

"How?"

King looked over at Brogan. "Are you kidding me? There's only one way."

"I guess so. Just wanted to see if you had an alternative to increasing the body count."

"Hey, bad guys who do bad things are better off dead."

"I s'pose. Just not my cup of tea."

"Well, maybe you should put some of that Tullamore Dew shit in your tea, sport."

King and Brogan had circled around behind the two unsuspecting men.

"Okay, sport," King whispered. "You take the guy on the left. I'll get the big guy. We're using blades, old boy," he continued, handing a knife to Brogan. "No need to draw attention or a crowd."

As they crept toward the men, they could hear them speaking in Russian. Having already encountered similar operatives in Birmingham, they felt no qualms about a preemptive strike. King attacked a split second before Brogan, but neither victim had a chance to scream or do anything in self-defense. They plunged their weapons into the men several times. They dragged the lifeless bodies around a corner and threw them down a nearby stairwell in front of what appeared to be a vacant building with a sign on the door indicating the facility was available for lease. Brogan saw a tarp nearby and flung it down the stairs, where it blanketed the dead Russians.

They hoped the bodies would not be discovered until well after daybreak, which was still hours away.

∗

Their mission to see Churchill's casket unsuccessful, Thompson and Murray did not want the men Winston Fleming mentioned to know about their visit. Thompson said, "We'll be on our way then. Could we ask something of you as a favor to Lady Churchill?"

"Why yes, of course. How can I help?"

"Please don't tell the men with the casket about our inquiry. Mrs. Churchill would not want any official feathers ruffled and all that."

"Oh yes. You can count on me," Fleming replied with enthusiasm.

Thompson winked and added, "I'll make sure you get an autographed copy of my book."

"I have my copy of your book with me. I was just reading some of it again, in light of what is happening and my little connection with history these days. I'd be honored if you'd sign it." Fleming disappeared into a side room for a brief moment, returning with the book.

"Not a problem." Thompson took the book from Fleming, and he flipped to the inside cover, where he wrote: *"To Winston Fleming, a wonderful young man named for a great man. – All the Best, Walter Thompson."*

Winston Fleming teared up as he read the inscription.

*

As Thompson and Murray walked away from the funeral home, they had only progressed half a block before they saw Harvey King and Tiernan Brogan standing on a corner across the street. "Friends of yours?" Murray asked Thompson.

"Indeed, but new friends. They're the men sent by President Johnson."

Harvey King spoke up as the men approached. "We need to get you men out of here. Had some company. Friends of the same gentlemen who tried to stop us in Birmingham."

"Where are they?"

Harvey King smiled and said, "They're sleeping. Who's this man, Thompson?"

"This is Mr. Edmund Murray of Scotland Yard. He's been taking care of Mr. Churchill for many years."

"Oh, so you took Thompson's old job," Brogan said.

Murray looked annoyed. "Yes. Something like that."

Harvey said, "What's the situation, Walter?"

"Well, Mr. King, it seems that many people in high places are interested in Mr. Churchill's casket. There are some men from MI-5 guarding it now. Let's just say that we were never here."

"Son of a bitch. Now what?"

Thompson replied, "If I were in charge of this operation, I'd start thinking about how to find the person with the trigger."

*

Thompson, King, and Brogan arrived at Walter Thompson's flat shortly after eleven. Edmund Murray went back at Hyde Park Gate. Mary was waiting up for her husband and sprang into hostess mode when she saw the guests. "My, oh my, what a pleasant surprise. I've made some dinner for Mr. Thompson, but there's plenty—will you men be staying for a bit?"

"Well, that's mighty fine of you, Mrs. Thompson. We'd love something to eat. But we have to leave soon thereafter. We have to find a new hotel—had some trouble at the Dorchester."

Mary looked over at Walter, who simply nodded.

"I wouldn't hear of it—you two will stay here for the night. It's far too late to be hunting a hotel room."

"Are you sure?" Brogan asked.

"Of course I am. You fine gentlemen represent the President of the United States. What kind of hostess would I be if I didn't help you?"

The men smiled at Mary. Then King said, "Walter, speaking of the president, I need to place a call to one of his men. You'll be reimbursed for the call. Might I use your telephone?"

CHAPTER TWENTY-FOUR

THOMPSON CLOSED THE DOOR as he left the small study, giving Harvey king privacy for his telephone call to Allen Dulles. The former director of the CIA answered on the second ring.

"This is Little Harry," King began, using the codename he and Dulles had chosen. "Problem complicated."

"How so?"

"We're not going to be able to get to the package. We're going to have to come at this from another angle. The mission has now changed from neutralizing the threat to finding a way to stop it. I could use a few more hands."

"Yes, of course. Have any recommendations?"

"You know I do. I'd start with a mutual friend who fancies himself a writer and build it out from there. But quickly."

"Ah, yes. I know that man. Consider it done. I'll have some boots on the ground to meet up with you in less than twenty-four hours."

"Roger that. Little Harry signing off," King said.

"Good luck, my friend."

Dulles immediately placed another call. "Hunt, this is Allen. I need you at my office in two hours. And I need you to bring four trustworthy friends."

"Absolutely, Allen. What's up?"

"I'll brief you at the office. Oh, and make sure you and your friends pack your bags. You're going on a trip."

"Might I at least ask for how long?"

"Long as it takes, Hunt. Long as it takes."

Everette Howard Hunt Jr., a spy who always looked like someone sent directly from central casting, had been working for the CIA, on and off the books, since 1949. He was a rabid anti-communist with a gift for creativity. This served him well in his work, as well as his hobby—something that was occupying more and more of his time these days—writing. He was the author of several novels, including a few espionage pot-boilers. He had been the CIA station chief in Mexico City in the early 1950s, supervising a staff that included a young, would-be writer named William F. Buckley Jr.. His way with words had won him a Guggenheim Fellowship in 1946. But cloak and dagger work was his real love. And Harvey King's call was just what the doctor ordered.

∗

Dulles got into his new Cadillac. There was little traffic on a cold Tuesday afternoon in January and the drive to the White House only took a few minutes. It was already dark before five.

As he approached the White House, Dulles wished he had better news for the president. He had no trouble getting through the gate even though he had not called ahead. His was a familiar face to White House personnel, having visited 1600 Pennsylvania Avenue more times than he could possibly count since his days as President Eisenhower's top spy. That was back when the Dulles brothers were at the top of their game, with Allen at CIA and John Foster as Secretary of State.

"Please ring the residence and have someone tell the president that I need to see him immediately," Dulles instructed the young man at the desk just inside the West Wing door.

"But sir—I'm sure the president is having dinner with the first lady," the young man protested.

"I'm aware it's suppertime, young man," Dulles said in a stern and condescending voice. "You know who I am, right?"

"Yes, Mr. Dulles, but I—"

"But nothing. You just do as I say. The consequences are on me." With that, the young man called up to the residence to pass along the message.

A few minutes later, Dulles was ushered into President Johnson's dining room. Lady Bird got up and gathered a few dishes. "Oh, I'm so sorry, Mrs. Johnson—didn't mean to interrupt your meal."

Lady Bird turned and smiled at Dulles. "It's fine, Mr. Dulles."

"Allen, come right in. Don't mind Bird—she has work to do. I imagine you have some news from our friends across the ocean. Am I right?"

"Yes, you certainly are. I got a call from Harvey King a bit ago. Our people on the ground there have not been able to get access to the bomb."

"You mean, the bomb is intact?"

"Afraid so, Mr. President. Which brings me to another point."

"Yes?"

"I think we need to send a few more hands over there as soon as possible to round up the people who are connected with this plot. That's the goal now. Someone has the trigger for the bomb."

"Do you have a recommendation?"

"I'd like to send Howard Hunt. In fact, he's assembling a small team to meet at my office in about an hour. I can have them in England, completely off the record and under the radar, by this time tomorrow, if not before."

"You trust this Hunt fellow? Didn't he work on that whole Cuba project with Bobby?"

"He worked on Operation Mongoose with Harvey King, but he has no love for the junior senator from New York. I trust him completely, sir. He also worked with us in the whole Bay of Pigs thing and is discreet as all hell."

"Well, that Bay of Pigs thing was a fiasco, Allen. You know that."

"Yes, of course. But I also know there was much more to that story than what meets the eye."

"I suppose. You spooks and your wilderness of mirrors. Just don't drag this administration down through any horse-shit looking glass, you hear me?"

"Yes, of course, Sir. I'll keep this clean and covert. But I think we're going to learn a lot about our enemies over the next few days. Churchill's funeral service is scheduled for Saturday. They plan for it to be interrupted by terror. Our team will see that it does not happen—or die trying," Dulles said, with the last three words uttered almost in a whisper.

"Go to it. When you go out, have that steward bring me a double Cutty."

*

Howard Hunt entered Allen Dulles's office in a building on K Street in Washington. With him were four men: Ferguson Matthews, Frank Sturgis, Howard Perlstein, and James McCord.

"You men ready for an adventure?" Dulles asked. He smiled and took a puff on his pipe.

"I can assure you, Allen, these guys are the best of the best," Hunt said.

"Or at least the best available on a cold as hell January night," Dulles countered.

"That could be true, too, Sir."

Dulles motioned for the men to sit down. "Pull up a chair, and I'll bring you up to speed. I'm sending you to England— unofficially—to help fix a problem for us. I want you to know the President of the United States is aware of your mission, but he can never be connected to it. It's off the books, boys. Understand?"

There was a collective, "Yes, sir!"

"Howard, how'd you round up this crew so quickly? You men work together before?"

"Yes, Allen. These men are experienced operatives. We last worked together on that Mongoose thing down in Florida. Before, well, you know."

"Yes, Hunt. I know. We both know," Dulles replied at the awkward and cryptic reference to the assassination of President Kennedy. Then he stood up abruptly. "Excellent. Now you men head over to Davis Field in Manassas. I've got a DC-3 fueled and ready for you. Crew of two. You'll fly into a small airport northeast of London. A colleague of mine will meet you there and get you to London, where you'll meet up with the leader of this mission, Harvey King. Brief the team once you're airborne."

The men looked at each other. The mention of King's name excited them. If he was a part of whatever it was they were going to do, it had to be both important and dangerous—real 007 stuff.

Less than an hour later, Hunt and the rest of the team were on board the large propeller aircraft. It lumbered down the runway and began to reach for the skies. Hunt immediately read the team into the story and the general parameters of their mission. About ten minutes after takeoff, the co-pilot, a fellow named Clark Williams, came back to the cargo area where Hunt and his men had made themselves as comfortable as such an aircraft would allow. "Okay boys, this particular bird is equipped with an extra tank of fuel, but we're gonna have to make a couple of quick stops to get over—one in St John's and the other in Iceland. We're on a tight schedule, so no more than fifteen minutes at each spot. You can get off and stretch your legs, but you'll want to avoid being noticed."

"Thank you, Clark. How long to St. John's?"

The co-pilot looked at his watch. "I figure we'll be there in a little less than five hours. So get some shut-eye. I don't know what you men will be doing in England, but I suspect you won't be sleeping much once we get there."

"You heard him," Hunt said with a wink and a smile. He wadded up his trench coat to use as a pillow.

CHAPTER TWENTY-FIVE

AT ABOUT THE TIME the team en route to England stopped to refuel in Newfoundland, Harvey King and Tiernan Brogan were awake and being served a fine full-English breakfast by Mary Thompson. Harvey, a man with a hearty appetite, was almost beside himself with anticipation as the early morning feast was spread out before him: fried eggs, grilled tomatoes, fried mushrooms, bacon, sausage, baked beans, and toast.

"Walter, you're one lucky lawman. Does she cook like this for you every morning?"

"Not every morning, but once a week or so. Most mornings it's just porridge and tea. But nothing is too good for men representing the President of the United States," Thompson replied proudly.

"Hell, I may need a nap after breakfast," King groaned.

"I always tell my husband what my mother told my father. 'Eat breakfast like a king, lunch like a prince, and dinner like a pauper.' This is why my Walter is in such great shape for his age," Mary said.

"You must be on to something, Ma'am. This looks delicious."

"How many men are coming from the States?" Thompson asked, changing the subject.

"I believe it's five, but not sure. I know the leader of the group. He's an old pal of mine in the business. A fellow named Howard Hunt. He's top shelf and knows how to run an operation and manage a team."

"When do you expect these men? Where will they stay?" Mary asked.

"I'm sure we can find some arrangements for them. They won't be here until close to noon. Long flight on a slow plane."

"I was talking to Walter last night about this. One of our neighbors, Mrs. Shelby, is on holiday in Greece right now. She'll be gone a month. I have her key. I look in on her cat every day. She has a nice flat—bigger than ours, actually. Now, if your boys can behave themselves—and if they don't mind a grumpy old cat—I'm sure her place would work for them for a couple of days. Nothing long term, mind you."

"That's very generous. I can assure you we don't plan to stay around long. Once our work is done, we'll be out of your hair."

"Fine, then. I'll prepare it all for five guests. But all the meeting, eating and drinking, will be done in this flat."

"Whatever you say, Mrs. Thompson."

*

After breakfast, Harvey, Tiernan, and Walter went into the living room area and talked about their next moves.

"Think the bodies of our friends have been found yet?" Brogan asked King.

"No tellin'. That building looked empty. If we're lucky no one will notice the stiffs. The real question is why they were there. Were they following Walter and Murray, or just watching the place?"

"What's the difference?" Brogan asked.

"A big difference. If they were assigned to follow them, then someone may be expecting them to check in. The bad guys would then likely know that someone was checking on the casket. If they were just there to observe and happened to see Thompson and Murray, they wouldn't have had enough time to report to anyone before lights out," King replied.

Brogan asked, "But when the bodies are found, won't that alert the Soviets that there was activity at the funeral home?"

"Yes, of course. A clock is ticking, we get that, sport. But we can hope the casket has an occupant before that happens—and is long gone from the funeral home," King said.

"So you and this Hunt fellow have some history?" Brogan asked.

"I should say so. We worked together on an operation south of the border back in '54."

"Guatemala?"

"Classified, sport," King said with a smirk.

"It's a pretty well-known story in our ranks. You orchestrated the overthrow of the government and helped install a regime friendly to the United States."

"And a great story it was. The commie was grabbing up all the land and nationalizing everything. Frankly, we should have done the same thing in Cuba in '61—at the Bay of Pigs—instead of abandoning all those brave men on that beach. Hunt was in that one, too. Eisenhower had the right idea and had no problem letting the CIA do what needed to be done. But Jack Kennedy didn't have the stones to finish what Ike started. He was a lot more profile than courage, frankly."

Brogan smiled at the reference to the Pulitzer Prize winning book written by Kennedy. "I heard he was working on something big for Cuba before he was assassinated."

"Yeah. He and brother Bobby really wanted to knock off Castro. Even roped the mob into the effort."

"Think that's what got him killed?"

Thompson was listening to this with great interest, missing the old days in harm's way. "For what it's worth, he could've learned a lot from my old boss," he interrupted.

"Actually, JFK had great admiration for Mr. Churchill. But he was more of a politician than a real leader of men. I think he died because he left too many missions unfinished."

"Care to elaborate?" Brogan asked King.

Harvey was lost in thought for a moment, like a man with a painful secret to tell. But he caught himself. "No. Not at all. Water under the bridge. I just hope President Johnson learns from his predecessor's mistakes."

Thompson remarked, "Well, the fact you two gentlemen are here—with more on the way—seems to speak powerfully to that point."

"I suppose so," King said.

∗

A buzzer on the desk went off, startling Roger Hollis for a brief moment. He found the device a source of constant irritation. He pushed the button and said, "Yes, Sean?"

"Might I have a moment with you, director?"

"Of course. Come right in."

Sean Welling was standing in front of Roger Hollis a moment later. "Sir, we have a bit of a problem."

"I'm listening."

"Two of our friends seem to be missing."

"Missing?"

"Yes. They haven't checked in for several hours. Some other friends are conducting a search, but because of what happened to the men in Birmingham, there is obvious concern."

"Concern?"

"Yes, director, at the highest levels."

A look of fear crossed Hollis's face. "I see. Thanks, Sean. Please keep me posted."

"Very good, sir. I will."

Sean began to leave the office, but Hollis called to him. "Sean, is there a way you could arrange another meeting with our guest at the Savoy?"

"Certainly, sir. I'll set it up. Lunch today?"

"Yes. But let him know we'll eat in his room."

*

"It's a manhunt now, Brogan. We need to go back to that building and follow the bad guys wherever they go. We need to find the person with the trigger," Thompson said.

Brogan replied, "Think the target is Westminster Hall? That's where the body is going today. And according to the paper, the public viewing will start early tomorrow morning."

"No. I think the target is St Paul's on Saturday. That's what our intel says. The attack is supposed to be designed to kill some major players on the world stage. Take 'em out so the Russkies can gobble up Europe. No bigwigs will be in town and all in one place until the funeral service itself. So that's the place we need to check out."

"Think they have someone on the inside there?"

"I sure as hell would," King said.

"Well, that scenario buys us some time. We'll have reinforcements tonight."

"And let's make sure we use the next few hours wisely. Once they're here, we need to know where to send the cavalry."

CHAPTER TWENTY-SIX

IT HAD BEEN SEVERAL MONTHS since his handler had contacted Henri, so he was overdue for a meeting. But this time there seemed to be some urgency. Generally, the man he knew simply as "Peter" gave Henri about forty-eight hours' advance notice. But the messenger Peter had used—the one with the enchanting female voice—called a few hours earlier to set up the rendezvous was clear, "Yes, he will meet you for coffee at the usual place in two hours." Now he waited at one of a dozen or so similar-looking places along the famous boulevard. The Champs-Élysées was now a bold, beautiful, and busy boulevard. Quite a contrast from the war years, when few people, and fewer automobiles, were present and moving about.

Henri Girard was good at his job, and he enjoyed his work. More to the point, he enjoyed what his work meant to the particular cause he had embraced since the days when the Nazis were ever-present in his beloved city of Paris. Back then he was a nineteen-year-old member of the French Resistance, fighting against Hitler's minions. He hated Nazism and Fascism in all its forms. That's what led him to a fascinating woman named Suzanne Spaak. She was from Belgium, but had moved to France in the 1930s. There she and her husband Claude, a successful playwright and art aficionado, lived a life of artsy luxury while the clouds of war were gathering over the continent.

By the time the Nazis were marching down the Champs-Élysées, Suzanne had joined what became the French Resistance. She was especially determined to do everything in her power to rescue Parisian Jews from Nazi persecution—and worse. On a day he would never forget, Suzanne introduced Henri to a man named Leopold Trepper. And before long Henri Girard had made the political journey to a view of history and politics shaped by the thinking of men like Marx, Engels, and Trotsky.

Trepper was the founder of an underground movement that came to be known as *The Red Orchestra*. And Henri was one of the boys in the band. *The Red Orchestra* was Josef Stalin's brainchild, part of a larger vision for the global spread of communism. Trapper himself, though of Polish descent, was a full-fledged agent for the NKVD, the ancestor of the KGB. Trepper, Spaak, and company worked as part of the French Resistance, being directed—at least to a point—by General Charles De Gaulle, the most dominant French leader in exile in England. But their real loyalty was to Moscow, and they made sure Comrade Stalin knew everything that was happening in Paris and with De Gaulle and his followers.

Henri spent his war carrying out guerrilla actions, not to mention the occasional assassination. By the time of the liberation of Paris in 1944, he was an experienced and skilled operative with a bright future. His exploits had caught De

Gaulle's attention, and when the general returned to French soil in triumph, he encouraged young Mr. Girard to serve in the emerging counterespionage service: *Service de Documentation Extérieure et de Contre-Espionnage* (SDECE). Such an appointment was just fine with Henri Girard, who emerged from the war as a fully vetted and valuable spy for the Soviets.

By 1959, the Fourth Republic in France had given way to the Fifth Republic, and Charles De Gaulle was president. Among the first things he did when he assumed office was to orchestrate Henri Girard's job at NATO. Though decidedly anti-communist, De Gaulle was less than enamored of NATO. He particularly resented the fact that the organization's headquarters were on French soil at Palais de Chaillot in Paris, yet his influence was not equal to that of his British and American counterparts. His prima donna propensities had changed little since the French patriot was annoying Churchill and Eisenhower in London during the war.

So the Soviets had a double agent at NATO Headquarters, with a tip of the late Josef Stalin's peaked cap.

Henri was mildly curious as he sipped his cafe au lait. His jet-black hair was slicked down close to his scalp, and his pencil-thin mustache was heavily waxed. He was wearing a dark business suit, complete with a starched white shirt adorned by cufflinks bearing the NATO logo. After he had finished reading the first few pages of *Le Monde*, he looked up and saw "Peter" approaching. They shook hands and ordered coffee, Henri's third cup.

"Thank you for meeting on such short notice, my friend," Peter began. "There's a matter of great importance I need to share with you."

"Of course," Henri replied. "I have some time. I took a few hours of time off from the office."

"Ah yes, the office. This is what our people are interested in. The time is fast approaching for a moment of great importance—something unprecedented."

"Sounds intriguing. What can you tell me?"

"Of course you know that our friends have a propensity for compartmentalization."

"Yes, yes. I'm well aware that they are not fans of the right hand knowing everything the left hand is doing. I've been working with them for more than twenty years, you know."

"Certainly. I know your case very well. We have an important assignment for you as part of a great plan that will change the course of France, Europe, and the world."

At that, Henri took a sip of his coffee and folded his newspaper, carefully. "I'm listening."

"You are aware of Mr. Churchill's death and the upcoming funeral in London?"

"Yes, of course. About half this newspaper is about this," Henri said, pointing emphatically at the folded copy of *Le Monde*. "But our friends have no great affection for the life, let alone the memory, of the famous anti-Bolshevik. How does his death translate into some kind of master plan?"

"It's called KOBA." Peter filled Henri in on the basic details of the plan.

"KOBA? That's Stalin's old name from pre-revolutionary days."

"Yes, of course. That's right. And now it adorns a bold plan in honor of the late leader. In a way, it began with him. You remember the days of the Comintern?"

"Of course I do. I played wonderful music with *The Red Orchestra* back in the day. Your file on me should mention that."

"Yes, well you know our late leader had a grand vision for taking control of all of Europe on the way to global communism."

"That seems long ago now, Peter. And far away."

"Not as far as you might think," Peter replied. He then gave Henri the basic details of the plan.

Henri was impressed, but a bit skeptical. "And where do I fit into this?" he asked.

"Simple, my friend. We need you to activate your old skills and eliminate your boss, Manlio Brosio—the Secretary General of NATO."

"My, oh my—that *is* quite a plan. And how do you propose I pull this off? He's surrounded by several layers of security."

"We leave the details to you. But one thing: it would be best if his death looked like an accident at first, so as not to hint of a conspiracy. We just want our enemies to be off-balance and distracted at the crucial moment."

"Anything else?"

"Yes. Please find a way to give us the most recent details about NATO troop placements."

"Good God, Peter. You want me to climb the Eiffel Tower while I'm at it?"

Peter smiled and lit a cigarette. "No need for that. There will be plenty of time for such things once the Soviet Army controls this decadent city."

"What about President De Gaulle—any plans for him?"

"Were you not listening, Henri?"

"I don't follow."

"He will die with so many others when that church is destroyed right in the middle of long-winded eulogies about Churchill's pathetic life. Think of it as Stalin's revenge."

*

The room service lunch—bacon sandwiches for two—was in place in Kim Philby's room a full five minutes before Roger Hollis knocked on the door.

"Late enough in the day for you yet, old man?" Philby asked as he held up a half-empty bottle of Black Label.

"Nothing for me, Kim. Except maybe some tea."

"Way ahead of you. Right there on the table."

As they began to eat, Hollis continued. "Two of our friends haven't been heard from for several hours. I'm concerned about what it means."

"Where were these 'friends' supposed to be?" Philby asked.

"Last we knew, they were keeping an eye on the Kenyon building."

"Ah yes, the favorite of the royals," Philby said.

"That's where the casket is right now. A bit later today, it'll be taken to Churchill's home at Hyde Park Gate. From that point, the body will be in it, and there will be no access."

"So I'd imagine you're concerned the package may not be all that secure?"

"Yes, and I need you to communicate that to your bosses. But please make sure they understand that we have no confirmation the secret has been discovered. But they should know."

"All right, my f-f-friend. I'll pass the information along and let you know the reply," Philby said. He took a large bite from his sandwich and smiled. "I've missed food like this. Nothing like it in Moscow."

CHAPTER TWENTY-SEVEN

A BLACK ROLLS ROYCE HEARSE pulled up to the service door at Kenyon funeral directors shortly after three that Tuesday afternoon. The timing of this had not been made public, as officials thought it best to avoid significant crowds and traffic. In spite of their best efforts, however, several hundred curious Londoners had been waiting for several hours.

Largely hidden from the onlookers, several men worked quickly to load the large, lead-lined casket into the back of the vehicle. Once it was secured by braces, the back door of the hearse was closed. A single car from Scotland Yard pulled out and the hearse fell in behind. The vehicles turned left and went around the building. When the vehicles came into the view of the crowd, several people rushed toward them, but they were waved back by the driver of the first car. The vehicles then turned right onto a narrow street, passing an empty building and its stairwell. That particular stairwell was the temporary resting place of the two missing Russian operatives.

∗

Harvey King and Tiernan Brogan were in the crowd outside of Kenyon's at that hour. They had returned to the scene to make sure the bodies were still covered and undiscovered. They waited for the crowd to disperse, which it did in short order. Walter Thompson had arranged for them to use a vehicle to transport the bodies of the two operatives. He had also cleared some space in a large freezer in the basement of his building— just enough room to put the two men on ice for as long as necessary.

Trying to avoid notice, Brogan walked carefully down the steps of the stairwell. He removed the large cloth covering the bodies, then wrapped it around one body at a time for transport to the back of the waiting vehicle, which King had pulled up to the stairwell in a way that blocked most of the view from anyone on the street or sidewalk. Brogan worked fast to load the two bodies in the back.

"These fine gentlemen are gonna have to stay back there until dark, sport—which is a couple of hours from now. Then we can put 'em on ice," King said as Brogan climbed through the vehicle, contorting his body to get into the passenger seat.

"You're the boss," Brogan said.

∗

The hearse turned onto the block near 28 Hyde Park Gate. Several hundred people were there, but no one rushed the vehicle. In fact, it was quite the opposite—the crowd respectfully allowed the vehicle to proceed and park in front of the Churchill home.

Many wept, men and women, as several men off-loaded the large casket and walked toward the front door. Edmund Murray opened the door and the casket disappeared quickly into the famous town home.

Once inside, the casket was taken to the back of the house and into Winston Churchill's bedroom. The great man was dressed in full military uniform. Three men carefully lifted his body and placed it in the large casket as Lady Churchill wept.

"How long before we must leave?" Clementine asked the man who seemed to be leading operations.

"We don't plan to move him until it is well past dark, ma'am. We'll be out of your way in a minute or two, that I promise. And if you need anything from us, please don't hesitate to ask. We're here to serve you and honor your wonderful husband. There likely wouldn't be much left of England were it not for him," the man said.

The comment clearly moved Mrs. Churchill. A slight tear appeared in her eye. After a moment, she asked, "Will you and your men be escorting him to Westminster Hall?"

"No, ma'am. A military honor guard will be here for that later on."

For the next few hours, Clementine stayed in the room. Members of the family and close friends took turns sitting with her before her husband would leave his room and their home for the last time.

About half past six, the honor guard from the Royal Navy arrived. Clementine watched as the casket was closed. The men then carried the it through the house and back out the front door. A slight drizzle had started to fall, but the crowd remained large and very quiet. The casket was placed in the back of the Rolls Royce hearse, now flying the insignia of Buckingham Palace.

The hearse slowly moved away and made its way toward what would be Winston Churchill's home for the next several days—Westminster Hall. There were eight cars in the procession, three of which carried members of Churchill's family. They rode along Knightsbridge, down Constitution Hill, and past Buckingham Palace. The journey took a mere five minutes because all traffic in the area had been stopped.

Once inside New Palace Yard, eight Grenadier Guards took the large casket into the Great Hall. They were led by an officer with a drawn sword. Clementine Churchill, along with her children and grandchildren, followed along. The casket was placed on a large catafalque draped in black velvet with braided silver edges. The catafalque measured forty feet long, seventeen feet wide, and seven feet tall. A Union Jack flag was then draped over the coffin. Dr. Michael Ramsey, the Archbishop of Canterbury, received the casket and offered a brief prayer.

Five officers took up their watch positions, one at each corner of the catafalque and another on the steps. After a few minutes, Lady Churchill and the rest of the family returned to their vehicles for the short ride back to Hyde Park Gate. Westminster Hall remained empty for the night, except for the vigilant guards. They served throughout the night—and week—in twenty-minute shifts.

CHAPTER TWENTY-EIGHT

A FEW HOURS LATER, the dc-3 carrying Howard Hunt and the rest of the team coming to the aid of Harvey King and Tiernan Brogan descended through the clouds. It circled once before landing on a dimly lit runway at the Stapleford Aerodrome near Essex about thirty miles northeast of London. After the aircraft taxied and stopped near a hangar, the men exited the aircraft to see an older man with a white beard. He was smoking the last inch of a cigar.

"Welcome, Gents! Name is Lithgow, Blair Lithgow. I hail from up north—a little place we call Scotland. Mr. Dulles and I have an arrangement, so here I am. Your host for the next few days. Exciting they shall be, am I right?"

"I can't say for sure, Mr. Lithgow," Hunt replied for the group. "But we have a job to do which just may raise our blood pressure a point or two."

"Of that I'm sure, Mr. Hunt. Now, you men need to visit the privy before we make the trip over to London? Your chariot awaits," the old man said, pointing to a gray panel truck nearby.

*

Lithgow made great time, arriving at Walter Thompson's flat shortly before noon. His driving, however, left something to be spoken for. Two of Hunt's men—McCord and Perlstein— became violently ill, vomiting on some bushes outside Thompson's building. They were struck by the irony that they had managed to keep their lunch and dinner down while on a bumpy trans-Atlantic flight in the cargo hold of an airplane, but a forty-five-minute truck ride had made them retch.

By the time they joined the rest of their party upstairs in the flat, Mary Thompson was pouring tea and serving sandwiches. Both sounded great to the two men who had left the previous contents of their stomachs a few feet away from the building's main door.

Harvey King briefed Hunt and his men about the latest and they agreed to get a few hours of sleep before they plotted strategy. Mary Thompson led several of the men over to the vacationing Mrs. Shelby's flat, where she had prepared sleeping arrangements. She gave the men a few ground rules. "No eating over here. And please pick up after yourselves, gentlemen. We don't want to leave a mess."

"Yes, Ma'am," Howard Hunt said.

Mary left the exhausted men alone. To a man, they were asleep within five minutes.

*

President Lyndon Johnson sipped his third cup of coffee from behind his desk at the Oval Office. It was the same desk he had used for years as a US senator and as vice president. When he took over in November 1963 in the aftermath of the Kennedy assassination and the myth of Camelot, Johnson had been determined to mark his territory and make the famous office his own. The first thing he'd done was to remove the famous Resolute Desk used by Jack Kennedy. It had been specially chosen by Jackie Kennedy when she found it in storage at the White House. The desk became part of a traveling exhibition about the Kennedy years and eventually found a home, for at least a few years, at the Smithsonian, before being put back into presidential service years later.

There were two telephones on Johnson's desk. One was a simple rotary model. The other was a special creation with six buttons and an attached speaker device. Johnson forcefully punched one of the six buttons and Bill Moyers came on the speaker. "Yes, Mr. President?"

"Get in here, Moyers, and make it snappy," Johnson barked.

Moyers was through the door in a few seconds. As he walked toward the president's desk, he noticed that Johnson's televisions were on. The president was obsessed with telephones and television and had requested a specially built cabinet with three monitors. He insisted on being able to watch all three networks—ABC, CBS, and NBC—simultaneously. He had a voracious appetite for information and opinion, for good or ill. The president's aide also noticed that his boss was not dressed in his customary suit and tie, but was still wearing his pajamas and a large silk robe, with slippers on his lanky feet.

"What can I do for you, Mr. President? How are you feeling, sir?" Moyers asked.

Johnson's eyes were glued to the screens and he ignored the small talk. "Did you see Hugh Downs's interview of Richard Nixon on that *Today Show*?"

"Sorry, sir. Don't have a television in my office."

"Gotta fix that, Billy boy. That son-of-a-bitch Dick Nixon had the gall to criticize me for not going to the Churchill thing. Says a common cold is no reason to miss it. That Churchill and the Brits went through hell to keep the world safe for democracy and all that shit. Kennedy was right about him. He's a cheap bastard."

"Are you rethinking your decision, Sir?"

"Hell, no! I'm still sick. In fact, I'm not even sitting here in this office at this moment—for the record. I'm in bed with a raging fever. Got that?"

"Of course, sir."

Johnson began to squint. It was his "tell"—the way aides knew he was about to either explode or ask something uncomfortable. "But the situation over there is growing. The threat has not been removed. There is likely a bomb, and our people haven't been able to disable it."

Moyers measure his words, "The world knows you aren't going—that's a done deal for good or ill. Better to have you here, safe and ready to lead the world if anything bad happens over there. I'm sure of it."

"Okay, Moyers. You go back to that office of yours and have someone find you a television, you hear?"

"Yes, Mr. President. I will."

CHAPTER TWENTY-NINE

HUNT AND HIS TEAM squeezed around a small table in Walter Thompson's flat and were not disappointed by what they found there. The hearty breakfast was a repeat of what King and Brogan had partaken of a day earlier, and was accompanied by lively and constructive conversation. And each man received an assignment.

"Do we have a good read on all the official activities related to the funeral?" Hunt asked.

Brogan pulled a page from his pocket. "Yes. These things have been published widely so the public can figure out where to go and what to do," he said. "For example," he continued as he scanned the page, "this morning at nine o'clock, people will start moving past the catafalque in Westminster Hall to pay respects. There are estimates that more than a quarter of a million people will do this between today and early Saturday. It'll be around the clock—but for an hour each day, they'll halt the queue for the staff to spruce things up."

"Okay," King said. "So we need a couple of you men to head over there this morning and check it all out—keep your eyes peeled for anything unusual. Tiernan—you should take one of these men with you. You know what some of the suspicious looking folks look like. We need to split up, since we're the only ones who could recognize any of the faces in the crowd. We are pretty sure that the target is St. Paul's on Saturday, but that doesn't mean that the big boom couldn't happen at Westminster."

"Fine, but I'd like to focus on St. Paul's," Brogan replied.

"Why? Nothing happening there until Saturday," Hunt interrupted. "At least that's what I thought I read in the paper."

Brogan looked over at him and said, "I'm well aware of that, Mr. Hunt. But you see, that's when all the world leaders will be in one place. If that's the target, they must have someone on the inside."

"Of course," Hunt said. "That would certainly follow."

"Well, you see, I've seen some faces. There's this lady I know from some of my hush-hush work when I was undercover for Five. She knows me as Sean Walsh from the IRA."

"How well does she know you?" Frank Sturgis asked, speaking up for the first time. His suggestive question drew some throaty laughs.

"Well, um, we had our moments back in the day," Brogan replied, then felt a bit ashamed for embellishing things. Any relationship with the red-haired beauty had only been in his fantasies.

"Bet you did, old boy," King said with a hard slap on the back.

Brogan caught his breath and continued. "Missing my point, gentlemen. Name of Kaitlyn Dorcey. I saw her the other night at a pub with an interesting crew."

King added, "That's right. And that led us to Birmingham and to clues, which led us to the bomb in a big box. What're you thinking, Brogan?"

"Just one of the blokes there. His face is imprinted on my brain. He was quiet—almost afraid, when I met him. It was just a brief thing, but something in my gut says that guy is in this thing up to his eyeballs. All I'm saying is I'd like to check both Westminster Hall and St. Paul's to see if this Higgins fellow is anywhere around."

"Okay, sport. How about you head to St. Paul's first—let me and a couple of these guys head over to Westminster Hall. Take Hunt with you," King instructed.

"Sounds like a plan."

"Great. Okay—let's head out in a few. Not all at once. Stagger it. Watch your backs. Tradecraft, men. Tradecraft. Walter, you come with us to Westminster." King hoped the presence of Churchill's former bodyguard would come in handy.

"Splendid. Now, do you men have weapons?"

The Americans chuckled. Hunt spoke for them. "One of the benefits of flying below the radar, sir. We've brought our arsenal with us."

As the men finished their breakfast and began to prepare for the morning tasks, Harvey said, "There's a pub called McRory's 'round the corner from St. Paul's. Let's meet up there half-past eleven."

Two of the Americans looked at their watches and realized they were still set to Eastern Time back home. They made the leap five hours forward.

*

Thousands of mourners had spent the night in the queue as Tuesday gave way to Wednesday. They braved the cold and the occasional rain for a few brief moments to pass by Winston Churchill's casket to pay their heartfelt respects.

Among those camped out were Adam Wilkinson and his ten-year-old son. The boy's name was Paul. Adam had flown Spitfires back in the war and often told his son about the day Churchill paid a visit to his squadron at Uxbridge in Hillington.

"Tell me about it again, Father," Paul said.

"Ah, my son. I've told you so many times you must know it by heart," Adam replied. He then reached into the nearby basket and handed his son a boiled egg. "Here. Peel and eat this—your mother will ask me. We don't want to disappoint her, now do we?"

"No, sir. How long before the line starts to move?" Paul replied.

Adam pulled out his watch and shielded it from the light mist that had started to fall once again. "Less than twenty minutes now."

"So plenty of time for the story once again," Paul said with a smile.

"Fine. Let's see it was back in 1940, in August. Hitler's air force—"

"The Luftwaffe."

"Yes, son, the Luftwaffe. They were bombing the city every day. Even these buildings—Parliament and all—suffered much damage. We were tasked with the aerial defense of the city. It was important work."

"Did you fly every day?"

"Not every day, Son. No. Many days I was in the Operations Room working with Number 11 Group helping to make sure our boys in the air had the best information about the enemy's movements."

"And that's where Mr. Churchill came—and where you met him, right?"

"Yes it is, son. On the sixteenth of August. The Prime Minister came into our room and asked all sorts of questions."

"Was he smoking that big cigar?"

"Had it in his mouth, but he never once lit it the whole time he was with us."

"What did he say to you?"

"He asked me what I did. And then, he shook my hand and said the nation owed me and all those in the room so much."

"But he said more, right? He said that famous thing. The one we read about at school. Didn't he say it to you before he said it to the whole country on the BBC?"

"Yes, you know he did."

"Say it again, Father."

"Well, Son. As you well know—you've heard me say it so many times. In fact, I think you know it better than I do, my boy. Let me hear you recite those famous words."

"All right, father. 'Never in the field of human conflict was so much owed by so many to so few.'"

"Perfect. Word for word."

"You know what I was just thinking?"

"I haven't a clue, Son."

"You could almost say it like this: 'Never in the field of human conflict was so much owed by so many to one man.'"

Adam smiled, a tear appearing in his eye. "I'm proud of you, Paul. You are absolutely correct."

The father and son grew silent as the rain stopped falling. A few minutes later, the line began to move toward St. Stephen's Porch and the South Steps, where they, along with tens of thousands of others, would enter the Great Hall to pay their respects to the great man.

CHAPTER THIRTY

As THE LINE SLOWLY MOVED along the sidewalk toward the public entrance at Westminster hall, Harvey King, Walter Thompson, and four of the Americans surveyed the line from several vantage points. Nothing looked suspicious, but then they didn't really know what they were looking for. All they saw was thousands of quiet people, lost in thought, waiting to whisper a word of gratitude to a man whose passing signaled the end of an era.

Harvey King sat down on a bench across the road from the line of mourners. He took a couple of short sips from his near-empty flask and wondered how it was going with Brogan and Hunt.

In fact, it was going just about the same at St. Paul's. Nothing interesting. That is, until the moment Harry Higgins hurried down the front steps of the famous church and walked briskly down the block. Brogan came to life, directing Hunt around a corner.

"That's the guy Kaitlyn introduced me to the other night," he said, excitedly. "He must be their inside man."

"Well then, let's see what he's up to," Hunt replied.

Higgins turned left at one corner and a moment later slipped into a small establishment bearing a sign that read: AITKEN & CO. BOOKS – NEW & USED – COLLECTIBLES.

"Well, I sure as hell can't go in. Higgins knows my face. It'll have to be you," Brogan said.

"On it. I love bookstores, anyway," Hunt said. He made his way to the door and entered. The sheer display of books inside looked much more substantial than anyone looking at the store's exterior could have ever imagined.

A older man looked up from behind a counter. "Good day, sir. I'm Jonathan Aitken, the proprietor. How may I assist you?"

Thinking quickly, Hunt replied, "Yes, thank you, Mr. Aitken. I'll tell you what I'm interested in. I'm in the market for anything you might have by Dickens—collectibles, mind you. I'm especially interested in *A Tale of Two Cities*."

"Well, my good man, you've come to the right place. I may have exactly what you're looking for. I think I know just where to find it. Could I plead for a bit of patience? I'll be back with you in less than five minutes."

"Of course. I'll just browse a bit."

"Yes. That's great. Plenty of books for your browsing pleasure. Now, if you'll excuse me, I'll see to it," the proprietor said as he made his way from the room.

Hunt began to move from aisle to aisle, looking for his target. The store was small, but filled with shelves at all angles. Hunt made several turns, confronted by stack after stack of dusty volumes. He heard voices—almost whispers—and tried to navigate toward them, but there was no direct way. Finally, he caught a glimpse of Harry Higgins having an animated conversation with another man. The other man looked to be younger than Harry, but was dressed like a much older man in a conservative business suit. Hunt thought for a moment and then decided to head back out to Brogan. Just as he left the store, the old man came back with three old books. He was out of breath and very disappointed to see his customer depart.

"He's in there talking to some younger fellow in an nice suit. There's something about their body language that makes me think that the guy in the suit is the one we should be concerned about," Hunt said to Brogan.

"Think we should split up?" Brogan asked.

Hunt replied, "Well, the way I see it, we already know this Higgins fellow works at the church. Let's assume for the moment that he's the inside man. He probably has whatever device that was needed to activate the bomb. It may be stashed somewhere in the church. Or, it may be where he lives. Can't search the whole church, but we could find his flat and check it out."

"You think the younger man is the boss?"

"Maybe not the big boss, but he looks like Higgins's handler. I say we let Higgins go back to St. Paul's and we both keep an eye on the new guy."

"Agreed," Brogan said.

A moment later, Harry Higgins exited the bookstore and walked away in the direction of St. Paul's. Hunt and Brogan waited. After about two minutes, the young man in the fine suit walked out the same door and got into a taxi. Hunt and Brogan got into another one moments later and followed.

Apparently confident no one was watching, the passenger in the lead car did not direct his driver to do anything evasive. Instead, he traveled directly to his destination, one that became clear to the two men in the following car when they entered the city's Mayfair section. Brogan and Hunt were astonished when the lead car turned onto Curzon Street and then stopped in front of Leconfield House, the headquarters of MI5.

"Tell you what, Brogan. You take this taxi to the rendezvous spot back near St. Paul's. That pub, whatever the hell the name is."

"McRory's."

"If you say so. Head back there. I'll stay around here and watch. Tell Harvey to get his ass and his team over here. But discreetly. This thing just got a helluva lot more interesting."

"Not to mention more dangerous," Brogan said as Hunt got out of the car.

*

King and the boys were enjoying a pint at McRory's and looking at their watches. Brogan and Hunt were late and they wondered what it meant. Finally, Brogan came through the door.

"About time, sport. Where the hell is Hunt?"

"You're not going to believe this one. Hunt's keeping his eyes on the headquarters of MI5."

"What the hell?" King asked.

"You heard me. That Higgins bloke met with someone—a secret kind of thing in a bookstore. We followed the guy, we think he might be Higgins' handler."

"So you saw that Higgins fellow?"

"Yes."

"Where?"

"Coming out of St. Paul's. But that's not the point."

"Higgins at St. Paul's. Wouldn't that make him a great candidate as the inside man?"

"Probably. But this thing likely goes much deeper. Now just stop asking questions and listen for a change, Harvey."

King took the rebuke in stride and said, "Okay, sport. Fire away."

"Well, it's just that this serves to confirm an MI-5 connection—and that means a larger conspiracy. We know someone from five put the Russians on our trail back in Birmingham."

"But you said the guy in the bookstore was a younger man," King said.

"Yes. Looked to be no older than twenty-five, or so, though he was clearly trying to."

"Can't see some kid being the brains behind a major conspiracy," King said, skeptically.

Brogan looked King in the eye. "Yes, Harvey, but he may be connected to someone high up. He may be an assistant to a highly-placed mole."

"Damn!" Harvey barked.

In a flash, the men were out the door.

∗

Twenty minutes later, the entire team was in the vicinity of Leconfield House. They moved into covert positions in various places. From each vantage point they could see each other, as well as the main door and two other doors to the building. With no better options, they simply waited for the young man in the nice suit to emerge once more.

After about two hours, the target appeared. Brogan alerted the team with hand signals. The members of the team broke up, with Hunt and Brogan taking the lead on foot and the others blending in with dozens of pedestrians in the area. The target walked down Curzon Street and over to St. James Park.

Once in the park, the man sat down on a bench next to another older man and woman.

"Holy hell!" Brogan yelled in a whisper. "They're Michael and Molly Wheelan."

"Who?" King asked.

"Hell, Harvey. He's the man who works at the casket place in Birmingham, the man who likely put the explosive material in the casket."

"Holy shit," swore Howard Hunt under his breath, expressing the collective sentiment of the group.

*

Now convinced there was a very real connection between at least one man at MI5 and a Soviet plot to kill world leaders, Harvey King and the team tried to figure a way to find out the identity and position of the young man they had seen with Michael and Molly Wheelman. The MI5 connection suggested a deeply-entrenched conspiracy.

King remarked, "Doesn't surprise me a bit. The commies have been trying to get their hooks into our intelligence operations forever. And it didn't stop with Philby, that's for damn sure. Who knows how high up this thing goes."

Despite his age, Walter Thompson had managed to keep up with all of them. He spoke up now. "Mr. King, might I offer you and your team a suggestion?"

"Of course, Thompson," King responded in a deferential tone.

"Let me follow the lad back to Leconfield House., if he heads back there. I can come up with a reason to be visiting. Then I can do my best to find out who he is and what section he works for. I know my way around the place. Spent some time there in the old days. Still have a few friends there—much younger than me, mind you. But contacts from the old days. I'm confident I could leverage my name a bit and shake the tree to see what falls out."

"Anyone got a better idea?" King said as he looked at Hunt and Brogan.

They all nodded affirmation and separated, each man keeping his eyes on the three people on the bench about seventy-five yards away.

Finally, the young man hugged the woman and man and walked away. Harvey King motioned to Matthews and Perlstein to follow the couple. The rest of the team hung back while Walter Thompson fell in behind the young man. Thompson had good instincts and looked like any of a dozen other old men in the park.

Sure enough, the young man walked back to Leconfield House and straight in the front door. Thompson followed him. He was stopped before he got to the front door by a security man, who said rudely, "Excuse me, old man, might I ask who you are and what your business here might be?" The man put his hand on Thompson's lapel and pushed slightly.

"I beg your problem. I'm Detective Sergeant Walter Thompson, and I represent the family of the late Sir Winston Churchill. I need to speak to the young man who just entered that door," he said, pointing with emphasis.

The security man hesitated, slowly recognizing Thompson. "Oh, very sorry, sir. I've read your book. So very sorry for your loss."

"Thank you, my good man. Now would you be so kind as to tell me the name of that young man who just went in? He treated me rather rudely a few moments ago, and I plan to register a complaint on behalf of Lady Churchill."

"Oh my, sir" his tone now more respectful, "I'm sure Mr. Welling didn't mean anything by it."

"Welling, you say?"

"Yes, Detective Sergeant, that's Sean Welling. He's a personal assistant to the Director himself, Mr. Roger Hollis."

"Is he, indeed? Well, he needs to learn some manners. He's one arrogant arse of a young man."

"Would you like me to have any message passed along to him?"

Thompson paused, then brushed his left lapel dismissively with his right hand. "Well, I don't suppose it's all that important. I had no idea he was in such an important job. Must have a lot on his mind, what with all the people coming to town for my late boss's funeral and such. Let's leave it be for now. What's your name?"

"I'm Arthur Brisbane."

"Well, Brisbane, you've been very helpful. I feel much better now. If you want, I'll come back by in a day or so and give you an inscribed copy of my book."

"That would be remarkable, Mr. Thompson. But I'll just bring my own copy and have it with me as long as it takes for you to get back."

"Have a good afternoon," Thompson said. He quickly turned and walked away. The spring in his step reflected his quickened pulse. The Yanks needed to hear about young Sean Welling.

✳

Ferguson Matthews was back near St. Paul's, watching for Harry Higgins to leave for home. When the target finally appeared, just before dark, Matthews followed Higgins to a building a few blocks away. After Higgins disappeared into the building, Matthews waited and then saw a light come on—third floor, corner flat.

Matthews was back the next morning, this time with Howard Hunt. After they watched Higgins leave for work, they made their way to Higgins' flat.

"A light touch, Matthews. Leave no clue that anything has been disturbed. We're looking for a device of some kind. Hopefully we'll find and disable it," Hunt instructed.

But after about twenty minutes of carefully searching, they came up empty.

Hunt fumed, "The bastard probably already has the thing at work. No way we'll find it there."

CHAPTER THIRTY-ONE

As THE LINE OF MOURNERS slowly moved by the catafalque, several people jumped the queue. But no one minded. Some were members of the royal family—although the queen would appear later. Others included two former prime ministers, Clement Attlee and Harold MacMillan.

That first day, the widow, Lady Churchill, was there, along with her daughter, Mary Soames, to observe the guards change around six p.m.

While Lady Churchill spent time in Westminster Hall as her husband lay in state, there was another memorial service on the other side of the Atlantic at Washington's National Cathedral. Nearly three thousand people gathered to hear Adlai Stevenson, the former two-time Democratic nominee for president and current US Ambassador to the United Nations, deliver an unforgettable eulogy.

He didn't disappoint those in attendance, nor the millions watching on television and listening on radio. His rhetoric was worthy of Churchill himself. And after speaking for nearly thirty minutes, he finished his erudite remarks:

"In the last analysis, all his zest and life and confidence sprang, I believe, not only from the rich endowment of his nature, but also from a profound and simple faith. In the prime of his powers, confronted with the apocalyptic risks of annihilation, he said serenely: 'I do not believe that God has despaired of his children.' In old age, as the honors and excitements faded, his resignation had a touching simplicity: 'Only faith in a life after death in a brighter world where dear ones will meet again—only that and the measured tramp of time can give consolation.'

"The aristocrat, the leader, the historian, the painter, the politician, the lord of language, the orator, the wit—yes, and the dedicated bricklayer—behind all of them was the man of simple faith, steadfast in defeat, generous in victory, resigned in age, trusting in a loving providence, and committing his achievements and his triumphs to a higher power.

"Like the patriarchs of old, he waited on God's judgment and it could be said of him—as of the immortals that went before him—that God magnified him in the fear of his enemies and with his words he made prodigies to cease.'"

*

President Johnson didn't attend, still clinging to the cover of his cold and monitoring the intelligence operation in England. He watched Stevenson's speech in the Oval Office with Bill Moyers.

"That Adlai may be a pansy-ass, but he can sure put the words together. How come my guys can't write me speeches that sound smart like that?" Johnson asked Moyers.

The presidential aide had grown used to his boss's insecurities and had developed a measure of skill in managing and massaging the tall Texan's massive ego. "Mr. President, Stevenson has nothing on you. Your inaugural the other day was a masterpiece, and delivered with impeccable timing and tone."

"I s'pose, Bill, but I can't help thinking I should be the one in that church speaking about Churchill. Damned Russians. I'll never forgive 'em for causing me to miss this moment."

"What's the latest from our guys over in England, if you don't mind me asking?"

"They're following leads trying to figure out where the bomb is supposed to go off and who'll trigger it. I feel like hopping on Air Force One and hightailing it over there. I have half a mind to do it."

"Mr. President, of course you should do whatever you think is best. But I do think there is danger there."

"Danger? You think this is about me being a coward, Moyers? Is that what you think of your president?"

Horrified, Moyers replied quickly, "No, no, of course not, Mr. President. This is not about courage, it's about wisdom. It's about having a firm hand on the rudder if something happens that gives the Russians a chance to move on Europe. You may be the only thing standing between war and peace."

Johnson thought for a moment. Then he took a sip from his ever-present glass of Cutty Sark. "Ah hell, Moyers. I know that. It's just that it's a hell of a thing."

"I know it is, Mr. President. No doubt about it."

*

Around four o'clock, the team—minus Matthews and Perlstein—was once again seated around the table at Thompson's flat. It was time for tea, and Mary had prepared some wonderful items: cucumber sandwiches, smoked salmon with cream cheese, warm scones with clotted cream and preserves, and cake.

"This is called Dundee cake, Gentlemen," Mary informed the men as she served the tea. "It's a Scottish fruit cake. Mr. Churchill loved it. It pairs very well with this fine Earl Grey tea. It's Twining's—same as Her Royal Highness drinks at this hour."

"Along with her gin and tonic," Mary whispered, thinking no one could hear her. The men chuckled and she became embarrassed. "Oh my, I'm so sorry for saying that," she said.

"It was funny. Thank you so much, Mrs. Thompson. You're gonna spoil us and ruin us for America," King said. He picked up his cup and raised it. "Not sure if you're s'posed to toast with tea, but here's to Walter and Mary Thompson, two wonderful hosts."

"Hear, hear!" they all said.

Walter then raised his cup. "Since we're toasting, here's to our American friends who have come to protect the honor of the late, great Mr. Churchill."

"Well, I gotta tell you, Thompson, you're still a top-notch lawman and intelligence professional. That was a great bit of detective work getting Sean Welling's name for us."

Brogan interrupted, "You know, it just struck me. I told you I knew the Wheelans from an operation some years ago, when I was working undercover in the IRA."

"Yeah, I remember. What of it?" King asked.

"Well, I'm almost certain they have a son, and by my guess, he'd be about the age of this Sean Welling fellow."

"From Wheelan to Welling—that's not much of a leap," King mused.

Howard Hunt added, "This is adding up to a conspiracy of monumental proportions. King here knows that I write spy novels, and I can tell you that this is the stuff of an espionage classic."

"So you're a spy novelist, and Harvey here is the real James Bond?" Brogan said with a smile.

"Hey, truth is stranger than fiction, sport," King said. They all had a good laugh.

Thompson spoke up. "Let me see if I have this right. You're saying that a personal assistant to the Director of MI5 is secretly the son of two members of the IRA?"

"It's worse than that, Thompson," King said. "These Wheelan people are part of a plot we believe was put together by the Russians. This would mean that they are really *Soviet* spies. And their work for the IRA is just an assignment from the communists."

"Good God!" Thompson said. "Mr. Churchill never did trust the Russians, all that riddle, puzzle, enigma thing. But this is almost too much to swallow."

"The Russians have been in the mole business for decades. It didn't start with Burgess and Philby—and it sure as hell didn't end there, Thompson," King said.

Howard Hunt stunned everyone with what he said next. "I'll go even further, my friends. And I'm pretty sure Harvey here will agree with me. There are even some in our CIA who believe your Mr. Roger Hollis is himself a Soviet agent himself."

Harvey nodded and said, "Hunt's right. I was among the first to shine a light on Philby back in '51. After MacLean and Burgess flew the coop and high-tailed it for Moscow, Beetle Smith—he was running the CIA back then, Eisenhower's old assistant—well, he asked me and one other guy, Jim Angleton, to write reports about Philby. Mine was easy. I said the guy was a spy. Jim didn't agree. But J. Edgar sided with me had the guy run out of the country."

Hunt said. "And years later, Harvey was proven right."

"Too little, too late," King said with a pathetic tone. "Point is, they've been doing this shit for years. And we seem to be surprised every time some new conspiracy turns out to be true."

Thompson said, "Maybe we should be taking a look at the director himself."

Hunt and King exchanged a look.

"Let's have some more of this great tea, Mrs. Thompson. I think your husband is on to something."

*

By the time their teatime meeting was over, Howard Hunt had committed to being the point man on the Roger Hollis angle, while others on the team worked on a way to get at Michael and Molly Wheelan, as well as Harry Higgins. Matthews and Perlstein showed up after the dishes had been cleared and cleaned, but Mary had saved their portions. As they dug in, they briefed the rest of the team about Michael and Molly Wheelan.

"When they left the park," Perlstein began, "they headed over to a pub called the Tipperary, where they met up with a lady."

This got Brogan's attention. "What'd she look like?"

"Easy on the eyes, that's for sure. Bright red hair—even brighter than your mop, Brogan. About five feet two, maybe. Gorgeous green eyes," Matthews answered.

"That'd be Kaitlyn Dorcey. She seems to be in the middle of this somehow."

Hunt added, "We're certain this Wheelan couple is working for the Soviets."

Matthews asked, "How about the redhead? Is there more red about her than just her hair?"

Brogan shook his head defiantly. "Not a chance. She's IRA through and through. No way she's a commie. Only politics for her have to do with kicking the Brits off the Emerald Isle."

"What makes you so sure?"

"Because I know her. Watched her work on operation after operation for the IRA; none of them could've possibly had anything to do with the Russians."

Harvey spoke up. "You may have a blind spot, Brogan. But then again, you may be right. I've been around a long time, and I know for a fact the Soviets love to use proxies. It wouldn't surprise me at all if that was the case here."

Hunt added. "I agree. After all, if they've planned some big bang to change the world, they sure want it to look like the work of someone other than them. Classic cover. Make it look like an IRA job, then exploit the fallout. False flag shit. Which makes me wonder if this Kaitlyn girl may be a weak link for us to exploit." He paused and looked over at the Irishman. "And by us, I mean you, Brogan."

All eyes were now on their ruddy colleague. "I imagine you're right. And if you are, then I know the last thing Miss Dorcey would want is to be used by anyone—especially the Soviets."

"Hey, sport, you need to head over to that pub and see if she's there. Go work your Irish magic. You might just save her life."

Tiernan smiled. "Well, I guess I can suffer through a night with a beautiful woman for a good cause."

CHAPTER THIRTY-TWO

As BROGAN SPRUCED UP a bit and prepared to head over to the Tipperary, Hunt pulled King aside and said, "Harvey, think old Thompson here will mind me making another call home?"

"To Dulles?"

"No. Angleton. I could catch him just before lunch in DC."

"Yeah, better catch him quick. After his usual dose of martinis, he'll be slow on the draw."

Harvey King went over to Walter Thompson and whispered into the older man's ear. Hunt watched as Thompson nodded. King looked over at Hunt and thumbed at the door to Thompson's small office.

Hunt went in and shut the door behind him. He placed the call, using a private number that connected directly to James Jesus Angleton's office. It rang four times, leaving Hunt just about to hang up, convinced that the wizard of counterintelligence had already departed for one of his favorite

Georgetown haunts with some of the boys from the office. But on the fifth ring, Angleton answered. They quickly dispensed with the small talk.

"You know what I think about our friend Hollis, don't you Hunt?"

"Yes, Jim. I'm aware of your suspicions."

"More than suspicions. They're facts, Hunt."

"Well, if so, then I can probably help you make an airtight case. I just need some help. Surely you have a file on the guy. Dig it out and help me with some patterns—the guy's habits. Stuff like that."

"Gladly, my friend. Hold the phone." Hunt could hear some noise. File drawers opening. Papers rustling. Footsteps. Then, after a couple of minutes, he heard something slam shut and Angleton was back on the phone. "Okay, here we go. We've had some eyes on the man here and there. Nothing official, mind you. More of an off the record kind of thing."

"Of course," Hunt said. He was well aware of the broad latitude Angleton tended to take. His superiors usually just left the man alone with his mysteries, conspiracies, and endless intelligence webs.

"I think your best bet is going to be over at the Savoy. It's always been a favorite haunt for Hollis. He drinks and dines there at least four times a week, according to my notes. Mostly alone, by the way. Doesn't seem to have many close friends. Sometimes in the company of a young staff member, a fellow named Sean Welling."

"Got it," Hunt said. He resisted the urge to divulge what they had just learned about young Mr. Welling. "Thanks a million, Jim. I'll get back to you if I need more."

"My files can always use fresh material, Hunt," Angleton said.

*

Shortly before eight o'clock that Wednesday evening, Her Majesty, Queen Elizabeth, accompanied by her husband, Prince Philip, The Duke of Edinburgh, and her sister, Princess Margaret, entered Westminster Hall. The long line of mourners—which stretched for more than a mile, back across Lambeth Bridge—was halted. They had been moving slowly past Churchill's casket at the pace of about four thousand per hour all day long.

The queen and her party entered the vast room through the Star Court and the middle door across from the catafalque. They stood silently near the casket for a few minutes. Then they left through the same door, and the long line began moving once again.

*

Tiernan Brogan looked the room over as he entered the Tipperary, but did not see Kaitlyn Dorcey. He went to the bar and ordered a pint. Then he walked over to a corner table, where he had a good view of everything. He nursed his drink, but before long had to get another. He was prepared to wait the length of three pints for her to appear. She came in just as he was approaching the bar for his third pint.

"Fancy meeting you here, Sean," Kaitlyn said as she met him at the bar. To her, he was still Sean Walsh from the old days.

"Kaitlyn!" he said with a big smile. "What a lovely surprise. Let me buy you a drink. What's your pleasure?"

She was flattered by his passionate greeting. "Well, if you leave the weak stuff behind, I'll join you in a Tullamore."

He called up the drinks and they made their way over to his table. They clinked glasses. His goal for the evening was to get her to somehow open up about the operation she was working on. But he couldn't help thinking about a different goal, too—this one involving something much more intimate. He did his best to put that idea out of his mind, which was increasingly difficult as one drink led to another. He was impressed with her tolerance. Yes, Tiernan was Irish through and through, complete with an ability to drink prodigious amounts of liquor, but Kaitlyn's skills were at a whole other level.

Their conversation over the next few hours ricocheted from old missions, to life back in Belfast, to the reasons neither of them had ever married. Eventually, Brogan decided to turn the conversation toward his mission. "Quite the show this week here in London. Churchill's funeral and all."

Kaitlyn drained her glass and wiped her hand across her mouth. Then she gave the first sign that the alcohol was beginning to loosen her lips. "Yes, quite the show. And the best is yet to come," she said, a slight smile and gleam in her captivating green eyes.

Tiernan played dumb, attempting to draw her out. "Yes, I've been reading about it in the papers. The world is watching. Leaders from all over here. Quite a moment for our British 'friends,'" he said, emphasizing the last word with slight sarcasm.

"Oh, Sean, you can be so thick sometimes."

"How?"

"You go over there and get us two more glasses of this fine whiskey, and I'm going to tell you a story." Tiernan looked down at his glass. It was still half full. Kaitlyn grabbed it from him and finished the drink in a long swallow. "There," she said. "Now off with you, and be quick about it, Sean. It's not good to keep a girl waiting," she added, slightly slurring her words.

When Brogan got back to the table, he handed a glass to Kaitlyn. Then he raised his own, "To Kaitlyn Dorcey, the most beautiful girl in all of Ireland."

She smiled, "Why Sean, you bastard. You trying to charm me?"

"Is it working?"

She smiled again and winked. "We can talk about us, or we can talk about Sir Winston Churchill."

Brogan was momentarily torn between his mission and his passion. He quickly rationalized that the best way to get her to talk about her part in a great conspiracy was to continue to pursue her. So he replied, "Churchill who?"

"Good answer, Sean. But it's Churchill you're going to get, before you get me," she said.

"Um, well, okay…I…er," Brogan stammered.

"Why, Sean, you're blushing. Are you smitten?"

"I am and have been since we first worked together."

"Well, we shall get back to that. But these are days that are going to change our future. And I'm not talking about you getting all horned up."

"I'm fine, Kaitlyn. Been controlling meself for years," he said. They laughed. "Sounds like there's something you want to tell me."

"Well, it's a secret now, but soon the world will know."

"I don't follow."

Kaitlyn finished the new drink in front of her and looked around to make sure no one else was listening in. Then she said, "Sean, think of it. The great irony of something happening at the funeral of the great enemy of our cause."

"Something?"

"Some friends of mine are planning an *incident* at St. Paul's."

＊

Howard Hunt had been in the American Bar at the Savoy for more than two hours. He had a good view of the entire room, as well as the entrance of the nearby restaurant. He was watching for any sign of Roger Hollis. But the director was a no show. He decided to have one more drink before calling it a night.

He had taken two small sips when a bearded man with glasses and silver hair walked in and took a spot about ten feet away. There was something about the man that triggered Hunt's curiosity. First, the hair wasn't right. He could see a tinge of black hair and surmised that the man was wearing a wig. Then the large frames—well, they reminded Hunt of some he used on occasion when undercover. He would bet that a closer analysis would show that the glass was just glass, not prescription lenses.

"Welcome back, Mr. Henderson. Same as last night?"

"M-m-mighty fine, my good man. Yes, p-please."

"That room number again, sir?"

"312."

The stammer struck Hunt as familiar. He made a mental note of the room number. He thought about trying to strike up a conversation with the man, but ultimately decided against it.

He paid his bill and headed back over to Walter Thompson's flat to check in with Harvey King.

*

Kaitlyn Dorcey led Brogan to her nearby flat, having decided either to reveal more details about the so-called Churchill incident or to fulfill the operative's long-standing fantasy. He needed the former, but longed for the latter.

She telegraphed her immediate intentions the moment the door was closed behind them. She kissed him passionately. He smiled at the thought of telling the team all he was going through for this mission. They made love and both drifted off to sleep.

Brogan got up about thirty minutes later and did a little snooping, trying to find anything of value to his mission hiding in, or just out of, plain sight. Nothing. Then he found some coffee in the kitchen, as well as a percolator. He turned on the stove and within a few minutes the aroma of coffee filled the small flat.

Soon Kaitlyn appeared in the doorway. She was wearing his shirt, stretching and smiling at him.

"Sorry to wake you."

"No bother at all. How about we turn that pot off for now and head back to bed for another round if you're up to it?" Her eyes widened. "Oh, I see you are," she said with a wicked laugh.

The mission would have to wait a bit longer, as Tiernan Brogan took another one for the team.

CHAPTER THIRTY-THREE

WHEN HUNT RETURNED TO THOMPSON'S FLAT, he briefed king on his evening at the hotel bar. He also mentioned the interesting man with the ill-fitting wig and pronounced stammer.

"You mean like a stutter? You sure it was a wig—the guy was in disguise?"

"Just as sure as I'm sitting here right now. But the guy wasn't doing recon. Kept to himself. The bartender knew him from other nights. The man is staying in room 312."

Harvey King was lost in thought for a long moment. Then he broke into his own silence and said, mostly to himself, "No. Couldn't be. There's no way they'd do that."

"No way who would do what?"

"Well, this is a big Russian operation apparently, right?"

"Sure."

"And they have been in the spy and mole game big time for years. We've been talking about Hollis, right?"

"Yes. Not sure where you're going with this, though."

"Well, remember what I was talking about back in '51, and how Beetle Smith asked Jim and me to write up reports about a suspected mole?"

"Sure—Philby," Hunt said. Then his eyes lit up and grew large. "Son of a bitch! You think that stuttering bastard in room 312 at the Savoy is Kim Philby?"

"I sure as hell think it's worth checking out. I mean, think about it. The Soviets extracted Philby from Lebanon, what, two years ago?"

"Yep. January '63."

"Well, most of us from the old days assume that the commies had been grooming Philby to run MI6 one day. If he hadn't been discovered, hell, they might have moles running both MI5 and MI6 right now. Those guys play for keeps. And they take their time. Who knows, but what if this whole conspiracy has been in the works for a decade or more? That's the way they do things."

"So somehow Philby was sent back to run it?" Hunt asked.

"All speculation, but it's a hell of a theory. The story I've heard is that good old Kim's been drinking and depressed in Moscow. But what if that's disinformation shit? What if he's back to exact revenge?"

"We need to call Dulles," Hunt said.

"And Angleton," King added.

*

Manlio Brosio was the Fourth General Secretary of NATO. He had served in that post for less than a year. He was sixty-eight years old, but he had the energy and stamina of a man half his age. With a background in law and diplomacy in his native Italy, he was a skilled manager. Always impeccably dressed, Brosio had a serious-looking face, marked by thin lips and a receding hairline. His calm demeanor endeared him to those who worked around him.

Since his appointment, Brosio had learned to rely more and more on his aide, Henri Girard, whose cluttered desk was not far from Brosio's office door. What the General Secretary did not know was that his dependence on Girard had been deliberately orchestrated and cultivated. The assistant was now well positioned to do the bidding of his real bosses, the KGB and Politboro.

Henri was working late that Wednesday, although he had to create busy work to justify the extra time. He was waiting for Brosio—a man also known to work long hours—to leave for the night. And since Henri managed his boss's calendar, he knew that dinner plans had been made with the Italian Ambassador to France, an old friend. The dinner would go on for hours—the spy would have ample time to get his job done.

After Brosio left for dinner, Girard entered his boss's office. His mission? To find up-to-date information on NATO troop placements and overall readiness. Because Brosio had even trusted Girard with the combination to the safe on the wall—behind a painting of a picturesque scene in Tuscany— the Soviet agent knew just where to look. He found a stack of files and, using a small camera, took several dozen photographs. While he didn't stop to read each page thoroughly, he was confident any information held in the safe was current and relevant. As he left Brosio's office, he put the film in a small envelope.

Henri left the Palais de Chaillot a few minutes later and made his way to a small cafe near the Gare du Nord. There he met Peter, passing the envelope to the handler.

Peter developed the film in a dark room in his apartment. Soon the materials were en route to Moscow.

∗

Kaitlyn Dorcey came back into her bedroom with a tray in her hands. On it were two cups of coffee and some bread and butter. "Haven't been food shopping for a while, love, but this'll settle our insides a bit," she said.

"I'd rather have bread and butter with you than steak with anyone else," Brogan told her.

"Aren't you the charmer? Aiming for another go at it, are you?" she asked with a smile, sipping her coffee and curling up next to him.

"I think you've worn me out, honey."

"Honey, he calls me," she said saucily.

"What would you prefer?"

"It's fine. More bread?"

"Thanks. I was thinking while you were in the kitchen— thinking about what we talked about back at the pub. About something that might happen at the big funeral on Saturday."

"It'll sure make a noise," she said, her words slightly muffled through a large chunk of bread.

"What exactly is it that will make this noise?"

She took another sip of coffee and looked him in the eye. "You sure you want to know? Might be better for you to just ignore what I said while you were getting me drunk so you could have your way with me."

"Getting *you* drunk? I couldn't keep up with you. I think it was actually the other way around."

"You would!" she laughed, then paused. "I'll tell you about it if you really want to know."

"I do. What's happening?"

"Some friends of ours have rigged things so that right in the middle of all the nice things being said about that old devil Churchill, there will be a loud explosion. Not a large one, mind you, but enough to get the notice of all the television cameras, not to mention everyone in the pews. I doubt anyone will be seriously hurt."

Of course, Brogan knew the intelligence they had indicated an explosion designed to be much bigger than what Kaitlyn was envisioning. But he didn't let on. "To what end?"

"To what end? Is that what you asked? To what end?" she spat, annoyed.

"Sorry, honey—didn't mean to upset you. Of course, I understand it's designed to be a statement."

"Damn right."

"And will the IRA take the credit?"

"Of course. Why wouldn't we? Our feelings about Churchill and his imperialism are well known."

"Well, I was just thinking—"

"About what?"

*

It was long after dark in Arlington, Virginia when the black telephone in the small green house rang. James Jesus Angleton was working on some of his prize orchids—a near obsession. They somehow reminded him of the intricate patterns of

255

counter-espionage. Those people closest to him were certain his love for the flowers was somehow connected to his obsessive work in a psychological sense.

He put a small shearing tool down on a table and removed his gloves before he answered the telephone on the seventh ring. "Yes?"

"Jim? It's King. I assume this is a secure line?"

"It is, Harvey. I'm in the greenhouse."

"You're gonna turn into a damn orchid one of these days, old boy."

Ignoring the dig, Angle ton asked, "What can I do for you, Harvey? Find out more about our friend at Five?"

"Not quite. But in the course of our investigation we did stumble onto something that begs a second look."

"Why call now? Why not wait for more intel?"

"Well, it's just that if this is what we think it might be, it's something you'd particularly want to know about, Jim."

"Harvey, I'm a spy. You're a spy. But cut the cryptic bullshit. What the hell are you talking about?"

"There's a chance that an old friend of yours may be here in London. And you'll never guess who it is."

There was a brief pause and then Angleton said, "Philby."

"How'd you know?"

"I didn't. But you're a piss poor poker player. Besides, you said friend of mine, not friend of ours. So that narrowed it down. Tell me about it."

King briefed Angleton in detail about Hunt's encounter with the mystery man. "What we need—and can't really get it over here; don't know who to trust—what we need is anything we have on a Brit named William Henderson. Probably a fake. But worth looking at."

"I'll check it out first thing. What's your plan going forward?"

"Well, I sure as hell can't check it out myself. Philby and I have some history, as you well know."

"Understood. How about Hunt? He's a good operative. Do he and Philby have any history?"

"Not a bit. They've never met."

"Then let him run with it. But I'd put another man there with him."

"Done. Do we have anyone else here in country—anyone we can trust? I think we may need a few more hands."

"I'll see what I can do. I know that we can't work through the official channels on this, so our station there in London needs to be kept in the dark," Angleton said.

King thought for a moment, then he said, "How about I call one of our old friends in Rome? Just saw him last week. We had dinner."

"You mean Romano?"

"Hell yes. Johnny Romano. He was prepared to do anything we needed back when the plan was to knock off Castro. I'm sure he can get us some muscle."

"I've no doubt that he can. But it needs to be discreet."

"Seriously? Hey, Jim, if there's any group that can keep a lid on things, it's the mob. And they're not bad at disposal either. We have the beginnings of a body count here."

"Okay, Harvey, make the call."

"Hell of a thing, Jim."

"Indeed."

✳

"Something's been bothering me for a few days," Tiernan Brogan said to Kaitlyn Dorcey. "And now that we've had this splendid time together, and you've told me what you've told me, it's bothering me even more."

"What the devil are you talking about?" she asked, as she sat up straight in bed and spilled some of her coffee on his shirt which she was wearing. "Sorry, love. I can wash this out in a bit. What's been bothering you?"

He wanted to break the ice, but he knew he had to work the edges. "It has to do with some of the people you had with you the other night at the pub."

"Who?"

"Michael and Molly Wheelan. I don't think you know everything about them."

"I've known them for years, and their son, Sean, too. Whatever are you talking about, Mr. Walsh?" she asked, her tone and body language noticeably defensive.

He forged ahead. "When I saw them—particularly him—the other night, he looked familiar, but I couldn't place him. Then it hit me. I recalled an operation over in Birmingham about four years ago. You weren't part of this one. But Michael was."

"I'm sure he's been involved in many things. What's your point?"

"Well, it's that I happened to observe him one night—totally by accident, mind you. He was talking with a man I knew to be an agent for the KGB."

"The Russians? What the hell was he doing talking to a Russian agent?"

"I haven't a clue. But I followed him twice more over the next week—this time on purpose—and observed him talking to the same man. One time he handed the Russian a large envelope."

"That makes no sense."

"Of course it does. Haven't you ever been approached?"

"Approached? By whom?"

"By a Russian?"

"Of course not! I've got nothing to do with those commie bastards. I'm an Irish patriot. My beef is with the crown."

"A true believer."

"That'd be me," she said, proudly.

"Well, I've been approached. In fact, I was once approached by the same man I saw meeting regularly with Michael Wheelan. I told the guy to go to hell when I realized he was trying to turn me. But it looks like your friend Michael may have made a different choice."

"'Tis hard to believe, Sean. Michael's been a big part of the plan I just told you about. In fact, he's the one responsible for the device—the bomb."

"You're missing my point, Kaitlyn."

"I'm not missing a damn thing, Sean," she said, angry. "My friend also works for the Russians. I get it."

"But do you get what it means? Who came up with the idea to put a bomb at St. Paul's?" Brogan asked. He was fishing, taking a risk.

Kaitlyn thought for a moment and then said, "Come to think of it, it was Michael Wheelan who started this whole thing. He brought me and the others in."

"Just as I suspected. And my gut tells me that Michael Wheelan got the idea from the Russians."

"But why?"

"I'll tell you why. Or better yet, let me ask you a question: what if the Russians are behind something bigger and are just using our IRA people to facilitate the plan?"

She listened and then said, resignedly, "And then will blame it all on us."

"I think so. With all the world leaders in one room on Saturday, it's possible that this 'incident' you've worked on could turn out to be bigger. Much bigger."

"Deaths?"

"Think about it. What if the Russians want to kill off dozens of key world leaders at one time—De Gaulle, Wilson—the whole lot? And what if they want to blame it on the likes of you and your friends?"

"But why would they do such a thing?" By this time, Kaitlyn was beginning to buy in to Brogan's premise.

"I can think of a few reasons. Mainly, though, if they create an unstable world political environment of that magnitude, they could exploit it for their own purposes."

"Such as?"

"Such as an excuse for making a move to take over all of Europe. They've wanted to do that since the days of Stalin."

"Oh my God!" she said, standing up. She was trembling. "What have I done?"

CHAPTER THIRTY-FOUR

GIOVANNI "JOHNNY" ROMANO spent most of his time in Sicily, but he had a nice apartment in Rome for when he was there on business. He missed America, but the terms of his deportation were clear—if he ever again stepped foot on American soil, he would be arrested and locked away for life. Part of him wondered if the American authorities would actually follow through on such a threat. After all, he knew things. Lots of things. Secret things about some ugly work he and some of his friends had done on behalf of the American government—unofficially, of course. Johnny knew where bodies were buried, literally.

His grandfather came to America around the turn of the century, landing in New Orleans, which became the first real foothold in America for what eventually came to be popularly called the "Mafia." The "official" family business was food distribution, but it was the "other" things that made them rich and powerful. Things like gambling, prostitution, and protection. By the time the 1920s exploded, along with Prohibition, the Romano family had moved into several major cities: Chicago, Philadelphia, Detroit, Miami, and New York.

Johnny was born the day the Titanic sank in 1912. His mother died in the influenza epidemic in 1920, so he was raised by his father and uncles. During World War II, he took over the business after his father was gunned down in a Brooklyn dry cleaners. He modernized the family work and became wealthy and powerful. Politicians were in his pocket. Law enforcement too.

Then came the fiasco in November 1957. Johnny Romano had allowed Vito Genovese and Santo Trafficante, two other powerful mob bosses, to talk him into attending a "summit" meeting in Upstate New York at the home of Joe Barbara in a little spot called Apalachin. Local law enforcement caught wind of it and raided the house. Johnny Romano found himself joining several other men, all in expensive suits and shoes, on a run through the woods, shedding rolls of money along the way. He was arrested, detained, and then released—but he'd been on the radar from that point on.

He hoped that trying to find a way to work with the CIA against Castro would enable him to continue to conduct his business as usual, but then came the Kennedy assassination. Johnny knew some of the evidence in that case led back to some of his friends and that there were secrets that could never come out.

Romano and Harvey King had known each other for a decade or so. They had become friends when King was working in and around Miami on Cuban organized crime. They had a mutual fondness for what they loved to laugh and refer to as "booze and broads." Miami was the perfect environment for both pursuits. South Beach was also a base for plotting and intrigue. The Cubans who had migrated there following the Castro takeover teamed up with members of organized crime, and the CIA exploited their collective hatred of the Cuban dictator.

＊

But after President Kennedy's death, it had all changed. King was exiled to Rome. So was Johnny. Both men were wounded warriors. So Johnny was glad to pick up the phone one day to hear from his spy friend.

"Johnny, it's Harvey King. I'm in London."

"What the hell you doin' in that place, paisano?"

"I'm on a case. And I think I need some help. You have any trusted associates anywhere near here?"

"What kind of case?"

"Something big. Can't go into it on the telephone. But I could use some muscle."

"Sure Harvey. I got some guys. Tell me where I should tell 'em to go?"

"Great. You're the best, Johnny. I'll fill you in when I can. Meantime, send them to me at this address."

Johnny Romano wrote down the address and hung up the phone. Then he yelled, "Tony, get Vince and Dom—I want you guys on the next flight to London. Go to this address. Then call and tell me what the hell is going on!"

＊

"Comrade Semichastny, you have the materials from your agent in Paris?" Leonid Brezhnev asked. The men around the table—

members of the Politburo, as well as several men from Department Thirteen in the First Directorate—anxiously awaited the findings. The large table was filled with plates of pastry and pots of coffee for the breakfast meeting in the Kremlin on Thursday, January twenty-ninth.

"Indeed, Comrade Chairman," replied the head of the KGB. "They tell quite a story."

"Does this story have a happy ending?" the Chairman asked.

"Yes, it does. It is clear from these documents that the nations of Western Europe, as well as the Americans, have made no unusual moves. There is no indication of any kind of NATO mobilization or even an increased level of readiness. It appears our enemies are sound asleep."

Brezhnev lit a cigarette. Then, in a gesture reminiscent of their late leader, Josef Stalin, he stood and began to slowly clap his hands. Everyone in the room joined in. After a few moments, the chairman sat back down and the others obediently followed his lead.

Brezhnev continued, "Now to the matter of our assets in London, what's the latest report from there, Comrade Semichastny?"

The mood in the room quickly changed with the revelation that three of their agents had been killed and two others had not been heard from for more than twenty-four hours.

"Who's responsible?" the chairman asked.

The director replied, "We believe there is some American presence and interest."

"Is this related to the fact that President Johnson will not be attending the service in that London cathedral?"

"No way to tell. The reports say he is sick. We have no one in a position to be able to verify this."

"Your recommendation?"

"Comrade Chairman, I believe we must move forward with this great visionary mission for Mother Russia and the Warsaw Pact nations. Our great cause is to liberate the remainder of the continent from the decadent grip of capitalism. I'm confident that if our enemies had any real suspicions, we would see a certain measure of military mobilization. They are indeed sound asleep."

All eyes in the room shifted from the Director of the KGB and back to the Chairman. Brezhnev finally said, "I agree." He once again stood and began clapping in that Stalinesque manner once more.

*

Shortly after noon on Thursday, Howard Hunt—joined now by Jim McCord—entered the Savoy Hotel. They had developed some hand signals for communication in preparation for what promised to be a long day of watching and waiting for Roger Hollis.

Hunt was more than surprised to see the man already in The Grill, having lunch by himself and reading some papers from a large folder. Hunt sent McCord over to a bank of pay telephones on the far wall. "Tell King that Hollis is here and we're going to watch him for any possible contact with the man in room 312."

Hunt took a table by himself, one with a good view of the director of MI5. He made sure to look as if he were immersed in working the *Times* crossword puzzle. He randomly filled in words in ink, impressing the waiter who filled his water glass.

"Just a bowl of whatever soup you're serving today," he said to the waiter, without looking up from the puzzle.

By the time the soup arrived—split pea, much to Hunt's chagrin—McCord had taken a table on the far side of the room. They made eye contact and Hunt wiped his mouth with a napkin, a preset signal that communicated: "If he moves, you follow."

McCord's server brought a glass of ginger ale to his table. At that moment, Hollis did a triple dab of his mouth with a folded napkin and walked from his table. McCord waited a moment and then followed. He watched Hollis head into the men's room, but decided not to follow him in. Less than a minute later, Hollis was back out and on his way to a lift. McCord made a split-second decision to try to catch the same elevator car—and barely made it. He noticed that the operator had pressed the button for the third floor and McCord indicated it was his destination, as well. Hollis gave him a long look. To escape his gaze, McCord fished through his pockets as if looking for something.

He followed Hollis off the lift and turned in the opposite direction than the one the director chose. McCord heard a door open and then close behind him. He turned and quickly walked back the way Hollis had gone. His impeccable hearing told him the door Hollis had used was on the left side of the hall and a few down from the lift. He looked at the numbers there and saw the room had to be either 310 or 312. Acting quickly, he took the lift back down. He briefed Howard Hunt.

"Has to be 312. That's the room our mystery man occupies. We'd better lay back and watch for a bit. If it's Philby's room, there's no way those KGB bastards would have him in a place like this without their own surveillance, so they gotta have some eyes 'round here somewhere. We need to be careful. You grab a paper and sit somewhere. I'll check in with King this time. Got a coin"?

McCord picked up a copy of *The Guardian* as Hunt headed for the phones.

"Yep. Room 312. Something's up in that one, old boy," Hunt exulted.

"You guys sit on this. Hang tight. I'll be by in a bit," King said.

"You'd better stay out of view, Harvey. If it is Kim, he'll see you coming a mile away. You're hard to miss."

"Yeah well, I know a thing or two about tradecraft, Hunt. Don't shit your pants worrying about me. Just don't get blown yourself."

*

A while later, as King walked up the Strand toward the Savoy, he saw Hunt walking from the site toward him. He stopped and waited. "What the hell, Hunt? Told you to stay put."

"I improvised—so sue me."

"This is my operation—"

"King, would you shut your damn pie hole for once? Listen to me. Hollis was here for lunch."

"No surprise. We know he's a regular," Harvey said.

"He left about ten minutes ago."

"Did you follow him?"

"I sent McCord with him. But that's not what you need to know. Just stop talking!"

"Okay, Hunt. No need to be a bastard about it."

"Philby—or at least the guy we think might be him—is back in the bar."

"Now?"

"As we speak."

Harvey King thought for a moment and then said, "Here's the plan, sport. You go back to the bar and keep an eye on him. Meantime, I'll get into that room. But here's the deal. If he makes a move, you pick up the nearest house phone and ring room 312 once—just once. That'll give me time to scram."

"Got it."

"Now you head back. I'll be thirty seconds behind you."

Howard Hunt turned and made his way back to the hotel. By the time he reached the bar, King was through the front doors and on his way to the lifts, looking every bit the part of someone who belonged there. He told the elevator operator, "Take me up to three."

The hallway on the third floor was vacant, except for a housekeeping cart. Harvey found room 312 and, using a device he kept in his pocket for just such occasions, he picked the lock in a matter of seconds. Once inside, he poked around, careful not to disturb things. He saw several glasses scattered around the room, but surmised the one on the table next to the bed would be the best bet to bear Kim Philby's prints—if indeed he were the occupant of the room. Using his handkerchief, King wrapped the glass and then put it in his pocket.

Just then the telephone rang—just once. King made his way out of the room down the hall and past the elevators. He hid inside a deep doorway and waited. When the elevator arrived, he saw the mystery man exit and walk straight to room 312.

"Kim Philby, you lying son of a bitch. We got you after all these years," he whispered under his breath.

CHAPTER THIRTY-FIVE

"PROBABLY GOING TO HAVE TO GET our friend detective Sergeant Murray to help with this one, Mr. King," Thompson said, as he looked over at the water glass now sitting on his kitchen table. "I'm sure he knows someone who can run a trace on the prints, but he'll have to know what it's about."

"He's played ball with us so far, Thompson. I trust him," King replied.

"Yes, he has. It's just that we've yet to talk with him about Hollis, MI5, and all that bloody rot. Not sure, but he might feel some need to speak to others higher up about our work in this matter," Thompson cautioned.

"Can't hurt to ask," King pressed.

"I suppose not," Thompson said. "Let me take this to him and see what he says. How do they say it in America on the television? I remember a phrase from my tour over there. Ah yes—stay tuned?"

King laughed and said, "Yeah. That's it. We're gonna stay tuned, Thompson. Just hurry every chance you get. The sooner we confirm our suspicions about the man in room 312, the better."

Mary came into the room. "Now, you fine gentlemen need to give me my kitchen if we're to have a proper tea. Off with you," she said with a gentle wave of her hand.

*

Kaitlyn Dorcey was uncharacteristically nervous as she nursed a pint of Smithwick's at the Tipperary. After hours of conversation with the man she knew as Sean Walsh, she was now convinced that Michael and Molly Wheelan were working for the Soviets. She had agreed to ring them at the building they had been using and told them that she had some information they needed to hear in person. Walsh waited nearby in her flat, joined now by Howard Hunt and Ferguson Matthews.

She had about an inch of ale left in her glass when the couple from Birmingham walked in the door and over to her table. "I'll get us a drink, and another for you, Miss Dorcey," Michael said.

"No. Let's not talk here," Kaitlyn said in a soft tone, looking over her right shoulder. "My flat's a block a way. Besides, I have a proper drink there—a nice new bottle of Tullamore Dew."

"Sounds splendid," he replied. The three of them left the pub and walked briskly toward her flat.

Once inside, the men waiting there surprised the couple. and quickly subdued them. Within two minutes Michael and Molly were bound to chairs. Matthews pulled out two syringes containing a powerful sedative that would knock the couple out for anywhere from twelve to eighteen hours. He injected Michael and Molly in their necks. As they drifted toward unconsciousness, they looked over at Kaitlyn with contempt. She returned the look with one of her own. She walked over and slapped Michael's groggy face.

"You bastard—working for the Soviets all along! We're going to find out all the parts of the story you've forgotten to mention."

*

Walter Thompson telephoned Edmund Murray and arranged to meet at Scotland Yard Headquarters on the Victoria Embankment overlooking the Thames. They rendezvoused outside the buildings.

"Whatever prints are on this glass may turn out to be quite revealing and important, Murray," Thompson said, handing him a small bag.

"All very cloak and dagger, Thompson. You turning into Sherlock Holmes?" They laughed.

"If our suspicions are correct, it will be important that this go no further than you and him—at least for now. Understood?" Thompson looked closely at Murray. "You look down—something on your mind?"

"Yes, actually. I think it's time to put in my papers and retire," Murray said.

"The devil you say. Why?"

"It's time. I can't go back to normal police work after what I've been doing for so long. Surely you understand?"

"Indeed I do. But retirement is not all it's cracked up to be, old boy."

"You and Mary seem to get on quite well. I owe my love some good years—never even been on a honeymoon. It's time."

"Well, first thing is to get us those prints. After we learn who the mystery man is for certain, you may want to stay on for another bit of time."

Murray went into the building and found his way to the area where his friend worked. Ninety minutes later, he had the confirmation. He trembled as he read the name on the small slip of paper: Harold Russell Adrian Philby.

"Good God!" he said. He left the building and headed straight for Walter Thompson's flat.

*

Hunt used Kaitlyn's telephone to call Walter Thompson's flat. He informed King that they had the couple in custody and asked for instructions.

"Leave Brogan and Matthews there, and get back over here."

"On it. Matthews made sure the man and woman are asleep for the next half day at least. Be there in twenty minutes."

A few minutes later, Murray showed up and broke the news.

"You blokes didn't tell me that the fish was going to be this big. Holy hell—Kim Philby? What the devil are we into here?" he asked.

King replied, "Well, we weren't completely sure. But now we know. Thanks for running the prints, sport. Did you have any problems?"

"Well, my friend—the one who did the trace—he saw the name, of course. Not sure how long it will be before the whole thing starts to make noise."

"Did you tell him to keep his mouth shut?" King asked.

"Not exactly, though I did mention the Official Secrets Act. That's always good for slowing someone down."

"Good. Now we need to figure out how to play this interesting hand we've been dealt. One thing's for sure. All roads now lead to and from our old friend, Kim Philby. I need to check in with Washington."

*

Kaitlyn had been quiet for the better part of an hour, which wasn't like her. Her waters were seldom still. Brogan, aka Sean went over to where she was sitting, staring out a dirty window.

"Not like you to be so quiet, love. I know this is an awful lot to think through."

She looked up at him. "None of this makes any sense. I've worked with them before. We've been friends. Betrayal hurts, Sean."

"I know. I know."

"I find me-self wondering if there are now other things I don't know."

"Other things?"

"Yes. Who can I trust? Do I even know you, Sean? Have you been truthful with me all along?"

"Of course, I have. You're just shaken. Give it some time."

"What are we to do now—just sit here and wait forever?"

"No. I'm waiting for word from the blokes I'm working with on this one."

"And about them, Sean. I may not be keen as mustard, but it's clear even to me that you're working with the Yanks. What are the Americans doing here, and how did you get to throw in your lot with the likes of them?"

"It's a long, complicated story."

"Well, love," she said with a sparkle in her eye. "It appears we have some time on our hands."

*

"Jim, it's definitely Philby. He's here in London and involved in all this Churchill funeral mess. Not sure what his role is, but it must be significant."

"Fascinating," Angelton said. He was at his desk and smoking another of his ever-present cigarettes. "What's your plan?"

"We're going to catch him in his room this evening—if we can."

"Now listen, Harvey. I want to be there for the briefing."

"I'm thinking more like interrogation, Jim."

"Whatever the case, I want you to hold him until I get there. I'm catching the afternoon flight to London. I'll need someone to pick me up at London Airport in the morning, your time."

"Roger that. I'll send a guy. By that time, we'll probably be set up in Philby's room at the hotel. By the way, our friend in Rome sent us three of his 'associates,' so we've got plenty of talent for whatever we need."

"Great. Glad to hear it. Now, I'm going to book a room there under one of my legends—Marco Renaldi. We can move Philby to my room when I get there. Keep my plans from him. I can't wait to see the look on that lying bastard's face when he sees me."

CHAPTER THIRTY-SIX

FOR THE BETTER PART of that Thursday evening, Howard Hunt was at the Savoy waiting for yet another appearance of Kim Philby. He read a paper in the lobby. Nursed a drink in the bar. Ate a sandwich in The Grill. Then back to the lobby. Every half hour or so, he walked out the front entrance carrying a newspaper. This was a signal to Harvey King, who was lurking nearby, that thus far the old spy hadn't popped up.

Finally, King saw Hunt emerge once more from the hotel, sans newspaper. Philby was in the bar. He was wearing the wig and beard, as well as a dark sport jacket and light blue striped shirt with an open collar. King made his way over to Hunt.

"Just sat down and ordered a drink. If his pattern holds, he'll have another, then back to the room. I give it fifteen minutes," Hunt said under his breath. "I'll ring once from the house phone when he's on the move."

As they walked through the lobby, Hunt split off and moved toward the bar, while King headed to the lift. Within five minutes, King was inside room 312. He took up a position out of sight from the door, pulled out a gun, and waited.

True to form, the man in disguise drained his second glass of scotch and settled his bill. Hunt was already by the house phone by the time Philby walked out and toward the lift. Hunt picked up the phone and said, "Ring room 312, please. But just the once." Once the door was closed on Philby's lift, he hurried over to the stairs and made his way to the third floor.

King heard the telephone ring and was instantly alert. A few moments later, he heard key noise at the door. Meanwhile, Hunt was watching Philby from around a corner. As soon as the door opened, he quickly and quietly walked to the door in time to catch it before it closed behind Philby.

"Hello, Kim," King said.

Philby was startled. "W-what the h-h-hell?" By this time, Howard Hunt was in the room behind Philby, holding a gun at his back. "Harvey K-King—is that you?"

"One and the same, Kim. And please meet a friend of mine, Howard Hunt."

Philby glanced over his shoulder, then turned back to face King with false bravado. "You old devil—what are you doing in London? You assigned here these days?"

"Cut the bullshit, Philby. The question is what are *you* doing in London these days?"

"Yes, old boy. I s'p-pose it is."

*

"I was doing some freelance work, investigations and such, and this American approached me in Belfast about doing some work for his company. Small stuff. Surveillance. Photographs. Men misbehaving," Brogan told Kaitlyn.

"You're a bloody Peeping Tom? That's what you've been doing all these years?" she asked with a mischievous look in her eyes.

"Much more dignified than all that," he tried to protest. "But eventually the same man approached me to help with a different kind of investigation—this one."

"And you agreed?"

"Not right away," he said. "But they were very persuasive—they made it clear that I'd have a problem with them and Five otherwise."

"What kind of problem?"

"A lock the door and throw away the key problem."

"When was all this?"

"I started helping the 'company' last year, but this current thing is only a couple of weeks old. They were working on a tip. Once they told me what it was they were looking for, I had misgivings. I mean, we all bloody hated Churchill, but the idea of the Russians using our cause as a cover for their power-hungry plans, well, that was too much. So I signed on."

"I'm not sure what I would do in the same situation, but I surely understand, Sean. I feel better now. Are they asleep for a while?" she asked, nodding at the Wheelans.

"Michael and Molly shouldn't stir until the middle of tomorrow. Why?"

"Gives us some time to make up and make love. Come with me," she said, taking by the hand and leading him to the bedroom.

Brogan felt a measure of guilt, but he pushed through it in anticipation of a night of pleasure. He did wonder though if he would ever be able to be completely honest with her.

*

True to his word, Jim Angleton was on a flight to London from Dulles International Airport later that afternoon, scheduled to arrive shortly after seven a.m. local time. He brought a large satchel containing many of his Philby files and spent most of the time over the Atlantic reviewing the infamous spy's case, making notes for the upcoming interrogation. Adrenaline, coffee, and countless cigarettes kept him alert in the First Class section of the Pan Am Clipper. He was inconspicuous, but not just because he was a spy. No one was paying attention to him when a former President of the United States—Dwight D. Eisenhower—was seated two rows in front of him.

It took Angleton a short time to clear customs. He was met by Howard Hunt, who brought Angleton up to speed on the ride to the Savoy. He assured him that Harvey King had followed his wishes and had not engaged Philby at all in serious conversation.

Angleton checked into room 408 at The Savoy and freshened up. The phone rang. "Welcome to London, my friend," King said. "Ready for some company?"

"I've been ready for this since 1951, Harvey. Bring the prisoner to me."

*

King and Hunt, gun in hand, escorted Kim Philby up the back stairwell to the fourth floor, careful not to be seen. They then walked down the length of the hall, and past the lift, to room 408. King knocked twice on the door and it opened. They entered the room.

"That cigarette tobacco smells vaguely familiar," Philby said, as he sniffed the otherwise stale air in the room. He turned and saw Angleton positioned behind the door he had just opened. Breaking into a big smile, he said, "I'll be d-d-damned, if it isn't my old friend, Jim. How the h-hell are you, old man? Still smoking those wretched weeds?"

Angleton stared at Philby for a brief moment. Then he nodded for King to deposit Philby in a chair that sat alone in the middle of the room. He said, "It's been a long time, Kim. Too long. We have much catching up to do. Can we get you some water or tea?"

"I know it's quite early, but I'd love a scotch, if I m-might?"

"Sorry, Kim. You're gonna need a clear head."

"Jim," he replied, drawing the name out with humor. "You remember those four martini lunches at Harvey's in Georgetown? We managed to survive those with our w-wits about us."

"That was a long time ago, Kim, though I'm sure I still can't keep up with you when it comes to the sauce." Angleton's body language, which had been stiff up until that moment, began to relax. "We're going to have a long talk. If it goes well, we'll have that drink."

"Promise me two and you can fire away, old b-boy. I'm all yours."

Philly almost seemed relieved to be in the company of Americans.

CHAPTER THIRTY-SEVEN

THOUGH HE HAD SERVED two terms as president of the United States, Dwight D. Eisenhower preferred to be called "General Eisenhower" after he left the White House behind in 1961, to live out his days on his Gettysburg, Pennsylvania farm. He had been a popular president and remained a beloved figure in America. When his successor John Kennedy got into political trouble in military and foreign policy matters, one of his early moves would involve a photo-op with Ike—one that usually showed him listening carefully to the old man's sage advice. Johnson followed suit.

So, it was yet another inexplicable oversight on Johnson's part that he didn't tap the General to be America's official representative at Churchill's funeral. After all, Ike and the British wartime Prime Minister had worked closely with each other during what the General called "The Great Crusade"—the build up to D-Day and the ultimate liberation of Europe from Nazi tyranny.

A few days earlier, Bill Moyers had tried to make the case for sending Eisenhower to London. "It just makes sense, Mr. President," he told his boss. "If not you, if not the Vice President, a former president is the obvious choice."

"Not gonna do it, Bill. I have my reasons and you're just gonna have to take my word for it." Of course, the bewildered Presidential assistant had no clue as to Johnson's real motives at time. There was no way the President wanted to put one of America's greatest heroes at risk. Moyer suspected that his boss was hiding something, but he knew better than to press the issue. "Yes, Mr. President. So should I arrange for McNamara and Rusk to represent us?"

Johnson paused and thought for a moment. "Add Warren to the list. And tell the Chief Justice he'll be leading the delegation."

It was only after Moyers had organized the official delegation that Johnson decided to take him into his confidence. Then the young presidential aide found himself feeling very guilty about his role in possibly putting some great men in harm's way.

*

What Lyndon Johnson did not know—at least not until well after he was able to do anything about it—was that Her Majesty the Queen herself had invited the former president on behalf of her nation and according to the wishes of the Churchill family. They had even made arrangements for Eisenhower to be involved with the coverage to be provided by the BBC.

When the General told Johnson about all of this—as a courtesy, always a man for protocol—the President was tempted to warn him off, but knew doing so might jeopardize Harvey King's operation. He gave Dulles a heads up about Ike's trip and ordered extra measures—covert ones—be taken to protect Eisenhower. He also had a message sent to the embassy in London that extra security precautions should be in place for their famous guest.

When the Pan Am Clipper carrying James Angleton landed in London, several agents got off with the passengers and remained nearby to wait for the former president to deplane. They watched the crowd as the great general, adorned in a dark top coat and matching hat, strutted down the stairs from the aircraft. His famous smile was in full bloom. He was greeted by dignitaries as the conquering hero that he was.

Among those greeting him that Thursday night, was David Bruce, U.S. Ambassador to Great Britain. He led Eisenhower to a waiting car, and they traveled to the American Embassy, where a grand room was ready. The "official delegation" was scheduled to arrive on Friday.

"Thank you so much, Mr. Ambassador. This is very kind of you," Eisenhower said as his luggage was being brought in. "Now, I'd like to visit Westminster Hall first thing in the morning to pay my respects to my old friend."

David Bruce was certain that President Johnson didn't want the General to make any public appearances before the funeral. He pushed back gently, "Sir, I'm not sure that's the best thing. The crowds are very large and the logistics might be difficult."

"Well, Mr. Ambassador, I'm sure you have a point. But I'm going to pay my respects there even if I have to walk there all by myself," Eisenhower said, reminding the man just whom he was talking to.

"Understood, sir," Bruce replied. "We'll take care of it. How about we leave here around eleven?"

"Splendid. And thank you, Mr. Ambassador. I'm well aware that President Johnson is concerned for my safety, and has likely given all sorts of instructions about my security, but I'm an old hand at these things, as you know," Ike said. Then he flashed that famous smile.

*

The line of mourners passing by the catafalque slowed for a few minutes late Friday morning as word began to be passed back that General Eisenhower was in the Hall. There were whispers. Mostly, parents pointing and telling their children about Mr. Churchill's famous friend.

Eisenhower removed his top coat—and of course the hat, too—as he entered the large room. He stood for several minutes with his head bowed in reflection and prayer. This was interrupted when another famous man from those war-torn years came and stood about ten feet from Eisenhower. It was the French president, Charles De Gaulle.

The man who led the "Free French" during the war, and whose relationship with Churchill was stormy at best, did not bow. He stood at attention as his way of remembering and showing respect. One man standing nearby whispered to his wife. "You remember what old Winnie said about that French bastard, right?"

His wife was horrified and shout-whispered back, "You keep your tongue!"

"He said, 'That De Gaulle thinks he's Joan of Arc, but I can't get my bloody Bishops to burn him!'"

"I'm warning you!" his wife scolded. Several people overheard him smiled at the spat, and at the memory.

Eisenhower left and returned to the American Embassy. It was then and there that he sprang a surprise on his host—one that was quickly reported back to Washington.

As he sat down to an early lunch with David Bruce, he told him, "I'm not actually going to attend the service at St. Paul's."

"Sir?" Bruce asked. He was clearly surprised.

Eisenhower smiled. "I was keeping this news close to my chest, but people from the BBC have asked me to be in a studio with them throughout the day, offering commentary on the events. So rest assured and pass it along to President Johnson that I'll be safe and secure. Not to mention warm and dry."

Ambassador Bruce raised his water glass. "A bit early for anything stronger, but this water will do. To President Eisenhower and the BBC."

Eisenhower smiled and raised his glass. Then he smiled and said, "My navy friends tell me that it's bad luck to toast with water. Good thing I'm army all the way. This chicken salad is delicious. Sure wish Mamie was here."

CHAPTER THIRTY-EIGHT

JIM ANGLETON HAD MADE a thorough review of his material about Kim Philby on the flight across the Atlantic, but there was little need. His interest had grown into an obsession over the years since the Brit had been sent packing back in '51. And Kim's eventual defection to Moscow from Beirut in '63 had only led Angleton to redouble his efforts to try to understand the man he once thought of as a friend. But nothing could have prepared him for what Philby said a few minutes into their interview.

"Jim, old, b-b-oy, I'm ready to come in from the cold."

Harvey King was sitting across the room reading a newspaper, but he heard Philby's words and tossed the paper onto the floor. He crossed his arms and looked intently at Angleton, who was lighting yet another cigarette.

"I'm not sure what you mean, Kim," Angleton said.

"I'm telling you that I would like to d-d-defect to the States. I've been in M-Moscow for two years and I miss the

West. When they sent me here I couldn't believe my l-l-luck. Been waiting to make a move. Now you Yanks have made it easier f-f-for me."

Harvey King said, "Holy shit, Philby. You're a lying bastard. Always have been. I had you pegged before any of 'em."

"My oh my, Harvey, you still m-mad about that drawing B-Burgess made of your wife at my house in Washington?"

"Ex-wife. And I couldn't care less about that. But I do care about the people you've betrayed. You have blood on your hands. Lots of it."

"All part of the great g-g-game, old boy."

"It's no game, you piece of shit!" Harvey yelled.

Angleton interrupted, "Okay, Harvey—enough. Let me do my job here. Capiche?"

King nodded, bending over to gather up the newspaper he had thrown.

"Now, you say you want to come to America? Not back to England?" Angleton asked.

"They'd n-n-never take me b-b-back here. I'd be thrown in prison. But across the p-pond, well, put it this way—I have m-m-much to offer you and your friends."

"Such as?" Angleton asked.

"N-not so f-f-fast," Philby said. "I'd need some assurance that I'll be safe."

"I'm sure we could work something out, but we'd have to have some information to start with—something we could verify."

"Still t-t-trying to figure out who's the real defector between those fellows Golitsyn and Nosenko?"

Angleton smiled and lit another cigarette. "I think I have that one figured out."

"Yes, but do you know for sure?"

"All right. Tell us and we can get started."

"No. I'll save that for when I'm s-s-safe in the States. But I can help you with w-w-what's about to happen here in London quite soon."

＊

The weather was not being very cooperative that Friday morning, a full day before Mr. Churchill's funeral was scheduled to take place. Harry Higgins was watching some of the preparations for the service at St. Paul's from a perch outside the building where he was sheltered from the falling sleet.

He smoked several cigarettes while Royal Navy sailors practiced pulling a large gun carriage up and down the block in front of the church. Because he worked at the famous church, he was privy to many details about the procession. And he knew the gun carriage would be carrying Churchill's coffin through the streets of London, coming and going. Of course, based on what he was certain would be happening at St. Paul's the next day, he smiled. *Not gonna be going anywhere from the church,* he thought.

Meanwhile, tens of thousands of sober and silent people from all over the realm braved the dreadful weather without complaint for hours on end, before making it into the dry and warm confines of Westminster Hall.

*

"We m-must not w-w-waste too much time, Jim, old boy. Can't let some of my f-friends get concerned about my whereabouts," Philby said.

"If you're serious about all of this, Kim—and I'm not at all sure that's the case—you've been a master of deceit for so long. But if this is the real deal, then we need to have a taste of what you have to offer. Then we can work out the details about how to move forward. How about you tell us about what's planned here in London?"

Philby stared straight into Angleton's eyes, which was unusual for him. In the years since Philby left America, Jim had thought long and hard about his former friend and remembered that eye contact was a rarity—a sign of duplicity he had overlooked back in the day. So he paid attention to Philby's directness now. "I find myself wondering what drew you and your team here to London at just the moment I made my dramatic return," Kim said.

"We had some intelligence."

"What kind?"

"Sorry, Kim, that's not how this is going to work."

"P-pity. But couldn't hurt to try," Kim said, flashing a mischievous smile. "Let me start with the b-b-ig item on the agenda. There's a plan to d-disrupt Winston's big sendoff tomorrow."

Harvey King had been uncharacteristically quiet as he watched and listened. But his patience was wearing thin. He interrupted, "Hell, Philby, I think you may want to rethink your use of the word 'disrupt.' Tell us everything about what's supposed to happen."

Philby looked over at King and then back at Angleton. "First off, my good m-men, I must have your assurance I will be protected. When what is p-planned does not happen, I'll be under immediate s-suspicion."

"We'll cover you, Philby," Angleton said. "Now what's the plan? Who's involved? Who's behind it?"

Kim Philby lit another cigarette and took a long puff. "A bomb has been planted at St. P-P-Paul's. It's set to kill as many world leaders as possible in one place."

"Whose grand idea is this?" Angleton asked.

Philby was struck by how matter-of-factly King and Angleton had received his bombshell. But he continued, "The Politburo—Brezhnev and the whole l-lot. They want to destabilize the continent and make a military move."

"How long has this been planned?"

"As I understand it, the original idea came from Stalin. He h-hated Churchill and thought he'd outlive him. But after his death, some of his associates—those called 'h-hardliners' here in the West—kept the idea alive for when the old man finally kicked o-o-off. The plan has a c-code name: KOBA."

"Ah yes," Angleton said thoughtfully, "Stalin's boyhood nickname."

Harvey King stood up abruptly and walked over to the prisoner. "Okay, Kim, here's what we're gonna do. We'll put you back in your room while we check out your story. In the meantime, to show more good faith, you'll write down everything you know about this plan. Names, places, anything that can help us. You have that done in one hour. Then you call this room as if you're calling room service and order some coffee. You put your info in an envelope and hand it to the man who brings the coffee. Got it?"

"Yes, Harvey. It's all very str-str-aightforward."

"Well, you'd better be straightforward yourself, Kim. Or we'll hand you over to the gangsters you've been working for all your pathetic life."

CHAPTER THIRTY-NINE

THAT AFTERNOON, THE AMERICANS—minus Tiernan Brogan, who remained with Kaitlin and the sedated Wheelan couple—met at Walter Thompson's flat. Edmund Murray was there, as well. Jim Angleton and Harvey King had brought along a two-page document in Kim Philby's own hand. It contained a treasure trove of valuable and actionable intelligence.

"Yes, the man came through. I think we must operate on the assumption that Kim very much wants to come to America," Angleton said.

"I agree," King added, grudgingly. Everyone in the room seemed to agree.

Mary Thompson brought another tray of sandwiches.

Howard Hunt spoke up. "We need to get some help—some more hands."

"Already on it, Hunt," King said brusquely. "I have some friends on the way."

"Who are these 'friends'? Some of our boys?" Hunt asked.

"Oh, we've worked with them a few times—like back in Florida a few years ago," King said, grinning.

Looks of recognition spread throughout the room, with the cryptic reference to some of their previous activities to undermine Castro in Cuba. Angleton then said, "Excellent, Harvey. But let's make sure to task them compartmentally."

"Way ahead of you, sport," King replied.

*

The document written by Kim Philby was very detailed. The Americans knew about the bomb threat, but the man who sought safe-haven in America had filled in many vital blanks. Many of these had to do with Soviet operations in other European cities. Accordingly, two of Johnny Romano's men were quickly rerouted to Paris and assigned the task of making Henri Girard disappear at the crucial moment in order to protect Manlio Brosio.

Other men were sent to Berlin and Brussels, Philby having given the names of two other conspirators who were part of the Soviet plan for coordinated disruption. And all of this was far out of view when it came to official law enforcement and intelligence channels. No paper trail. The Soviet plan involved very few people at first. A handful of operatives in key roles and places. This was designed to help ensure that their fingerprints would never be found on the foul deed they hoped would set the wheels of revolutionary conquest in motion.

∗

As Friday afternoon gave way to evening, Lady Churchill and her daughter Mary appeared at Westminster once again, this time with Randolph Churchill, who brought a large party for a lengthy visit. This was the loudest moment during the entire period of mourning, as Winston's son—known for excess and flamboyance—acted true to form.

In the car on the way back to Hyde Park Gate, Detective Sergeant Edmund Murray spoke to Lady Churchill. "I've decided to retire after the funeral. I'm sure you don't need the likes of me lurking about anymore. But I want you to know that it has been such a privilege and honor to serve your husband and your entire wonderful family."

Mrs. Churchill took the officer by the hand and said, "Mr. Murray, the honor has been ours to have you in our lives. Please give our best to your dear wife, and thank her for all the precious sacrifices she has made on our behalf. I surely know what it is to be married to a man on a mission." She smiled and he nodded respectfully.

∗

By this time, and in spite of the increasingly foul weather, the line of people still seeking access to Westminster Hall stretched back over Lambeth Bridge and along the South Bank of the Thames. Throughout the day, the everyday people wanting to pay respects to their fellow "commoner" were interrupted by monarchs and dignitaries, including The Duke of Edinburgh, Prince Charles, Princess Anne, and the Kings of Denmark, Norway, Belgium, and Greece.

About half-past ten that night, Prime Minister Harold Wilson led a delegation that included his Conservative party counterpart, Sir Alec Douglas Home, as well as Liberal Party leader Jo Grimmond. The group stood silent and motionless for several minutes. The great and famous came in a few at a time, but the next day they would all be in one place.

*

Far out of public view, an army of security men from Scotland Yard and other agencies searched buildings along the route the procession would follow, from Westminster Hall to St. Paul's to the Tower Bridge to Waterloo Station. Much earlier—long before the great man's final illness—the name of every person in every building in a position to watch the procession had been supplied to the police. Every name was checked against a current list of what they called "politically uncertain" persons, those who might have an ax to grind.

The security plan also called for nearly four thousand soldiers, sailors, and airmen to line the route. The thinking was that the best chance for any kind of attack or action would be outside and in plain view. Little thought had been given to the funeral venue itself, and the Russians were aware of this because of Harry Higgins. Every report from him was the same: "no unusual security measures inside."

As he tried to sleep that night before the big event, as he liked to think of it, Higgins was restless. It wasn't just the fact he was the trigger person for a moment that would change the world—that part excited him. No, what was bothering him is that he hadn't heard a word from anyone else in the circle of conspirators. Nothing from Michael and Molly Wheelan, and nothing from Kaitlyn Dorsey.

After a few hours of tossing and turning Higgins convinced himself that going dark right before a major operation was the usual rule, though this particular long silence had come without warning.

He drifted off to sleep thinking about a small box he had carefully hidden at St. Paul's Cathedral. The box contained the device he would use to activate a timer on the bomb in the casket, giving him enough time to quietly slip away to safety. He knew he would become more famous in history than Gavrilo Princip in Sarajevo all those years ago—the triggerman for the global war that started in 1914. At least that is what he thought. In fact, the device in his possession would bring about the immediate explosion, followed by carnage. The Soviets wanted no loose ends.

CHAPTER FORTY

LONG BEFORE DAWN ON SATURDAY, January 30, 1965, Operation Hope Not was well in motion, and thousands of people from all walks of life had already mobilized for duty. No one allowed the foul weather to bother them one bit. They had a job to do. They wanted this to be one of those days that could be later described as their finest hour.

Harvey King, Jim Angleton, and the others on the team also worked long into the night and wee hours of the morning on their plan of action. They reviewed the funeral arrangements and surmised that the conspirators would most likely try to detonate their bomb after everyone was in place inside St. Paul's, for maximum damage. That meant that the window for the explosion would be between eleven and eleven-thirty that morning.

Churchill had insisted on a relatively short church service. Years earlier he had picked the hymns and plotted the order of things for his eventual funeral. Edmund Murray was charged with watching Harry Higgins at St. Paul's. Because of the tight security, he was the only man in the group—with the possible exception of Thompson—who even had a remote chance of getting inside the church at the appropriate time. Murray was determined that his last day of service on behalf of Winston Churchill and his family would be one to remember. He might never be able to tell anyone about it, but he would know in his heart he had been part of something historic.

*

Edmund Murray arrived at St. Paul's about seven-thirty that morning, using his security credentials, as well as his well-known status among law-enforcement professionals, to gain entrance. He was able to move about freely and examine everything unimpeded. It took only about fifteen minutes to lay his eyes on Harry Higgins. He began following from afar as the workman attended to his various duties. Murray watched to see if Higgins looked to be recovering any hidden item. But there were no such signs. After a while, Murray assumed that the device had already been retrieved and was in Higgins' possession.

Eventually, Higgins wandered away from the other workers and assumed a fixed position standing out of sight in a loft area overlooking the main room. Murray watched his prey for about twenty minutes, but he did not approach him. He concluded that Higgins was where he wanted to be for the big moment. Murray found a nearby spot where he could continue to observe unnoticed. At one point, he saw Higgins remove a small box from his pocket, which he then quickly put back. Murray assumed it contained the triggering device.

That was all he needed to know. Rather than wait and run the risk of acting too late, Murray pulled his pistol out and quietly moved into position behind Higgins. While pushing the pistol into Higgins' back, Murray said, "Hello Harry. I'll be taking that item in your pocket, and you'll coming with me."

Higgins made a move for his pocket, but Murray put the pistol to the side of the triggerman's head. "Not a smart move, Harry. We're on to you. Now let's move." Then Murray reached into Higgin's pocket and retrieved the small box containing the device.

He had noticed an empty room behind him around a corner. It looked like a small office. He led Higgins there. There was a telephone on the desk. Murray pulled out a set of handcuffs and secured Higgins in a chair in a corner of the small room. Then he found a small slip of paper in his pocket and dialed a number on telephone.

"Murray here. I have our Mr. Higgins nicely tucked away here in a room at St. Paul's."

Thompson was on the other end of the line. "That's splendid! When you can find a way to get him here unnoticed, bring the rascal back to my flat. The Yanks will figure out what to do with him."

"Who the devil are you?" Higgins asked, clearly afraid.

"Name's Murray. I'm with Scotland Yard and assigned to Mr. Churchill and his family. Your treachery has failed and you are about to answer for your crimes. We're going to wait here for the church to empty, so you just sit tight."

*

Big Ben tolled at nine o'clock that dreary morning, as it had every day in memory. It would chime three more times that hour. But after nine forty-five, the great iconic symbol would remain conspicuously silent until midnight, to honor Mr. Churchill. For several hours, roads in the city had been closing down. Eventually, vehicles would be banned from eighty streets in the surrounding sections of the city.

While Big Ben was striking nine, several cars appeared at Hyde Park Gate. Family mourners, led by Lady Churchill, were transported to Westminster. When she got out of the car, Clementine saw the Royal Navy gun carriage, complete with its cannon attached, waiting for the coffin.

After the family entered the building, they watched in silence as a group of Grenadier Guards draped the coffin with the Union Jack. Then one of the Guards laid the insignia of Churchill's Order of the Garter on top. The Guardsmen then carefully lifted the flag-draped coffin and made their way to the waiting gun carriage. Lady Churchill and her family walked ahead of the coffin to its vehicle, then made their way back to their own cars. After everyone was in place, the Duke of Norfolk gave a quiet signal to the commanding officer for the processional to begin the journey to St. Paul's. More than two thousand military personnel walked slowly behind the gun carriage and vehicles, the pace about sixty-five steps per minute. Along the route military bands played somber funeral marches written by Chopin, Beethoven, and Mendelssohn.

The crowd lining the route was six rows deep at most places. When the processional neared St. James Park and Tower Hill, artillery began firing—the first of ninety such outbursts to be spread throughout the day. One for each year of Winston Churchill's life.

*

Even before the funeral procession was underway, the world was watching. It was hours before dawn in Washington and New York, and approaching midday in Moscow. More than three hundred and fifty million people worldwide would tune in to at least part of the coverage—the largest television audience in history to that point, surpassing even the number who watched the funeral of President John F. Kennedy. It was a testament to how much the world had changed in Churchill's lifetime that the funeral of a man born in Victorian England, decades before the flight of the first primitive airplane and the invention of the automobile, was being viewed via space-age satellite technology. People seemed to sense that what they were watching was more than just the funeral of a political giant. It was almost like the lights from a long-forgotten age were being extinguished forever.

President Johnson was up early and tuned in. He knew few would ever know the real reason he skipped the funeral. And even if they ever learned the truth, he knew many might then question his courage in the face of danger. However, he was in the Oval Office because of an act of terror that had removed a world leader, and he knew first-hand how unsettling it was to a nation. *If the worst happened, the world would need at least one great commander to handle the chaos and actually lead,* he told himself. But the thought was little solace as he watched the three networks on his specially built television console.

All three screens carried the same image, that of a somber procession slowly making its way through the streets of London. And when he turned up the volume Johnson heard Eisenhower's voice. LBJ felt very left out, and terribly alone.

*

A world away, in a large conference room in the Kremlin, the men who had planned, and activated KOBA were also watching the coverage. A fire blazed in a large fireplace. There was a buffet spread for a celebratory luncheon. Vodka was on hand for the toasts. Caviar, too. They were waiting for the event, the explosion, and the beginning of change across Europe. One man suggested a toast to the success of KOBA, and all agreed, despite the fact it was not yet noon. They anticipated their plan would be a fait accompli in a little more than one hour. They raised their glasses and drank.

CHAPTER FORTY-ONE

As THE GUN CARRIAGE carrying Winston Churchill's coffin slowly made its way toward St. Paul's, world leaders had arrived and were already seated. Ambassador David Bruce and Supreme Court Chief Justice Earl Warren led the American delegation. The delegation was also supposed to include Secretary of Defense Robert McNamara and Secretary of State Dean Rusk, but both men were noticeably absent, citing sickness.

It was the Soviet delegation that raised the most eyebrows as a steady stream of official vehicles deposited dignitaries and diplomats at the famous church. Even though the Soviets and the United Kingdom had been allies during the war, and much of that war had been conducted by Churchill working with Josef Stalin, the delegation representing Moscow did not include any familiar Kremlin names. Instead, it was up to a deputy Prime Minister named Konstantin Rudnev, and Ivan Konev, who had been instrumental in the suppression of the

Hungarian revolt in 1956, to be the official faces of Soviet respect.

Around ten-thirty, the Queen, Prince Philip, and Prince Charles left Buckingham Palace in their maroon Bentley limousine for the short ride to St. Paul's. They arrived at the destination a few minutes later. Being in the church before the casket arrived was Her Majesty's deliberate show of respect for the Churchill family. Sir Lionel Denny, the Lord Mayor of London, met her on the steps in front of the church, holding London's velvet-handled mourning sword. They walked up the steps and were received at the door by Michael Ramsey, the Archbishop of Canterbury.

General Eisenhower was in a television studio off site with the veteran BBC broadcaster Richard Dimbleby, providing commentary. At one point, the former president pointed out one man in the crowd, who was smoking a pipe and failed to remove his hat as the gun carriage moved past his position. Eisenhower was offended by what he saw as a clear expression of disrespect.

$*$

Roger Hollis, now under the watchful eyes of the Americans, paid a visit to Philby's hotel room that morning. He wanted to brief Philby about everything being in place, knowing Kim was the man in charge of things in London for the Kremlin. But Philby was long gone. Hollis surveyed the room. It looked like there had been a struggle. He noticed some scraps in the waste can near a desk. He retrieved them and left the room, nervously reading them as soon as he was on the lift heading down to the hotel lobby. What he saw on the small pieces of paper made him ill. He couldn't make out several of the words from the chicken-scratch writing. But all he needed was two: KOBA and Angleton.

Hollis now feared that Kim Philby was playing both sides to the middle. But he didn't know what to do with his suspicion. He was glad Alex was on duty in the men's room downstairs. Hollis broke with protocol and told Alex that Philby was gone and likely with the Americans. Alex was instructed to warn his superiors, and soon alarm bells—stealthy ones, of course—were going off near and far.

$$*$$

At ten forty-five, the gun carriage arrived at the bottom steps of St. Paul's. The steps were lined with Household Cavalry. Also present were the Ceremonial Pallbearers. Eight Grenadier Guards would actually lift and carry the lead-lined casket, which weighed more than four hundred pounds, up the steps and into the church.

There was one brief moment of potential drama as the pallbearers moved carefully up the steps. Eighty-two-year-old Clement Attlee, the former Prime Minister, struggled up the stairs and had to pause halfway up, causing the movement to stop and the brunt of the weight of the casket to fall to the guards at the rear. But they managed to stay steady, and after a moment, Attlee—possibly aware of what his hesitation meant to those carrying the load behind him—resumed his climb. Once inside the church, the casket was carried toward a black and silver catafalque centered directly under the iconic dome of the church. It was then gently placed on the catafalque, which was offset by large candlesticks at each corner. These particular candlesticks had last been used at the First Duke of Wellington's funeral in the same place in 1852.

*

Soviet operatives were soon going over room 312 with a fine-toothed comb. They had no idea that the former resident of the room was still close by—up one floor, in room 408. Harvey King had ravaged Philby's room on purpose, leaving a few telltale hints in the process. Nothing too obvious. Just enough to make the Russians smell the scent of the Americans.

As for Philby, he was sitting with Jim Angleton and watching the funeral coverage on the television. Both men were quiet. Philby checked his watch every few minutes. Finally, Angleton broke the silence as strains of Beethoven's Funeral March Number Three played from the television. "I suppose in a few minutes that your friends in Moscow, who must be watching as we are, will know whether or not their plan has succeeded. But what if there is no explosion?"

"They m-may think it was a mechanical thing, at first. But I know these men. They're absolutely p-paranoid. And when they realize I'm in the wind, they'll as-s-sume the worst."

"Then they'll be looking for you, Kim."

"Indeed. So, w-why am I still here?"

"We have some people to round up and deal with first. No loose ends here before we head home. This entire episode must never see the light of day."

"The same could be said of y-yours t-truly."

CHAPTER FORTY-TWO

THREE THOUSAND MOURNERS FILLED the seats in St. Paul's. As the casket and the procession moved toward its place in the room, a choir sang a song called "The Sentences," which began with words from the Gospel of John, chapter eleven: *"I am the resurrection and the life, saith the Lord. He that believeth in me, though he were dead, yet shall he live: and whosoever liveth and believeth in me shall never die."*

Winston Churchill had planned his own funeral service with exacting care, down to the last song and scripture. He also intended for the service to be colored with the theme of Anglo-American unity. This was indicated most clearly with the singing of "The Battle Hymn of the Republic," a uniquely American song written during its Civil War a century earlier.

The Apostle Paul's words to the Corinthians were read: *"O death, where is thy sting? O grave, where is thy victory?"* And the service included the entire congregation reciting "The Lord's Prayer." Once the national anthem was sung, the strains of

"Last Post," Great Britain's equivalent to the American "Taps," was sounded from a silver trumpet played by a Corporal named Wilson. He had played it hundreds of times before, but was still quite nervous. Some of his friends had teased him about not making the same mistake his American counterpart had made during the burial of President John F. Kennedy, when the bugler sounded a flawed note. But Wilson's tribute was flawless. Then, to the surprise of everyone—but specifically requested by Mr. Churchill—another trumpeter played "Reveille." The great man believed a great morning of resurrection would one day come.

Soon the crowd rose to sing the hymn, "O God, Our Help in Ages Past," the coffin was lifted and those bearing it began to move toward the exit. It was a beautiful service, and everything went according to plan.

The British plan—not the Soviet plan.

*

The men seated around the large conference table in the Kremlin grew increasingly quiet as they watched the service at St. Paul's via satellite hookup. About the time when the congregation began to sing "The Battle Hymn of the Republic"—hardly a favorite of the hardliners in the room—a young assistant entered with a dispatch from their embassy in London. It informed them that Kim Philby was blown and likely in the hands of the Americans. The message also indicated it was possible that the Americans had information about KOBA.

Most of them drank more vodka. But there were no more toasts. Just disappointed silence.

After a few minutes, Leonid Brezhnev spoke up, taking charge of the moment. "Comrades, it is clear our plan has fallen short. We must now make sure it never becomes public. Pass the word down the line for everyone to stand down. And get Philby back."

An hour later, Henri Girard got the word to stand down—just five minutes before he had planned to murder his boss. He and the other assassins around the world would never know how close they had come to vanishing from sight at the hands of Johnny Romano's goons. Nor would Manlio Brosio and scores of other diplomats in various cities in Western Europe know how close their world came to a massive upheaval.

By the next day, the Italians were back in Rome reporting to Romano. He scratched his head and asked, "What the hell was that all about?"

*

Tiernan Brogan received instructions from Harvey King, who had called to share the news that Murray had Harry Higgins in custody and was going to bring him to Thompson's flat after the crowd in St. Paul's moved out. Tiernan Brogan was to bring Kaitlyn, as well as Michael and Molly Wheelan, to Thompson's flat, too. That would be the staging area for the team's end game and exit. He also told Tiernan that he had to figure out what to do with the girl. She was a potential complication.

After watching the service at St. Paul's, Kaitlyn was drinking a cup of tea and pondering it all while sitting at her kitchen table. She looked over at their prisoners. They were still unconscious. Brogan poured himself a cup and sat down across from her. "That call was from one of the men I've been working with. I have the instructions about our sleeping friends. He also told me that they have Harry Higgins."

"Ah, very cloak and dagger, love. You're quite the handsome man of mystery," she said with a smile.

"Well, it appears we need to prepare to move out."

"Out where?"

"There's a flat that's being used by the team. From there we'll be moving to Essex and Stapleford Aerodrome. There's an airplane there waiting to get us out."

"And where, pray tell, is this mysterious airplane going to be headed?"

"America."

"You're going to America?"

"Yes, for now, I must. That's where this whole story resolves. Our orders are to make sure none of this sees the light of day here in Britain."

"Isn't MI-5 working with your friends?"

"Actually, no. Not at all. This is strictly a Yank operation."

"And what of me? I know all about it."

"Yes, and that means you need to come with us to America for now."

"The devil you say? I'm not getting on any airplane to the United States, I can tell you that for sure."

"I'm afraid I must insist."

"I was thinking maybe you cared about me. You've just been using me? You bastard!"

"Calm down, darling—"

"Don't darling me! I can't believe I allowed me-self to get taken in by you and this bloody plot."

Brogan realized that he had to come up with an alternative. So, thinking quickly, he provided another way.

"Kaitlyn, I do care for you. If you don't want to come to America, I don't want to force you. How about I set you free and you go back home to Belfast. And I was thinking I could meet back up with you in a month or so, after this all settles down."

Kaitlyn's scowl turned swiftly to a smile. "Now, that's the man I've been loving. 'Tis more like it."

"Great. So, I think you should make your way from this place quite soon. Do you have money? I have some you can use."

"Aren't you the gentleman? I'm fine. Save yours for when you come to Belfast. We'll have a proper fling. Let's meet at Bittles Bar one month from today. I'll be there waiting."

"It's a date."

A few minutes later, Kaitlyn had packed a bag and was on her way. Her plan was to make her way by train to Manchester, catch a ferry there, and be in Belfast early the next day.

Neither Kaitlyn nor Tiernan was aware that Michael Wheelan had woken up just enough to hear all about their plans.

CHAPTER FORTY-THREE

As Winston Churchill's casket, complete with the plastic explosive material hidden in its lining, was carried down the steps of St. Paul's, members of the Cathedral Guild began to ring the church's bells. There were twelve of them, but it took thirteen people to ring them. The tenor bell weighed more than three tons. French President Charles De Gaulle stood tall, wearing a large khaki greatcoat. He was flanked by the Queen of the Netherlands and the Duke of Luxembourg. After the casket began to move away from the famous church, Queen Elizabeth made her exit and returned quickly to Buckingham Palace, where she would host a luncheon for foreign dignitaries, who joined her shortly thereafter.

The gun carriage carrying the large casket made its way to Tower Hill via Cannon Street, then to Tower Pier, a journey that took not quite twenty minutes. There was a nineteen-gun salute. The casket was carried on to the MV Havengore, a teak and oak framed vessel built in 1956. Others went aboard, a host of family and friends. The launch journeyed up the Thames, escorted by several other launches. It was at this point that General Dwight D. Eisenhower read his tribute to Winston Churchill, which quoted from Alfred Lord Tennyson:

"Upon the mighty Thames, a great avenue of history, move at this moment to their final resting place the mortal remains of Sir Winston Churchill. He was a great maker of history, but his work is done, the record closed, we can almost hear him, with the poet, say--'Sunset and evening star. And one clear call for me! Twilight and evening bell and after that the dark! And may there be no sadness of farewell, when I embark."

The General spoke for several more minutes before ending his remarks with an emotional, "And now, to you Sir Winston—my old friend—farewell!"

*

Edmund Murray escorted Harry Higgins to Thompson's flat, where the Americans were getting ready to head to the airfield. Higgins would be joining them on the flight to America. Jim McCord was currently on his way to meet Brogan to help with the transport of Mike and Molly Wheelan.

Harvey King chose the waiting moments to thank his hosts. "Walter, Mary—you have been so gracious to us. I want you to know that I will personally commend you to the president of the United States. Now, because this whole mission has been top secret, there's not much that can be done publicly to thank you. But I assure you that all of us 'across the pond,' as you like to say, will make sure you are rewarded for your efforts."

Thompson replied, "Mr. King. Nothing for us. Please no. We have served our nation and history. You have given an old man one more moment of service to my nation and Mr. Churchill. For that I will be forever grateful."

Howard Hunt added, "You are a remarkable man, Mr. Thompson. A real hero. It has been an honor to serve with you."

"Hear! Hear!" the Americans all said, with respectful laughter.

"Where the hell are Brogan and McCord?" King said, interrupting the mood.

*

Kaitlyn had left the flat, and Brogan went over to the Wheelans to prepare them for travel. Working in a kind of daydream about Kaitlyn, he was oblivious to the fact that Michael had been awake and working on his restraints for some time now. As Brogan bent down, Michael came up with an elbow to his chin, knocking him to the ground. Brogan's gun was on the kitchen table and Michael lunged for it, beating Brogan to the weapon. The gun went off. Suddenly, Tiernan Brogan was on the floor, clutching a fresh gunshot wound to the shoulder. He watched through the quickly increasing fog of pain as Michael managed to rally Molly to consciousness. Quickly, the couple was out the door.

Less than five minutes later, McCord came in and saw Brogan. The Irish operative was still alive, but he had lost a lot of blood. He was conscious enough to report what had happened. McCord called Harvey King at the Thompson flat, who told him to leave immediately for the airfield where they would meet up.

"How the hell do I know how to get to Essex?" McCord asked. "Especially with a man who needs a hospital?"

"Stop the bleeding the best that you can and get out of there. We're blown. Who knows what this couple knows? And find a map. Just be there—you got that? I'll try to figure a way to get a nurse or doctor to the airfield."

"Roger. We'll be there."

Harvey then placed a call to Allen Dulles in DC. "We're blown," he said. "Heading back to the airfield now. Brogan's been shot. Not sure of his condition."

Dulles replied, "I'll let the president know. Is Philby with you?"

"Yes, we have him. The Russians probably know this and are on the trail."

"Is there any way they know where you're headed?"

"Well, two bad guys escaped—the ones who shot Brogan. It's possible that they may have picked up on our plans before they ran. We'll operate on the assumption that the Russians are not far behind us."

"All right. Get a message to us when you can. And be careful."

"I plan on it."

Meanwhile, McCord was attending to Brogan's wounds and readying him for travel. He grimaced. "Come on, Brogan, you're gonna have to stay with me. We're heading to the plane. It's gonna be a bumpy ride. And I hope to hell that one of us knows the way to Essex."

"I know the way," Brogan gasped.

King kept his word. It turned out that Blair Lithgow's brother was a doctor. It took one discreet telephone and medical help was soon waiting for Brogan at the Stapleford Aerodrome.

∗

As the Havengore passed a place called Hay's Wharf on the South Bank of the Thames, thirty-six crane drivers decided to pay their own unique respects to Mr. Churchill. These men had shown up for work on a Saturday, but not for pay. As the vessel bearing the casket containing the former Prime Minister came into view, the workmen, in well-practiced synchronization, dipped their jibs in a powerful and public gesture of respect and salute. Their boss was so moved that he gave the workers overtime pay for their act of homage.

The Havengore journeyed under London Bridge and Waterloo Bridge before arriving at Festival Pier, where the casket was taken ashore. The next stop was Waterloo Station, where the funeral train, a Pacific steam locomotive, Battle of Britain class, waited. The train left from Platform 11 for Churchill's final journey to Hanborough, not far from the great man's final resting place.

The train was named, appropriately, "Winston Churchill." The front of the locomotive bore three large white discs in a V formation., which customarily meant a train had broken down. But on this day of days, the discs were there to remember Churchill's famous "V" for victory.

CHAPTER FORTY-FOUR

SHOWING UP AT THE SOVIET EMBASSY was a risky move, but Michael and Molly Wheelan had nowhere else to go. They needed to report what had happened, and they also saw it as a safe harbor. It took a few minutes, and several phone calls from the guard station, but soon they were inside. Their information set off a scramble of activity, and a helicopter was dispatched to the Stapleford Aerodrome. The Russians hoped they would get there before the Americans. Their goal now was the retrieval of Philby at all costs.

*

McCord drove like a madman toward Essex, trying to keep Tiernan Brogan conscious and engaged in conversation. The bleeding had stopped, which was a good sign. The bullet had missed any vital organs and was lodged toward the bottom of his left shoulder.

"Hang in there, Brogan. You need to stay awake."

"No one could possibly sleep with you driving," Brogan replied weakly.

McCord smiled.

*

The hastily assembled group of five Russian operatives were now on the ground, well ahead of the Americans. Their helicopter had landed in a clearing just beyond a wooded area near the perimeter of the property. They made their way toward the airfield and saw the DC-3 near a hangar next to the administration building. The crew was not in sight, and the Russians assumed the pilot and crew were already on board, waiting for the American team.

They made their way to the main building and entered from the rear, out of sight from anyone in the DC-3. They observed two men working in the facility, one sitting at a desk in an office adjacent to a lobby area and the other man standing behind a counter. The Russians moved with practiced swiftness and quickly subdued the two workers. They dragged them into a nearby storage room and undressed them. Two of the Russians were soon dressed in the workers' clothes. One man, using a pair of binoculars, spotted the Americans' vehicles approaching. The Russians did not speak, merely waited for their arrival. They seemed to communicate with each other intuitively.

Blair Lithgow pulled his gray panel van up to the main building at the Stapleford Aerodrome. He didn't expect to see much activity, seeing as it was Saturday and the nation was transfixed on events surrounding Churchill's funeral. But as soon as he entered the building he sensed that something was not quite right. "Afternoon, gents," he said to the man behind the counter, who simply looked at him. "Where's Alfred? I expected to see him today. He sick, or just watching the telly somewhere?" Still no reply. As he walked closer he looked over to the office and saw another unfamiliar face. All at once, he noticed that their clothes didn't fit all that well. When he was close enough to read the name tag—Alfred—on the shirt of the man behind the counter, he knew. Lithgow turned to run back toward the door. He yelled, "Russians!" But that was all he could muster before a bullet got him in the back.

The men getting out of the van and car did not hear Lithgow scream. But they did hear the gunshot and instinctively went for their weapons. As they did, the other three Russians appeared from the side of the building firing their weapons, forcing Harvey King and the men to find cover.

Meanwhile, the two Russians from inside the building had exited out the back way. They went around the other side of the building, hunting the vehicle carrying Kim Philby. And as most of Harvey's team hunkered down to fight it out, these two Russians spotted two men in the second car. One was Ferguson Matthews and the other was Kim Philby.

Matthews and Philby watched the firefight. The shots were flying away from them, so they weren't ducking. And for all his training and better judgment, Matthews had left a blind side for the two Russians to exploit. They wasted no time on nuance. One man shot Matthews in the head through the window, while the other man dragged Philby from the vehicle and back around the corner. The two Russians did not wait for their comrades, but moved swiftly across an open field and back toward their helicopter. They had what they had come for.

✳

As McCord neared the airfield, he noticed another vehicle trailing about three hundred yards behind him. He had no way of knowing who it was, but he was concerned. "May have picked up a tail," he said to Brogan.

"Russians?"

"No way to tell, but the car has turned with me three times now."

"How far to go?"

"Should be to the airplane in less than five minutes, barring any problems."

"Yeah, well, let's try to do this problem free, old man."

"I'll do my best, Brogan. You hold on."

In a few minutes they could see the airfield and their plane. It was about then that they heard the gunfire.

"Tell me that you're seeing fireworks," Brogan struggled to say from his position on the back seat.

"I wish. It's definitely gunfire, coming from the airfield. Holy shit!"

"What are you going to do?"

"Get as close as I can to see what's going on."

As they came close to the scene, McCord saw the van and the other members of his team pinned down. The sound of the gunfire muffled the sound of his car approaching. He pulled as close to the far side of the building as he could. Then he looked back in his mirror. The car that had been following him was nowhere in sight.

"You stay put, Brogan. I'm gonna take a look and see how I can help our guys."

"Look at me, McCord, you asshole. Do I look like I'm going anywhere?"

"Roger that," McCord replied, as he quietly exited the vehicle. He walked the length of the building and then looked carefully around the corner. He could make out three shooters, presumably Russian. He knew that if he made a move, they would shoot him on the spot. Thinking quickly, he noticed a ladder to the roof of the single-story building. He climbed up and carefully positioned himself in view of the shooters. He knew that he could get one good shot off before he was noticed. He took aim and took down one of the Russians with a single shot. In the confusion, as the other two Russians looked around to see where the shot had come from, he managed to take another man down.

The remaining Russian operative ran back behind the building, where he caught sight of the car where Tiernan Brogan was. The Russian moved cautiously toward the vehicle. Harvey King, Howard Hunt, Frank Sturgis, and Howard Perlstein slowly came out into view as it became clear that somehow, someway, their attackers had been neutralized.

"Go check on Philby and Ferguson," Harvey barked to Howard Perlstein.

Perlstein, gun drawn, walked gingerly around the side of the building. As he did, he saw a Russian near the vehicle and a body lying next to the car. But before he could act, the Russian turned and fired a single shot, hitting Perlstein in the right arm and knocking him down. By this time, McCord had crossed to the other side on the roof and was trying to catch a glimpse of the shooter. But the car was parked too close to the building.

The Russian looked in the car and saw Brogan in the back seat. He needed the car as a getaway vehicle, but he didn't want a hostage. He raised his gun to finish Tiernan Brogan off, but as he did, McCord got enough of a bead on the man to graze him with a shot, knocking the Russian to the ground. The wounded man quickly dragged himself up, got into the driver's seat, and began to back the car away.

By this time, the other members of the American team could see what was going on and they all opened fire on the vehicle that was now racing across a field toward where the Soviet helicopter was waiting. After a few moments, the vehicle was out of range.

"Get in that van and chase that car," King barked out to no one in particular. Howard Hunt raced to the van and was soon in pursuit. As the vehicle the Russian was driving raced across the field, another vehicle appeared, as if out of nowhere. It drove directly toward the racing vehicle.

"Who the hell is that?" Howard Hunt muttered to himself.

As the mystery vehicle came close to the Russian, a single shot was fired and the Russian slumped over the steering wheel and his vehicle plowed into a small hill. Hunt and the other Americans now following approached the scene carefully. They watched a woman get out of the mystery vehicle. She opened the back door and disappeared from view.

"Identify yourself," Howard Hunt yelled as he walked toward the scene with his pistol drawn.

"Brogan, Tiernan Brogan," a voice replied.

"Brogan? You all right? Who is that with you?"

"An Irish angel—that's who."

*

Kaitlyn Dorcey had not gotten far along on her escape before she had second, then third thoughts. She turned around and went back to her flat to talk to Brogan further. But all that was there was a bloody scene. She feared the worst, but there were no bodies. Then she'd remembered Sean talking about the airfield at Essex and thought he might be in serious trouble. She borrowed a car from a neighbor—well, she had left a note and taken it, really—and drove off toward the Stapleford Aerodrome. She had no idea what she was getting herself into, but she had been part of enough operations to know trouble when she saw it. When she arrived, she trusted her instincts and decided that the one car racing across a field was the bad guy.

As Kaitlyn tended to Brogan's wound, she said, "If I'd known you were going to be in this bad shape, love, I might have thought twice about leaving. It's clear that you need me. You know I used to be a nurse, right? Back in Belfast?"

"I had no clue," Brogan replied.

"Well, me father used to ask, 'You know where you find clues, don't you?'"

Brogan just stared at her. "Like I said, no clue."

"You find clues in the clues closet."

Brogan laughed and then cringed in pain.

*

As the rest of the Americans made their way to the scene, they saw a helicopter flying off in the distance. "Son of a bitch," Harvey King exclaimed. "I'll give you ten to one that Kim Philby, that bastard, is aboard and already spinning a tale about us trying to kidnap him."

The Americans—plus one—made their way back toward the main building and began to put the pieces of the puzzle together. Howard Hunt said, "As I see it, the Russians got wind about our whereabouts from that Wheelan couple. The bad guys scrambled over in that chopper, beating us here. Their target was Philby, and they got him."

"Well, this is a royal pile of shit. But I don't think there's much left for us to do. Our work here is done," King said.

"I can get some people to clean up here; I doubt the Russians will be back. They have what they wanted. I guess it's a consolation prize, considering they didn't get their big-ass explosion," Hunt added.

"We need to be airborne in fifteen minutes. Did that doctor get here?"

"Yeah. He's taking care of Brogan," McCord said. "The guy's is in rough shape, but he'll make it. The girl is in there with him now. Last I heard, he was trying to explain why he never told her his real name. Probably better that he has a bad wound when breaking news like that, especially to that broad. She's working on Perlstein, too, but he was just grazed."

"What about Ferguson?" King asked.

"He never had a chance, poor guy. We'll put his body on the plane. By the way, Brogan's new girl is a trained nurse, so she can watch Brogan on the flight back," McCord said. "Don't want to lose another good man."

CHAPTER FORTY-FIVE

THE "WINSTON CHURCHILL"—the train carrying the casket—pulled up to Hanborough station shortly before three-thirty. From there, the hearse and other cars made their way to St. Martin's Church at Bladon, a tiny hamlet about two miles away.

The rector of St. Martin's met the coffin and the funeral party. He and his son went straight to the graveside, where the rector recited a brief word of committal before the simple and private burial. After the casket laden with both occupant and secret was lowered into the ground, Lady Churchill remained, looking into the grave for several minutes. The conspiracy called KOBA was also interred beneath the sacred soil. The plastic explosive was buried with the great man, never to be disturbed.

Once the grave had been backfilled with earth, wreaths were placed on it, including one from the queen. It was made of various flowers: lilies, carnations, and freesias—all white. It bore the words:

"From the Nation and the Commonwealth in Grateful Remembrance, ELIZABETH R."

*

Howard Hunt called in some cleaners, CIA contract workers who asked no questions. For the promise of a handsome fee, they had the area around the airfield sanitized by the time the DC-3 was at cruising altitude over Ireland.

On board that plane was the entire American team of operatives, including Harold Higgins, as well as the body of Ferguson Matthews. Higgins was on his way to a future of secret and protracted incarceration. Kaitlyn Dorcey mostly tended to Brogan's gaping wound, but she also kept an eye on Perlstein. Somewhere over the Atlantic she decided to give Brogan and America a chance.

As the Americans were making their way across the Atlantic, another plane, this one a much larger DC-8, was making much better time. It was chartered by *Life Magazine*. It had been converted into a flying news office, complete with a photo-lab for a staff of forty, a ten by fifteen-foot darkroom, tables for typists and writers, and a small reference library of books by and about Winston Churchill. It was all designed to put out a very special edition of the magazine at thirty-three thousand feet, one that would be a gem for collectors down through the years.

None of the workers on the *Life Magazine* charter had any idea of the plot that had been foiled by elements of American intelligence. If the Soviets had been successful, they would have been working on a very different kind of story.

∗

James Jesus Angelton stayed in London for another week. He wanted to make sure there were no loose ends. He arranged for the Russians who had been stashed in Thompson's freezer, as well as their comrades who did not survive the firefight at the airfield, to be delivered to the Soviet Embassy. A truck pulled up to the main gate and the driver told the security men that he had some sensitive items for the ambassador. At least that's what the bill of lading said. When shipment was searched, the security men recognized the dead men and quickly accepted the delivery. There was a unsigned card with the shipment that said: *"With Sympathies for KOBA."*

Angelton also arranged for Blair Lithgow's body to be sent back to Scotland. Allen Dulles wired funds sufficient for a proper burial just outside of Edinburgh. The family was told that he was killed trying to stop a robbery at Stapleford Aerodrome. No one seemed curious about why anyone would think to rob a small airport office.

Aboard a commercial flight home, Angelton wrote a detailed memo about the entire affair for his files. Years later, after his forced retirement, most of his files, including material about the assassination of JFK, Watergate, various highly secret operations, and, of course, KOBA, were destroyed.

In the aftermath of the failure of KOBA, the Soviets whisked Kim Philby back to Moscow. Because he was good at what he was—a trained prevaricator—he was able to convince his superiors—at least some of them—that he had been abducted by the Americans and had never really cooperated with them. He told them that the Yanks had somehow learned about the plot before they found him.

There were a few Kremlin hardliners who never got over their suspicions. They wondered if Philby was possibly a double agent working on behalf of British intelligence. They were never in the majority, but their influence was such that they were able to ensure that Philby would be on the sidelines of what he loved to refer to as "the great game" for the next decade.

Harold Adrian Russell Philby retreated to an uneasy exile in his Moscow flat, devoting himself to drink and depression. He would die more than twenty-years later, just before the system he served for so long spiraled down toward its demise.

*

Harvey King was personally congratulated for his efforts by Lyndon Johnson in a late-night, off the books, meeting in the Oval Office, about two weeks after he returned from Great Britain.

"Harvey, you *are* James Bond, after all," the president said, wrapping one of his long arms around the legendary spy.

"Just serving at your pleasure, sir," he replied, while trying to extricate himself from the awkward embrace. He and Johnson shared a few glasses of Cutty Sark as he briefed the President.

"Sad thing is this can never be known," Johnson said, shrugging. "It would be too easy to trace it all back to this office. Can't have that. Maybe one day the story will be told. But you and I will be long gone by then, Harvey."

"I'm used to working in the shadows anyway. I do have one request, though—something you may be able to help with," King said.

"Name it. If I can do it, I sure as hell will," Johnson replied.

"Get me the hell out of Rome, please?"

"Consider it done," Johnson said.

A few months later, Harvey King was appointed to lead a new division for the CIA. His office was in the new facility at Langley.

∗

The British Ambassador, David Ormsby-Gore, stepped down a few weeks after the events in London. He paid another visit to President Johnson in the Oval Office—this one on the record and covered by the press. The two would never meet again. Ormsby-Gore took a seat in the House of Lords as Lord Harlech, succeeding his father, who had died a year earlier. His wife died in a car accident a few years later, and David was often seen shortly thereafter in the company of JFK's widow, Jackie, prompting rumors of a romantic relationship. But she eventually chose another. Ormsby-Gore then became a media mogul, before being killed in 1985 in a suspicious car accident.

Roger Hollis quickly realized that his days running MI-5 were coming to a close and that his exposure as a spy was highly possible. He decided to retire, a move which surprised Prime Minister Harold Wilson and his cabinet. Soon he did come under suspicion, with several books written to try to prove Hollis's treachery. But Sir Roger spent the rest of his life denying he was anything other than a man loyal to Queen and country.

Howard Hunt went back to his life balancing the occasional CIA mission with his life as a writer of spy novels.

Several years after the Churchill funeral, he was recruited to help Lyndon Johnson's successor, Richard Nixon. Hunt, in turn, invited his friends Frank Sturgis and James McCord to join him in this effort. They were brought into the White House to help plug leaks of information to the press.

That operation would not turn out as well as the one in London in 1965.

As for Harold Wilson, he served as Prime Minister until 1970, then again from 1974-1976, before retiring from politics. Whispers about his political leanings and affiliations dogged him throughout his career and continue to this day. One fact, though, is clear—he was at St. Paul's for Sir Winston Churchill's funeral. So if he was a Soviet mole, they must have thought him to be expendable.

A few days after Churchill's funeral, President Lyndon Johnson, now fully "recovered" from his bad cold, held a press conference. He was prepared for the obvious question, but everyone in the room could tell he was more than a little bit annoyed at the members of the White House Press Corp. He was not anywhere near as skilled at handling the reporters as his predecessor. And his thin skin clearly showed.

"Mr. President, there has been some criticism both abroad and here because Vice President Humphrey was not sent to London to the Churchill funeral. Would you care to go into your reasons and what motivated you in selecting the American delegation?' a reporter asked.

Johnson replied, "Well, at first I thought I would hope that I would be able to go if my physical condition permitted. I asked that we defer final decisions until the doctors could act. But I had my staff contact President Truman and President Eisenhower and express the hope they could accompany me. President Truman was unable to go and President Eisenhower informed us that he had accepted the invitation of the family and he would be going and that he would be in attendance and would be doing other things there.

I urged that he go with us in our delegation and sent a plane to California to pick him up. At the same time I personally called the Chief Justice and asked if he would agree to go with me in case we made the trip. I also was informed we had Senator Fulbright, the chairman of the Foreign Relations Committee, and Senator Hickenlooper, the ranking Republican of that committee, and eight other Senators in London at the time, some of whom would be paying their respects as representatives of this country. I felt that with the former President, with the Chief Justice of the United States Supreme Court, with the distinguished Ambassador of this country to the United Kingdom, that we had a good delegation and a high ranking delegation.

I had no particular reason for not asking the Vice President to go, although the Vice President, as you may or may not have observed, was addressing the delegates from 50 States at noon the day the plane left at seven-thirty in the morning, on his new responsibilities in the field of civil rights.

I am glad to have the press reactions and the reactions abroad on the protocol involved in connection with funerals. I had served as Vice President for three years and it had never occurred to me and I had never had it brought to my attention so vividly that it was the duty and the function of the Vice President to be present at all official funerals. On occasions during the three years I was Vice President I attended one or two funerals representing this country, but there were many representatives from many walks of life. I did review the list of delegates representing their countries at the Churchill funeral and I did not observe that other nations sent in most instances either their top man or the next man necessarily. I thought we had a rather well-rounded delegation in the former President, the Secretary of State, the Senators who were present, the Chief Justice of our Supreme Court.

In the light of your interest and other interests, I may have made a mistake by asking the Chief Justice to go and not asking the Vice President. I will bear in mind in connection with any future funerals your very strong feelings in the matter and try to act in accordance with our national interest."

*

A few months later, a new term made its way into the American vocabulary—and it was first used by the media to describe how Lyndon Johnson tended to handle the truth. The term seemed to describe the new spirit of an age that had seen the death of a president under mysterious circumstances, as well as a growing military involvement on the other side of the world. An involvement that Lyndon Johnson was determined to guard by what Winston Churchill once described as "a bodyguard of lies."

That new term was, "credibility gap."

THE END

AUTHOR'S NOTE

The idea for this novel came to me as the fiftieth anniversary of the death and funeral of Sir Winston Churchill approached back in January 2015. I was struck—and disappointed—by how little the milestone was reported here in the United States. I remember watching some of the funeral when I was still in elementary school. I have been fascinated with the great man ever since.

I have always been intrigued by the "what ifs" of history, as well as those moments when something obvious did *not* happen. In one Sherlock Holmes story, the great detective asks, "why did the dog *not* bark?"

Indeed.

So I was curious as to why the President of the United States, Lyndon B. Johnson, a consummate and ego-driven politician, who had just been inaugurated for his own term, following a landslide election victory the previous November, would choose to stay home instead of grabbing the chance to make his presence known as the leader of the free world?

And why did the president not even send his new vice president, Hubert Humphrey, to the funeral?

And why did the Secretaries of Defense and State eventually travel to London as part of the "official" US delegation, only to be conspicuously absent from the actual service at historic St. Paul's Church?

It became "curiouser and curiouser" to me.

With these very true historical facts as a backdrop, I began to imagine a story, one that takes the reader through the "looking glass" into a murky world of shadows, mystery, and intrigue.

The cast of characters in THE CHURCHILL PLOT includes some familiar names from history including Lyndon Johnson, Bill Moyers, Allen Dulles, Clementine Churchill, James Jesus Angleton, Leonid Brezhnev, E. Howard Hunt, Walter Thompson, Robert Kennedy, Frank Sturgis, Queen Elizabeth II, Harold Wilson, Yuri Andropov, Edmund Murray, Roger Hollis, Kim Philby, and Dwight D. Eisenhower.

Then there are other fascinating (I hope) characters I have invented. Some of these are based, at least in part, on real. For example, readers familiar with Cold War espionage will recognize the character Harvey King as based on a real-life spy by the name of William King Harvey who led the construction of the Berlin Tunnel in the 1950s, and who was involved in "Operation Mongoose." President Kennedy was drawn to him because of the rumor that the spy was one of Ian Fleming's models for his creation—James Bond.

But at the center of the story is Winston Churchill himself. His accomplishments. His mistakes. His admirers. His enemies—even at the hour of his death.

The book is fiction, but it is rich in precise historical detail. You may wonder what is real and what is made up. You may also find yourself wanting to grab your smart phone to check a detail on Google.

Go for it.

David R. Stokes
Fairfax, Virginia
February 2017

ACKNOWLEDGEMENTS

I am indebted to a great number of people who encouraged and aided me during the research and writing of this book. I enjoyed working with Natasha Simons and the great people at New York Book Editors. Her input was invaluable, especially when I found myself struggling with a few plot points and the tendency to empty my notebook into the prose.

Rachel Walker, a wonderful freelance editor who happens to be the daughter of a college friend, was instrumental in bringing the story to its finished form. She excels both as a copy editor and as someone with an eye and ear for nuance.

A number of wonderful beta readers offered excellent feedback when the novel was still in its early formative stages. Thank you to Kelsey Nielsen, Billy Newman, Hunter Sherman, Lori Allen, Tim Downs, Sheila Schult, Beena and Tory McMahan, Eric Lynd, Blaine Gaudette, Joan Douglas, Jon Bergen, Debby White, and Al Donaldson.

Eowyn Riggins created the cover for this book—it's simple, yet compelling, with Mr. Churchill himself featured prominently.

Special thanks to Rachel Greene at Penoaks Publishing for the excellent interior design.

I am going to resist the urge to share a detailed bibliography of all the books and articles I devoured to make this book possible. I've been interested in Winston Churchill since I watched his funeral on American television live as it happened when I was nine years old.

Finally, I am, as always, inspired and refreshed by Karen—the pretty girl I first saw in a college speech class in 1975. She dropped the class because, well, she didn't want to give a speech. So I had to find other ways to connect with her. And when I did, I fell in love and married her. Now, after more than forty years of married bliss, we are surrounded in life by our three daughters and their families, including seven grandchildren.

Winston Churchill often said, "My ability to persuade my wife to marry me was my most brilliant achievement." I may not be able to speak with the great man's eloquence, or write with his erudition, but we share a common brilliant achievement. — DRS

ABOUT THE AUTHOR

David R. Stokes is an ordained minister, Wall Street Journal bestselling author, commentator, broadcaster, and columnist. He's been married to the love of his life, Karen, for more than 40 years. They have three daughters and seven grandchildren. And they all live in the great and beautiful Commonwealth of Virginia. He has served as the senior minister at Expectation Church in Fairfax, Virginia since 1998.

David's website is:
http://www.davidrstokes.com/

Follow David on **FACEBOOK**:
https://www.facebook.com/DavidRStokesAuthor/

Follow David on **TWITTER**:
https://twitter.com/DavidRStokes

Follow David on **AMAZON**:
amazon.com/author/davidstokes